PERFECT

UNYIELDING BOOK ONE

CHAOS

NEW YORK TIMES BESTSELLING AUTHOR

NASHODA ROSE

Perfect Chaos
Published by Nashoda Rose
Copyright © 2014 by Nashoda Rose
Toronto, Canada

ISBN: 978-0-9937023-5-8

Copyright © 2015 Cover design by Louisa Maggio at LM Creations
Cover Photo by Michael Stokes with Michael Stokes Photography
(http://michaelstokesphoto.com/index2.php#/home/)
Model Aron Abikzer

Editing
Content Edited by Kristin Anders, The Romantic Editor
(http://www.theromanticeditor.com/)
Editing by Hot Tree Editing
(http://www.hottreeedits.com/)
Formatted by Champagne Formats

*Any editing issues are my own. I'm Canadian and on occasion I may use
the Canadianspelling rather than U.S.
*A few timeframe liberties were taken regarding the Canadian military in
order to fit the story.

**Warning: This book contains offensive language, violence, disturbing
situations and sexual content. Mature audiences only. 18+**

Books by Nashoda Rose

Tear Asunder series

With You
Torn from You
Overwhelmed by You
Shattered by You

Unyielding Series
Perfect Chaos
Perfect Ruin (coming 2015)
Perfect Rage (Date TBA)

Scars of the Wraith
Stygian
Take

http://www.nashodarose.com/

DEDICATION

To the readers.
Thank you for all your support.
For the heartwarming messages.
For the friendships.
For making my journey as an author so incredible.
This book is for you.

PROLOGUE

Georgie

I SMOOTHED OUT the wrinkles on my bedspread then placed my stuffed brown bunny rabbit against the white-and-pink flowered throw pillow. At sixteen, I was a little old for stuffed animals, but it had been a gift from my brother the first time he went away to Afghanistan with the military.

I straightened, then saw the sheet hanging down in the right corner and quickly tucked it back into the mattress. Perfect. I liked … no, I was obsessed with being organized. Everything had its place, even me. I kept to the same bland, colorless clothes, the same schedule, and the same hair style. Why mess with what worked? My brother often teased me and said I should join the Canadian forces like him. I may like neat and tidy, but I hated fighting, blood, guns, and, unquestionably, any killing.

Connor knew that. He'd helped me bury my goldfish, Goldie, in the backyard when I was seven, then the hamster, Fiddlehead, when I was ten. To this day, there is a marked stone Connor had made for him near the back fence. I could see it whenever I looked out the kitchen window.

I jerked as a car door slammed, which sounded as if it was in our driveway. The sun had just peeked over the horizon; six in the morning was too early for any visitors, plus it was Sunday and Dad had the rule he and Mom sleep in. I always rose early wanting to get ahead of the day, another reason Connor said I'd excel in the military. Although, we both knew he'd never allow me anywhere near danger, which I was very content with. Danger to me was if my shampoo was missing and I had to use my brother's instead.

But Connor wasn't due back for another month, so that meant ... A sudden freeze hit my body, locking my limbs in place as I realized why someone might be in our driveway at six in the morning on a Sunday. My breath trapped in my throat as if clamped hands were strangling me.

No.

No. I shook my head back and forth. *Please, don't knock.*

It was the newspaper boy. Early. He was an hour early today. In a second, I'd hear the clang as the newspaper bundle hit the metal screen door.

Eyes squeezed tightly shut, I waited for the familiar sound.

Nothing. I sucked in large amounts of air for my starved lungs.

Not him. Please, not him.

Connor.

Connor.

My heart thumped harder and harder in its cage and tears pooled in my eyes. I couldn't hear his footsteps, but I knew his team leader's black combat boots were walking up the stone path toward the house.

I can't lose him. Please.

Run.

Run and it won't be true.

But I couldn't move. My legs were locked in place as I waited for the nightmare to begin.

Thump.

Thump.

Thump.

It was as if each knock was a punch to the stomach. No air. I couldn't breathe. I was silently screaming and nothing could stop the fear gripping my insides.

Please. No. I need him.

I heard my parents' bedroom door open and the shuffling of feet down the hallway on the hardwood floors. The distinct click as the lock turned and then the front door opened, followed by the screech of the screen door.

Then silence.

It felt like hours as I stood in the middle of my room, afraid to look out the window and see the car I didn't want to see. Afraid to run. Afraid to move. Hoping I was still asleep and this was all a dream.

Yes, it was a dream. I'd wake up any second. I'd call Connor today. I'd tell him how much I missed him and loved him. It had been weeks since we last spoke. I should've emailed him more often. Why hadn't I?

My mother's loud wail pierced the air, and my perfect world crashed to my feet. It was like I was being coiled in the death grip of an anaconda and dragged under the water.

I fell to my knees, my arms wrapped around myself, and I rocked back and forth as my mother's cries became muffled as if she was being held against something.

There were more footsteps. Not quiet and soft like my mom's. Not slow and lumbering like my dad's. Long, confident strides.

No. Go away. Just go away. It's not real.

The steps stopped outside my door, and I heard the click as the door handle turned. It was opening my soul and ripping out my heart.

I stopped rocking.

The door swung open.

I clamped my eyes shut, not wanting to see him. Unable to face him, face what he was here to tell me.

"Georgie."

Deck's gruff tone, I'd recognize anywhere. It scared me. *He* scared me but what scared me more was my body's reaction to him. The strange tingling between my legs, the warmth on my skin and the whirling in my stomach as if I was falling from the sky.

I sniffled as my nose dripped, and I felt the trickle of tears slip from the corners of my eyes.

"Look at me, Georgie." If I ignored him, it would all go away. "Georgie."

It was the hint of softness in his voice when he said my name which had me opening my eyes.

My gaze hit his legs first, the long, lean length covered in black cargo pants. There was a rip in the material just above his knee. Dirt. Smudges of dirt on his pants as if he'd come straight from whatever hell they'd been in.

3

They. In a second, the word *they* wouldn't exist anymore.

My gaze moved upward, hesitant, as if my brain was fighting every step. His hands were curled into fists at his sides, his knuckles strong notches which had felt the harshness of pounding into another man. It was odd because his hands were clean, and yet I saw the dirt on his tatted arms and the … blood? Was it his blood or—

"Georgie."

The loud, abrupt sound of my name made me lurch and my gaze flew to his.

His jaw was tense. Eyes hard and cold—unemotional. He looked directly at me, not an ounce of compassion in his unyielding stare. But I saw other things. There beneath his stoic solidity … the torment, the pain, the darkness which was soon going to become my own.

I started shaking violently, and my throat tightened against the sobs that racked my body. "No." It was the only word I could get out.

Please, no.

He stood and watched me tremble and cry on my knees in the middle of my room for several minutes before he said, "I couldn't save him."

His words cut into me with the finality of the truth, and my breath hitched as more tears pooled and slipped from the confines of my eyelids. I tightened my arms around my body as if that would help the pain ease.

It didn't.

Nothing would.

Connor.

He was gone.

I'd never hear his teasing. Feel the touch of his hand ruffling my hair. Hear his voice calling me 'Georgie Girl'.

He promised to come back.

Pain.

Hurt.

Devastation.

'Chaos'.

My head screamed with anarchy as Connor's image played across my mind. It was distorted and broken with bits of light being sucked apart by the darkness.

Destruction. I had to destroy. My perfect world was no longer. Nothing would ever be the same again. I'd never be the same again.

I scrambled to my feet, grabbed my duvet and tore it off the bed, the flowered throw pillow and bunny tossed to the floor. A strange sound emerged from my throat as I dove for my dresser and swept my arm across the shiny, neat surface—books, my jewelry box, and a vase crashed to the hardwood floor. I could hear glass shattering, and silver stud earrings, pearls, and rings scattered in every direction.

I didn't stop. I couldn't.

Destruction.

I grabbed my light off my nightstand and threw it across the room. The bulb made a loud pop as it hit the wall. I needed to destroy. Everything I'd made into a neat and tidy place was no longer. It was all gone. Nothing would be perfect again. My world had just burst open, and I was bleeding. It hurt. God, it hurt.

I tripped over my duvet as I went for the closet and fell to my knees. It didn't stop me … the physical pain was nothing, almost welcoming to the emotional pain taking me apart piece by piece. I got up, then staggered to the closet and threw open the doors.

I wrenched my clothes off the hangers—the pretty, soft-yellow dresses, white ones, black ones. Then the plain, button-down blouses and the black pants. The empty hangers swung back and forth on the metal bar as every single piece of clothing was thrown to the floor. When the closet was empty, I picked up whatever was in reach and began tearing. Buttons popped. Silk and nylon tore, sleeves ripped from the cores—like me. This was me being shredded apart.

Carelessly, I yanked and pulled at whatever my hands could get a hold of.

Rip.

Tear.

Ruin everything. Destroy.

I was breathing hard when I finished. Nothing was left alive. Just like me. I had nothing left except to run.

Run.

Run.

Run.

I ran for the door. I couldn't breathe. I had to get out of here. Away from this ruined perfect world. He was gone. Connor was gone.

My mind was whirling and frantic.

Escape.

I didn't even see him; my vision blurred from tears and anger and pain. He blocked the doorway, his broad frame preventing my path of escape.

I ran anyway, trying to dive past him.

He snagged me around the waist with one arm and my feet left the floor. I screamed and squirmed in his hold like a rag doll. He set me down directly in front of him, his hands latched onto my upper arms in a bruising grip.

"Georgie, look at me."

I kicked and yelled, trying to leave, but nothing would set me free. I knew I'd never be free again. My brother. My best friend. He was dead.

"Let me go. Let me go. Let me go."

Run. Get away.

"Look. At. Me."

This time his voice cut through my hysterical need to escape, and I stopped struggling, staring up at his unflinching eyes. How could he just stand there? He'd just destroyed my life, my family's life. And he was standing there looking at me without a trace of sympathy.

"I hate you."

"You going to stand still?"

Chest heaving and heart pounding, I realized Deck had watched me destroy everything in my room. He never did anything to stop it. The one thing I did know about this man was that he was unbending. Connor always said Deck was the best team leader, because no matter what shit went down, Deck would never yield to anyone. He'd stand by his word no matter what, and I guessed he wouldn't let me go until I bent to his will.

I stopped fighting.

He waited a second then released me. He reached into his back pocket and pulled out a small, leather-bound book with worn edges and a cracked spine. "He'd want you to have this."

I didn't move as I stared at what I knew was Connor's journal. Deck grabbed my wrist and shoved it in my hand, the hard surface abruptly hitting my palm.

Connor's name was written on the top in his familiar, messy handwriting.

I nearly fell, and probably would've if Deck hadn't grabbed my arm. He guided me further into my room, and I didn't object. All I did was stare down at the bound book. The last piece of my brother. It wasn't enough. It would never be enough.

I felt the softness of the mattress as Deck made me sit, and then the floor creaked as he started to walk away.

I looked up at the retreating figure. "I wish it was you, not him."

He gave no reaction to my words, and really, I hadn't expected any. It just came out. And I did hate that Deck was here instead of Connor. I hated that he could walk back to his family and laugh and hold them and my brother couldn't.

He turned his head and met my eyes. For a second, I thought I witnessed remorse, but it was so quick I could've imagined it or maybe I hoped to see it from my brother's best friend.

"Yeah." His whispered tone was barely audible as the door shut, and I listened to his steady, booted steps walk away.

The front door opened, and the screen door screeched. Both shut.

I had no idea why I did it, but I walked over to the window, parted the white sheer curtains and watched as he walked down the path. The tension in his back. The stiffness of his stride.

He stopped at the side of the car and stood still for a second. I couldn't see his face or what he was doing until he slammed both fists into the roof of the car. Then his head dropped forward and his shoulders slouched.

My fingers curled around the delicate material of the curtains, and I didn't realize how hard until they ripped from the rod and fell to the floor, leaving the window bare.

As if he'd heard it—but I knew that was impossible—Deck turned. Our eyes locked. It felt like he could see right into me with that direct gaze. I felt naked and vulnerable, unable to look away, trapped. He gave me these wounds. Wounds that would never heal. Deck was now part of the darkness inside me I'd never escape from.

His nod was barely distinguishable before he broke the connection and opened the car door.

I watched his lean form curl into the driver's seat.

The engine came to life with a loud purr.
Life. Something Connor had lost.
I turned away just as I heard the squeal of the tires on the street.
My perfect world had just been thrown into destructive chaos.

CHAPTER ONE

"RYLIE, LOOK! ULTIMATE cupcake of the day is here." Rylie snorted and looked over her shoulder at the guy unfolding from the blue Lexus. "Georgie, your *ultimate* is Deck Ryan and that is definitely not him. Secondly, Tristan is an arrogant arse with nothing going for him but a chiseled body and money. Total meatloaf." She pressed the button on the cappuccino maker and it hissed as the air spurted out and foamed the milk.

The bell on the door clanged.

I ran my tongue along my upper lip and walked to the cash register then placed my hands on the counter and leaned forward so my breasts were accentuated. They weren't anything special, but they were mine and I knew how to use them when needed.

Tristan was wearing his usual expensive business suit that clung to his striking form like bees to honey. When he started coming in a few weeks ago, he had a stick up his ass. Barely looked at me and sure as shit didn't take to my flirting. That was an issue because I needed him to look at me whether I wanted to or not.

I toyed with all the hotties to keep up appearances, but this guy was … special. I had to get his attention and a week ago, I got it. Now he flirted with me, and I suspected soon I'd have his number and a date.

Tristan strode toward me: tall, lean and with confidence written all over him. His looks matched his overbearing personality, short black hair, matching dark brows and a square jaw. Definite eye-candy except for the fact his intensity would scare the shit out of most women. Luckily, I wasn't most women.

"Tristan, you're looking make-out worthy, as usual." I lowered my voice so it sounded kind of husky and just loud enough for him to hear. "If only I could be your coffee cup."

He definitely caught what I said because his brows raised a minute amount and the corner of his mouth twitched. A blue streak of my hair fell forward over my shoulder and he reached out and lifted it, caressing the long, fine hairs between his fingers.

"Blue?"

Yesterday, I had pink streaks, but blue was Tristan's favorite color according to his choice in car and the dress shirts he always wore. I really didn't give a shit what color my hair was, except I'd never do orange. Didn't liked the color and besides, it would clash with my green eyes.

I winked. "Was feeling a little blue last night." Actually, that wasn't a lie. My friends Emily and Kat were out of town, and our usual Sunday brunch at my place was put on hold. And Deck … yeah, he was on some dangerous mission overseas which I hated. My life was supposed to be easier with him gone—and it was without him watching over me—and yet, it wasn't because I worried about him. I missed him constantly, but when he was here, it was … painful.

I glanced over my shoulder at Rylie. "Tristan's usual, babe."

"My girl can't be blue." My girl? That was new. He could call me whatever the hell he wanted as long as I got what I needed. "I may have to do something about that." My hair slipped from his grasp as he reached into his pocket, pulled out a five and slid it toward me. "Dinner?"

Finally. Progress. I put my hand on my hip and smiled. "You're smokin' hot, but dating you is against the rules of the establishment." Tristan was a challenge, and therefore he'd like a challenge. Kissing his feet, so to speak, just wouldn't hack it with this guy.

"Isn't this your coffee shop?"

How did he know that? I didn't have it posted anywhere and had never mentioned it. I was betting he had some poor sap with ankle-length dress pants sitting at a crappy desk in an office with no windows researching chicks Tristan wanted to fuck. "My place, my rules. Dating clients is at the top of the list of 'fuck no'."

He laughed and it was a rumbling sound which, if I was interested, would've done something for me. I wasn't. At least, not in any sexual capacity. "Clients? It's a coffee shop."

Asshole. A coffee shop was a business and mine was damn successful. I slid my hand across the counter and took his five, making certain my finger brushed against his. Then I hit the cash button and the drawer bounced open with a loud ding. "And I take pride in my work place. Besides, if you sucked in bed, I'd have to ask you not to come here again. You know … reminders and really awkward."

He placed his palms on the counter and his playful smile disappeared. "I *do* suck in bed, Georgie." His voice lowered as he leaned closer. "I suck until you scream and beg."

I bit my lower lip, the five-dollar bill still in my grasp now crumpled in a ball, and despite not wanting him, that was friggin' hot.

"That won't be happening."

I yelped at the deep, familiar voice behind Tristan and my heart took off at break-neck speed. My body became a fucked-up concoction of relief that he was back safe, sexual heat and nerves sparking. Deck being near me was a love-hate thing. Jesus, my life was a fireball rolling down a really dangerous path.

Rylie giggled as she slid Tristan's espresso across the counter then pinched my butt. I shot my gaze to her and glared; she smiled, her pearl-white teeth gleaming. She was laughing her ass off at me: One for yelping like a girlie-girl and two for being caught unaware by Deck. I hated that, but Deck could sneak up on a friggin' mouse. "You could've warned me," I mumbled to her.

She shrugged. "Could've, but that's no fun."

"Bitch."

She laughed then hesitantly smiled at Deck. "Hey, Deck."

Although his eyes remained on me, he nodded to Rylie. And when Deck looked at me, it was like he was touching my entire body with his hands—*penetrating*. Shit, that word and Deck *so* had to stay clear of one another.

11

I pushed the ball of money into the till, grabbed a coin then shut the cash drawer with my hip. I passed the change to Tristan who was now half-turned and looking at Deck.

Deck was about an inch taller than Tristan and more muscular, yet still lean and agile-looking. He had tatts running down both arms and a tribal design crawling up the side of his neck. His black t-shirt fit snug to the hills and valleys of his muscles, and I knew underneath that shirt was a plethora of hard abs. I had, after all, woken up in his bed after he'd hauled me out of some bar or party. Of course, Deck always crashed on the couch, but I'd seen him with his shirt off a number of times. Sometimes, I wish I hadn't because it certainly didn't make my life any easier.

Deck had that intimidating factor. Confident. Unyielding. And the guy hid his emotions like they were in a vault. Not knowing how to read him made him unpredictable like he was right now. He could either *let* Tristan walk away, or he'd *make* Tristan walk away and I'd lose a client and the date I needed.

"Sweetpea, you're back." Just looking at Deck made me want to kiss him. It took everything in me to just stand there and not leap over the counter and jump into his arms. In all the years we'd known one another, I'd never felt his lips on me. I never would, either. I knew that. I'd been told that. I'd been warned to keep it that way.

Deck had no interest in me anyway. I was a pain in his ass. If he only knew how much of a threat I was to him.

Tristan frowned and his eyes flashed with annoyance. "Boyfriend?"

I laughed. "Nope. Master." Tristan's brows rose and Deck's lowered even further. "Kidding." Well, sort of. "Badass is a friend—of sorts. You know, the kind of friend you can't get rid of. Kick him in the ass and he just keeps coming back like a lost puppy dog." But Deck was no puppy dog. More like a fire-breathing dragon.

Tristan pocketed his coin then curled his hand around his espresso, lifted it and took a sip like he always did. It was as if he wanted to be certain we hadn't fucked up his order which we never did unless it was on purpose. "Interesting analogy," he drawled. "Not sure it fits." Yeah, it was more like Deck was the bull and I was the red cape. Tristan nodded to me. "Like the blue. My number's on the five dollar bill."

And success.

A week ago, I'd messed up his espresso and loaded five tablespoons of sugar in it and half milk. That sip he always took ended up in my face in a spray of hot liquid. It was the first time he'd ever really looked at me; the guy always had his eyes on his phone. I had winked at him and the annoyance in his expression disappeared and was replaced by a scowl. I had calmly wiped the coffee from my face with a napkin then reached across and dabbed the corners of his mouth. I passed him his real espresso and said, "You have sexy-as-hell eyes. Might want to use them every now and then." At first, he just watched me intensely for a few seconds as if assessing me. I didn't flinch or waver, merely stared back at him with a half-cocked smile. I think he liked that because slowly, a grin formed and then he chuckled.

Now, he came in every day and made eye contact and conversation.

I glanced up at Deck who didn't look at all perturbed by Tristan's invitation. Typical. I lowered my voice but knew Deck could still hear me. "Just so we're clear, I don't do relationships. One-nighters only."

Tristan burst out laughing. "I can do that. Call me." And then he nodded to Deck and headed for the door. I was impressed; Tristan wasn't at all threatened by him.

I smiled, looking at Deck. Yep, he was clenching his fists and ready to throttle me. The guy was super-protective ever since my brother died. Well, two years after that actually, because Deck vanished the day he told me Connor was dead. I saw him briefly at the funeral, but he didn't stick around.

Every day, I expected him to come back. If I heard a car door shut outside my house, my heart would start to race and I'd run to the window to see if it was him. Or if I'd get an email from an unknown address, I'd open it with my breath held hoping it was from Deck. It never was.

Then things changed and I stopped waiting, and stopped caring.

When he did finally come back, I tried to avoid him, but avoiding Deck was like pushing away a cement truck with your baby finger. It just wasn't happening. We argued about it … okay, I argued while he merely ignored me. He said he left because he had to go back to his team overseas. I didn't fault him for that. What I was pissed off for was he never contacted me. Then I felt stupid because why the hell would he keep in contact with his best friend's kid sister?

Deck was fearless, something I completely lacked when I was sixteen, and it drew me to him. Despite him being intimidating with the

13

way he seemed to own an entire room, sometimes when he looked at me I saw a softness that made my heart pound and my stomach flutter.

Connor told me Deck had spent time in Juvie then on the streets. When I'd asked what he'd done, Connor shrugged it off and said nothing he wouldn't have done himself. That made him a bit of a mystery, which intrigued me.

The thing was I'd only technically met him three times before my brother died. Once, he stayed with us for two weeks when he and Connor were on leave from the Army. Then before he and Connor went for training with the JTF2: Joint Task Force, an elite anti-terrorist unit. And again when they came home from duty. I'd asked Connor why Deck always came to our place, and he told me he didn't really have any other place to go. I'd asked what about his family, but Connor just shrugged and said the team was Deck's family.

Then Connor died and shit changed.

I hated that Deck saw me break that day. I hated that he lived and my brother died, and I hated that I'd wanted him to hold me and take the pain away. Then I hated him more because he didn't. Deck was everything I wasn't that day—strong, controlled and unafraid.

Then he left and my life catapulted into the same darkness I'd seen in Deck's eyes. There was no question I was completely fucked up after that. My parents had been so caught up in their own grief they assumed I was just grieving, as well, and I was, but it was much more than that. It was the hell I suffered for months after Connor's death. Deck didn't know it, but it was thoughts of him which gave me the strength to survive what I went through. He was my solid.

The door swung closed after Tristan, and I watched him fold back into his car then drive away. Deck hadn't moved, and I felt the heat in my belly burn as he watched me. After all these years, he still unnerved me. The man could be standing on the other side of a football field and still make me quiver. I just wasn't sure yet if it was quivering with nerves or quivering because I was turned on. I was going with a blend, and that could—and would—destroy me if he got too close.

I glanced over my shoulder for Rylie, but she had snuck away to clean tables which didn't need cleaning. Tanner, an old friend of sorts, sat at a table tapping away on his laptop with his earphones in, hat pulled down low over his face. He glanced up at me, then at Deck, frowned and went back to typing. Tanner didn't really like Deck, although they'd never formally met and never would.

Deck approached me. He was my only weakness and no matter what I did, I couldn't get him out of me. And I'd tried.

I smiled. "Hey, baby, when did you get back?" He hated when I called him 'baby' and I knew this by the way the muscles in his arms tightened. "Kill anyone this trip?" I was gambling he had.

"You planning on dating him?"

Straight to the point, as always. I raised my brows. "Who?"

Deck scowled. "Georgie."

"Come on, Deck. You don't know already?" His brows lowered. "Well, he's been coming here for three weeks." Deck's security cameras would've told him that. When I'd bought the coffee shop, he'd had them installed, said they were a deterrent for burglars. I knew it was another way for Deck to keep his eye on me.

His men came and collected the footage randomly and I was betting Deck had them research every regular customer who walked in my shop. Last week, I gave them all a treat. After I closed, I blared the music and did an erotic dance standing on the counter right in front of the camera. My guess, Deck hadn't seen that yet or I'd have heard about it.

"You know who that guy is?" he asked.

I crossed my arms, more to cover my nipples, which I knew were erect from the shivers coursing down my spine. "In what context? Because my guess is who he is in the bedroom is entirely different than who he is when he walks in here." I let my voice trail off at the end, which was probably a good idea because Deck's scowl was pretty menacing. "Guess I'll find out now that I have his number." I pressed the button on the till, and it dinged and popped open. Then I took the five-dollar bill Tristan gave me and smoothed it out. "Maybe a threesome would be—"

"Not in the mood, Georgie."

I rolled my eyes. "You're never in the mood."

He knew exactly what I was referring to as I teased him all the time about us having sex. Of course, I was off the menu.

He went to grab the bill from me and I quickly shoved it in my pocket. "That's this week's one-nighter."

"You don't have one-nighters and if you did, I'd be stopping them." True, sorta, kinda. I'd never had a one-night stand, but really that was my choice, not his. But I let him think what he wanted. I scrunched my nose then went and poured him a black coffee. "Vagina blocker," I mumbled, but he heard because I saw the corners of his lips twitch when I looked over my shoulder at him. Nice to know he liked some of my humor.

I'd dated several men over the years, and Deck did his overprotective thing and checked them out. He probably knew more about the guys I dated than I did. The thing was I had to be careful about the men I didn't want him checking into. Tristan … well, as far as I knew, there was nothing on him except he owned Mason Development and dated a lot of women.

Deck placed a five on the counter when I came back with his black coffee. I never took the money. Well, I did because he insisted, but I placed it in a pink elephant piggy bank I kept under the counter. There was no reason why I did this except I didn't want his money and he refused to take free coffee. So, I put it in the piggy bank and saved it. He knew I did it—shit, Deck knew just about everything I did … except what was the most important. What bothered me was being *bothered* in a way I couldn't ease except with a battery-operated device named Deck.

"You off work now?"

"Is that a question, Deck? Really?" Deck didn't ask questions he already knew the answers to and he knew exactly what time I left the coffee shop on Tuesdays. "You must want something from me. Ah, I know, you've missed carrying me out of bars these last few weeks you've been away? Well, I'd let you do it here, but my one customer might think you're kidnapping me."

"I want you to stop drinking." No bullshit, Deck. Straight to the heart of what was pissing him off, and as usual, it was me. "What the fuck, Georgie? Every night? What the hell is going on with you?"

"Not every night. And I like to go out." I'd been overdoing it lately because my girls were gone and Deck or his men had been watching me closer than usual. Tanner had warned me to cool it on the drinking thing.

"What was with last weekend?" He must have heard already about my little episode at Avalanche on Saturday.

"I wasn't that drunk. And the band asked me to get on stage and sing with them." Semi-sort of truth. The band *had* asked me to get on stage, but the singing part was all me. I'd been seeking the attention of a guy who was alone drinking in the back of the bar. I knew the type of guy. He wouldn't go for a chick who threw herself at him, so I got it another way. And I was good at what I did, but getting carried off stage by security was not in the plans.

"We need to talk," Deck said.

Oh, that couldn't be good. Deck needing to talk meant he was talking, I was listening and then he laid down more rules. Luckily, he hadn't yet tapped my phone or computer. I suspected if that happened, all hell would break loose. And it was a hell he wasn't going to be cool with. "Can't." I grabbed my purse from under the counter and made for the back exit. "Just scored a date. I have to wash my hair." A lie. I wouldn't be calling Tristan for at least a week.

"Georgie." That warning tone sent tremors down my spine. Yeah, I liked it. How totally screwed up was that? I was pretty immune to most men—I'd trained myself to be—and yet, Deck was my kryptonite. The worst part was everyone knew it, which made it dangerous for him and me.

I didn't want to talk about the drinking. It was a never-ending conversation, and one I wasn't going to fix anytime soon. But what I didn't like was that Emily had mentioned it before she left with her fiancé's band, Tear Asunder, a few weeks ago. Hearing it from her hit hard, because I knew her mom was a real shitty mom who'd been a drunk. I hated worrying Emily like that, but that was who I'd become to everyone. I liked to party, had a sassy mouth and lived under Deck's thumb. For now, it was staying that way.

I made it into the stock room all the way to the emergency exit before Deck grabbed my arm, hauling me to a stop. I didn't struggle, there was no point. He'd win.

I sighed and leaned against the door. "Okay, sexy. Let's get this over with."

Deck stepped in close. So close, I could feel the beat of his heart against my breasts and his warm breath tickled the fine hairs on my skin. He loosened his grip on my arm then his other hand came up and cupped my chin. My insides were having an all-out rave and I was wishing I hadn't worn my thong. I needed grannie panties with what was happening between my legs. No control when it came to Deck. Jesus.

"You're not going out with him."

I sighed. *Here we go.* "Why not?"

"Because he's an arrogant ass." And he obviously had checked up on Tristan.

"I find that kind of hot. Besides, *you're* an arrogant ass."

Deck didn't look impressed. Actually, he moved further into my space so his leg was between mine. "This isn't up for discussion."

"No, it's not." Because discussing anything with Deck just didn't happen.

"Babe." Jesus, I seriously hated when he called me that. It made me want to jump him. It also made him sound ... well, real and human, not cold and uncompassionate. But most of all, it made him sound like I was his. "I don't like the blue. Change it."

A squeak of outrage escaped my mouth, but I shouldn't have been surprised. When Deck spoke, he told you the truth. With him—no pretence. The complete opposite of me.

I went to smack him, but he got a lock on my upper arms. I struggled, wiggling pretty pathetically considering he was twice my weight and a head taller. "I'm dating him, and since when is my hair any of your business?" Deck had no filter, kind of like me. Except I talked fantasy and bullshit; he talked real-life honesty.

"Were you singing on stage drunk? Did security have to drag you off stage? Did Matt cut you off?"

Shit, total change of topic and not in my favor. "Tyler has a big mouth." He was one of Deck's guys from his company Unyielding Riot. The men who worked for Deck were either ex-military, ex-gang or ex-fucked-up and dangerous. Wherever they came from, they all had specialized skills of some kind needed for the work they did, and most of it was illegal. But from what I knew, it was eliminating this world of some of the worst assholes.

When Deck went away on a mission, most of the time one of his men would stay back and keep an eye on me. Overprotective, obsessive-compulsive control freak. Could've used that when he left me for those two years.

"You holler, pretty girl?"

Deck's hands dropped from me as the steady drum of boots came toward us. Tyler had a coffee in hand and a broad grin on his face.

He was a definite cupcake—no second-guessing or wondering if you should take a bite or pass. He was a 'grab it and taste while you had the chance'. And chances with Tyler would be quick considering he wasn't the type to stick around for breakfast in the morning.

"Told you I'd be out in five," Deck said.

Tyler shrugged, ignoring Deck's frown. "Five, two, ten; it's all the same."

I laughed because that was such bullshit. Tyler had also been in the elite JTF2, and one second off could mean the difference of life or death. There was no half-assing the time. "Tyler, hon. I was just going to tell Deck about us." I saw him visibly swallow and his bright-blue eyes widen with alarm as I playfully smiled and winked at him. Deck's gaze shot to Tyler and I sweetened the pot. "It's nothing serious, Deck. Just a few nights of us fooling around."

Tyler stepped back and his hand tightened around his cup, which made the lid pop off and coffee spill over the top. He yelled as the hot liquid burnt his skin and he dropped the cup, black steaming liquid splattering onto the floor.

I watched with amusement, biting my lower lip to stop from laughing aloud because I wanted to play this out a little longer … until I saw Deck's face.

"Deck." I grabbed for him as he dove for Tyler. "Deck. I was kidding." Whoa, I wasn't expecting this reaction. Deck was always in control. Tyler moved too late as Deck slammed his fist into his face, and he staggered backward, landing hard on his ass.

"Fuck." Tyler shook his head. "I never touched her, boss."

"Deck." I ran up and stood in front of him, placing my palms on his chest. "You look smokin' hot, all badass and shit, but Tyler and I … yeah, so not happening. I was just kidding around." I looked over my shoulder at Tyler still sitting on the ground, rubbing his jaw. "You didn't have to tell him everything that happened Saturday night."

"Pretty girl, you know I have to."

Yeah, I did. I moved away from Deck who was silent and still looking from me to Tyler. "But, you said you wouldn't mention the security thing."

"And you really remember our chat that night?" Tyler said, brows rising.

I did, but of course, he wouldn't think that. I had been slurring my words and stumbling. "Rylie said—"

He huffed. "Rylie was drunk off her ass, too." Yeah, she was the perfect partner, and she didn't even know it. Tyler got to his feet and before I saw what was coming, he hauled off and shot Deck one in the jaw. Except Deck didn't go down, just staggered back a step. "I know the fuckin' rules."

A Deck rule—no messing with his dead best friend's sister. I'd overheard him telling his men this when he first came back when I was eighteen … well, just turned nineteen.

He'd been in the back of my coffee shop with Josh, Tyler and Vic after installing all the security cameras. I was bringing them coffees when I heard him say, "Connor's sister is off-limits."

Tyler had laughed. "Damn, are you claiming her, Boss?"

"Fuck no," Deck replied. "She's off-limits to all of us."

The coffees ended up on the floor as the churning mix of emotions threw me in a dark, closed cistern while his words echoed in my head.

At that time, I'd still had hope for Deck and me, even though it was a dangerous thought because I knew better for a number of reasons. But just hearing him say that, the reality of Deck and me never becoming anything more than what we were—and I wasn't even sure what that was—came crashing to the ground and disappeared beneath the rubble of cement.

It broke me. And here I thought I had already been broken.

I remember the second our eyes met, locked, and then his cool mask of unemotional glare seeped into me.

I must have looked a sight with coffee spilled down the front of me. It had burned my skin, yet I didn't feel the pain; only emotional pain was filtering through me. Then came the pissed off, and I kicked one of the empty coffee cups next to my foot.

"Why the fuck not?" I'd yelled.

Deck, in his usual calm manner, merely said because he said so—period. Well, the period became an abrupt dash when I freaked. My control on my emotions was still a work in progress at the time. I walked straight up to Josh who'd been standing beside the stock shelf and kissed him.

Josh's hands came to my hips and I felt the slight push, but then his mouth eased under mine and I heard him groan. It only lasted a few seconds before we both pulled back at the same time.

I had no interest in Josh or any of Deck's men. It was the point. It was then my anger turned to disgust with myself for being so weak when I'd been trying hard for the last two years to get past these feelings I had for Deck.

The guys had made themselves scarce as Deck and I stared at one another and then he said, "My men are off-limits to you because every mission we go on, there is a good chance one of us might not come back. Your brother never wanted that for you." Then he left and we never discussed it again.

Deck ran his hand over the top of his head, then down his face. The flicker of uneasiness in his eyes was unusual for him. Steady as a rock, but something was different in him. I noticed it over the last few months. He was gone most of the time and when he was here, he was distant. Well, he was always distant, but something wasn't sitting right and I had yet to figure it out. What worried me was if it had anything to do with me, and I wasn't talking about the drinking.

Deck shook his head. "Jesus, this shit is fucking with me."

"What shit?" I looked between both men, but they remained quiet. Fear skidded like little skipping pebbles across my skin. I hated this. I hated that Deck could be taken away from me just as quickly and suddenly as my brother. It fucked with my head ... the only thing that still did. "What's wrong?"

Tyler put his hand out as if to pat Deck's shoulder and backed off, lowering it again. "We'll get it done." What would they get done? He nodded to a camera up in the corner of the stock room. "Oh, and the security feed ... nine pm last Monday. We can watch it on the plane later. I'll bring popcorn."

Shit. My dance. Tyler winked at me then grabbed his empty cup and walked back out to the front of the coffee shop where I heard him asking Rylie for a refill.

"I'm not going to like it, am I?" Deck said.

"No." Deck hated my choice in clothes, hair, and the way I flirted. He was really going to hate me doing a sexy dance for the camera knowing Tyler had watched it. "You're leaving again? You just got back." I asked, but I already knew he was going to New York.

"Just a couple days."

"You mean you can track down, torture and kill a guy in a couple days? Impressive." Whenever he came back from something bad, he had a dark, cold look in his eyes, which took a few days to get back to normal. I knew this trip to New York wasn't like that.

"No. Just business. I need Tyler with me and the others are still overseas, but they're meeting us there. So that leaves you alone."

My brows rose. "Seriously, Deck. I'm not a kid anymore."

"Then act it."

Jesus, sometimes I just want to... Before I could react, he reached for me and cupped the back of my neck, drawing me in close. My breath hitched and I knew he heard it because his dark walnut eyes blackened.

"The drinking, partying ... you're right, you're not a kid. That shit has to stop and ..." He sighed and his hand on my neck tightened. "Georgie, things might be changing. I need you to be ready."

Fuck. Did he know? I didn't think he did. He couldn't. I was careful. "What's that supposed to mean?" I shivered as his fingers slid into my hair and for a second, I was thinking he was going to drag me up against him and kiss me. Stupid thinking. I should be thinking of what the hell he meant by things changing.

He suddenly let me go and stepped back. "It means I need all my men with me, and we can't be around if you get into trouble. So get your shit together." He paused and I was still reeling from his words. I hate my life. "And I find out you dated Tristan, things will change more than you may want them to. The fuckin' guy has a revolving door of women coming from his place. Stay away from him."

"Tristan? Who's that again?" I asked innocently.

He half-smiled then shook his head and turned, striding toward the door back into the coffee shop.

"I can date whoever I want, Deck." I liked Deck's protective side. Sure, it made my life difficult and sometimes pissed me off, but it made me feel as if he cared about me and I was holding onto that with both hands.

"Try me," he shot back.

I grabbed the closest thing to me, a can of coffee grinds, and threw it at him. It hit the doorframe beside his head and he didn't even flinch as he walked through the swinging door.

22

I heard a loud bang and the bell of the front door rang. A second later, Rylie came running into the stock room. "Shit, what the hell was that? Oh, my God, Deck's face. Georgie, he was pissed. I've never seen him hit anything before. He's always so … together."

I plopped down onto my ass on the floor then lay back, putting my arm over my eyes. "I'm friggin' exhausted." I'd had it. I couldn't do this anymore. I had to get Deck out of my head.

"Umm, Georgie? You okay?"

"We still on for tomorrow night?" I asked. It was Wednesday night, and I had to go to Avalanche where I knew there was a good chance someone was there I wanted to meet. Well, wanted was the wrong word. I *had* to meet.

"Ah, about that."

I sat up. "Jesus. He talked to you?"

Rylie nodded. "I wouldn't use the word 'talk'. After he punched the side of the espresso machine, he told me to lay off the bars with you."

"Bullshit. What did he really say?"

She held out her hand; I took it then she pulled me to my feet. "'The fuckin' bars are off-limits for Georgie'."

"Him and his off-limits."

Rylie put her arm around my shoulders and I knew she was bailing on me for tomorrow night. Deck really did scare her and I guess if you didn't know him like I did, then she had the right to be scared.

Rylie was the same height as me, five-foot-five, and she was conservative as much as I wasn't. Her hair was always perfectly pulled back tight in a ponytail while mine was all over the place, hadn't seen scissors in years and had been every color of the rainbow. I wore skimpy clothes I found in Kensington market downtown, which never matched and she bought smart sets from the mall.

But we got along with one another. We'd connected instantly when I hired her a few months ago, I think partly because I used to be a lot like her. With my best friends busy, Emily horse-whispering and Kat painting, both with their men who were in the hit band Tear Asunder, I needed another cohort to party with. Rylie may be straight-laced, but she liked to dance, drink and party, which was exactly what I needed.

"Deck doesn't own me. And I'm going out. You can come or not. Either way, I'm drinking Deck out from between my legs." It was time.

I had to get him out of me and stop holding onto something he'd never take—me.

Rylie winced. "Maybe we should cool it for a few days. We've been partying hard for weeks. Besides, I'm low on cash. Unless you intend to give me a raise?" She smiled.

I laughed. "Babe, I love you, but you just had one. And now, I'm out of here. Patrick will be in any minute for the evening shift." Her cheeks flushed and I happy-danced my eyebrows. "And you need to fuck that man. Seriously. He likes you and he's in the cupcake club, so he's totally allowed to be shagged in the back of the shop after close. That's if you don't mind being on camera."

Rylie giggled then shoved me away. "I'm not sleeping with him. He's slept with every hot chick who's walked in the place."

"Well, then he must know what he's doing."

"I'll sleep with Patrick the day you sleep with Deck."

"Oh, I sleep with Deck every single night."

Rylie laughed and walked toward the front. "Vibrators named Deck don't count."

I stuck my tongue out at her before she disappeared from view. She laughed.

Grabbing my purse off the floor near the fire exit, I opened it, took out my cell and dialed *his* number.

DECK

I FUCKED UP. With this shit going down and now leaving without a man on her … I didn't like it. Not when I had a job in the works, which could affect her. If there was any leak of who we were after, she could become a target. The last time she became a target, Georgie had nearly gotten herself killed by leaping out of the attic on top a guy who had a fuckin' gun on her best friend, Emily. The sick fuck, Alfonzo, trained girls then sold them into the sex trade. Georgie had been drugged up and taken to a warehouse where the transporter was going to ship her, Emily and this girl, Raven—real name, London—off to God knows where. Jesus, if that had happened … girls rarely ever came back from that shit.

They disappeared.

That day had been the second worst day of my life.

I was on edge and rarely did I lose it. Today, I did. I fuckin' punched Tyler. The rage that tore through me after hearing he fucked her … it blew my mind apart. Control completely obliterated at the thought of Georgie screaming Tyler's name as he plowed into her. Losing control was not something I let in. I couldn't. I lost it once and it landed me in Juvie for six months and then on the streets for two years until I hit eighteen and joined the Canadian armed forces.

I walked outside the coffee shop Georgie called Perk Avenue, and the summer air hit my heated skin, doing fuck-all to cool the anger simmering inside me.

Tyler was leaning against the brick wall, a blade of grass in his mouth, one leg cocked with his foot resting on the wall. He pushed away and approached me, spitting the grass onto the sidewalk.

"All good?"

I looked at him and he smirked. Asshole. He knew damn well nothing was ever good with Georgie. And now it was worse. This wasn't just a young girl partying and drinking anymore. This was Georgie having a drinking problem.

At least she'd never had a boyfriend—thank fuck. I checked out every guy she had dates with, which was as Tyler said, 'fuckin' shit-ass crazy', but I made a promise to her brother and I never broke my word.

Some of the men were pansies or in serious debt or had shit jobs and I wanted to stop her from dating them. But I kept my opinion to myself—most of the time. When I didn't was when guys like Tristan, who had a different woman every day of the week, wanted to date her.

This was about protecting her against the scum, the assholes and the womanizers. And yes, men like me. Men who had a fuck of a good chance of not coming home.

Of course there were times like now when I didn't have a man on her and had no clue what she was up to, and Georgie was often up to no good.

I couldn't figure out what the fuck she was doing lately.

The drinking … fuck, I couldn't understand it or stop it. It was the one part of Georgie I had no control over. At first, it had been hard partying on the weekends then slowly over the last few months, it became

25

more often until I found the little bottles in her purse.

What was really fucked up was it didn't fit who she was. I knew she was better than that. She was too stubborn and determined, too fuckin' sure of herself to be an alcoholic, yet I dragged her ass out of bars too many times to recall.

The thing was, Georgie thought she was indestructible. And she was because I was there, or one of my men, to haul her ass out of whatever trouble she landed herself in.

I opened the door of my Audi and got in. Tyler hopped in the passenger side and I started the car and headed to the airport. I'd been staying away from Georgie for the last few months, getting some distance. I didn't like who she was becoming and I hated seeing it. I felt like she was slipping away and yet I didn't know how to stop it.

"I don't get it. The way she looks at you ..." Tyler sighed shaking his head. "She loves you, Boss."

I tightened my hands around the wheel. "She loves the idea of me saving her ass all the time so she can drink herself into a fuckin' coma. She doesn't know shit about who I am."

"Sure she does. She may not know the bad shit, what you're capable of ... but she knows you care about her. She knows you protect your men with your life. Boss, Georgie met you before you started Unyielding Riot. That girl fell for you eons ago and Connor knew it, too."

I directed my eyes on Tyler. "You hear what you just said?"

Tyler leaned his head back and closed his eyes. "Piss on it. Connor isn't coming back. All the leads are dust. Don't know why we're chasing a ghost."

"And you hear what else you just said?"

Tyler sighed, shaking his head.

Whether Connor was dead or alive, I wouldn't break my promise to him. My word was one part of my soul which hadn't been tainted by the shit I'd been around over the years. Every day was getting worse. I felt the numbness leaking into me when I tortured some sick fuck that had pissed off the wrong people.

When I watched Vic pull out a man's teeth or rip off his fingernails, I didn't hear the screams, or smell the urine, or see the suffering. All I saw was a scumbag, and I wouldn't yield to anyone.

But I did.

I yielded to Georgie.

I'd let her seep into my veins and take hold, and no matter how many men I killed or women I fucked, I couldn't get her out of me.

"You sure it's safe?"

I knew exactly what Tyler was talking about. Was the location in New York safe? Was the guy we were meeting safe? "No." I didn't trust the bastard. Kai was elusive, had a hell of a lot of money and a non-existent history. That meant it was hidden, and hidden was dangerous. "But I owe him." Kai had helped me with the situation involving that sex trafficker. He'd shown up looking for the transporter responsible for shipping the women. We collaborated because he had already set up a meeting with Alfonzo. Led us right to the girls and the transporter. Kai told me he'd ask for a favor in return for the help that day.

Two days ago, he asked.

"What do you think he wants?"

"A guy like Kai …" Kai was known to be the hired man in the underworld to do the jobs no one else wanted—even me. I didn't risk my men without a fuck of a good reason, even for a shitload of money. I knew the jobs to take and the ones to pass on. Kai was the unknown, his morals shaky, and that was dangerous. "Fuck if I know."

CHAPTER TWO

Georgie

"**M**HMM, SWEETNESS," I purred beneath his mouth. He put his hand in my hair and tugged me in closer so my body was against him, breasts pressed into his hard chest.

He backed me against the bar. I heard the beer topple over then the slow drip of liquid as it spilt to the floor.

I groaned at the pressure, but the pain against my spine felt good. I liked pain, it breathed life into me as if … as if I was being set free. It was totally fucked up, but my entire life was fucked up, so it didn't really bother me.

He was a sweet kisser; no slimy wet tongue invading my mouth like a fish on steroids. Instead, he did it with finesse, the tip of his tongue pushing past my lips to play with mine. But sweet didn't do it for me.

"Gorgeous, let's take this to my place." He pulled back and his hand stroked down my back to my ass where he fondled with a slow, squeezing motion.

Bingo. I moaned, leaning into him then put my fingers in his hair at the back of his neck. It was time. It had to be tonight; Deck was gone and so were his men. I planned on getting two things accomplished tonight, and everything was falling into place.

I reached between us, slid my hand over the top of his jeans and felt the hard swelling. "Potential, definitely. Okay, sugar, let's get this done."

He chuckled. "Sounds like a chore."

He had no idea. He tightened his grip in my hair and drew me in for another kiss. It wasn't hard and demanding like I yearned for, but it would do until I had what I wanted. He let me go with a deep groan then took my hand and pulled me through the crowd toward the door.

"Georgie!"

I turned to see Matt coming out of the back of the bar, phone to his ear. Shit. I knew exactly who he was talking to, but there was nothing I could do about it. I couldn't hear what he said before he hung up and shoved his cell into his back pocket, but by the stiffness of his stride, he was pissed. Matt was my friend, Kat's brother, and owned Avalanche. It was my local hangout, and lately I was here more often than I was at home. Matt was in the hot group with his tall, lean frame and stark, square features. In all the years I'd known him, though, he'd remained single. I'd seen the girls slip him notes, no doubt their numbers on it, but if he did hook up he kept it private.

Lionel's hand tightened around mine as I came to a stop. He glanced down at me then looked up at the approaching Matt. "Don't tell me you have a boyfriend?"

"Relax, Luther—"

"Lionel," he corrected, frowning.

I flicked my hand in the air and laughed. "Whatever, sweets." I knew his name; I just didn't care. Besides, I was supposed to be drunk and slurring my words.

Matt stopped in front of us, took a second to eye the guy then looked back at me. "You need a ride home?" His lips pursed together tight as he looked at my hand in Lionel's. "Thinking you probably do. Give me five and I'll drive you."

Shit, that would fuck up everything I had planned. "Nah, I'm good." I winked at him. His glower deepened and his eyes narrowed in on my date.

"Georgie, you've had a lot to drink." Yeah, no shit, Inspector Badger. I'd ordered five shots and four rye and gingers from Brett, the bartender, although it didn't mean I drank them all. I had more than I usually did, but I was still sober enough to get the job done. I had made sure Lionel drank plenty of shots. When his eyes got that half-lidded look, I knew it was time to go.

Matt chin lifted to Lionel. "Listen, bud, think you better leave."

"Yeah, that's what we're doing," Lionel said.

And thank you, Lionel.

"Alone," Matt said.

Now, that pissed me off. Jesus, I just needed to get this shit over with. I wasn't usually nervous with what I had to do, but tonight was different and already I was having second thoughts. "Oh, go suck on some pussy, Matt. Just because you're not getting any doesn't mean you have to ruin my night." I turned away and started walking to the door, but Lionel's hand was still in mine and he was standing still, so I only made it two steps before I was sling-shot back into his chest.

"Georgie, not a good idea. You're drunk." Matt's voice had an edge to it, which I completely ignored.

"Yeah, well, I like not good ideas. Let's go fuck, Lionel." A shiver went through me at my words. Screw it. I was letting go of him—of Deck.

Lionel shrugged then looped his arm around my waist and ushered me outside and into a cab. Before Matt had a chance to do anything, we pulled away from the curb.

The cab ride was more kissing with his hand up my skirt. I suspected the cab driver was getting a real nice show of my black lace panties in the rear view mirror.

When the cab stopped, Lionel threw him some cash then helped me out. He picked me up in his arms, swaying to the side a bit, and I wrapped my legs around his waist and my arms around his neck. Our lips locked and I heard him groan.

He was drunk, wanted me and we were at his place—perfect.

My heart pounded as I heard the sound of his key, then the door opening and slamming behind us. I did a quick glance around, taking in everything then mentally taking notes. Before he noticed, I whispered in his ear. "Ruin me." And it would be ruining—completely. Pathetic, really, but I was finally doing something about my pathetic-ism.

"I plan to." He set me on my feet in his bedroom but kept his arm tight around my waist. I titled my head back and moaned as his hand went beneath my shirt, lifting my bra out of the way to play with my nipples.

"Oh, man, you're incredible." He rubbed my nipple and it felt … like a rough, wool shirt was chafing my nipples back and forth. Really, I wanted him to pinch them, make it hurt, but Lionel was all gentle and sweet. My stomach knotted. It was like every touch was tying up my intestines. I had to do this. I was fucked up anyway. What did it matter if I gave myself to some pussy? It was about time.

He lowered me onto the bed then straddled me. I took in the layout of the room: bed, nightstand, dresser, no computer.

Once he passed out, I could do what I was supposed to do by coming here tonight.

"Shirt, gorgeous." He helped me take off my black-knit V-neck then groaned as he leaned over me, taking my nipple into his mouth, suckling then swirling his tongue around the pinkish glow.

"Harder." I wanted pain. It was my reminder that I was real.

He drew it into his mouth, and I arched my back into him hoping he'd bite down, but he didn't. Instead, he placed kisses across my breastbone to my other breast and squeezed it like it was a friggin' stress ball.

"I need inside you." As soon as he said it, I knew this wasn't going to happen. I'd thought maybe I could, but not like this. This wasn't the right guy, right time or right reason.

I'd have to live with my pathetic a little longer.

He slid off the bed and for a brief second, I thought of running. Escape. But it was in that brief second before I got my shit together.

I leaned up on my elbow and watched as Lionel lowered his zipper. Shit, I needed Plan B in action now. "How about you wait here and get naked and I'll find us some drinks."

An image of Deck flashed before me. His disappointment. His glacier expression. The fucked-up thing was I was wet just thinking about him. It was how I got through this shit. Deck always made me feel safe and protected, and yet he had no idea I hadn't been safe since he left when I was sixteen.

I bolted off the bed the second I heard the front door to his apartment. "You have a roommate?" Shit, what the hell. I was told he lived alone.

He shook his head.

"Fuck." No roommate. That meant … I snagged my top off the floor at the same time the bedroom door burst open, the wood splintering where the faceplate met the door frame.

"Jesus." Lionel swung around and staggered back, hitting the bed and falling onto it.

I gaped at Deck standing in the doorway, his eyes scanning the room as he did recon. Always in military mode even when breaking in some poor sap's place to drag his dead best friend's sister out. Shit, what the hell? He was supposed to be in New York. This was planned for when he was in New York.

"Get dressed."

His voice was the usual deep, abrupt sound, but I noticed a slight vibration to it. I knew Deck. I was addicted to him and his darkness, the pain always lingering in the depths of his eyes matching my own. Yet, that rumble in his voice I'd never heard before.

Goose bumps blazed across my skin as if I'd just touched an electric fence. "Weren't you supposed to be in New York, sweetpea?" My guess, Matt had been on the phone to Deck the second I showed up at Avalanche tonight. It was only an hour-and-a-half flight back to Toronto. This was a total screw-up. A warning from *him* would have been nice.

"Ah, fuck. Boyfriend? Hey, man, I didn't touch her," Lionel said, like the wimp-ass he was. He crawled off the opposite side of the bed as far away from Deck as he could.

Shit, couldn't blame the guy. Deck was freaking intimidating and no doubt was carrying a gun and knife or two … or three. Deck never went anywhere without a gun, even if it was against the law to carry a handgun in Toronto. I didn't think Deck cared much for laws, though. Besides, he knew people and that gave him a pass.

"Now." Deck's voice thundered through the room.

I pulled my bra back down then tugged on my top. It was inside out and backwards, the white tag showing in the front beneath my chin. I was attempting to turn it around without taking it off again and was having difficulty because really, I was a little freaked out that Deck caught me half-naked with a guy. That wasn't supposed to happen. I was always careful.

Damn it. I had the top up over my face, blinding me, but I hadn't taken my arms out.

Knuckles brushed against the bare skin of my abdomen as the edge of my top was grabbed. I sucked in my breath. I knew his touch, his scent; I'd recognize it anywhere. It was embedded in my brain like the negative side of a magnet rolling around, searching for its positive side. It only calmed when he was near.

Suddenly, my shirt was yanked off. Then, before I could focus or say 'what the hell', it was back on.

Damn, he smelled good. In my fantasies, he did too, and I had a lot of fantasies about him. At first, I fought them, but now I begged for them to haunt my nights. It was the only way I could have him. Any girl would romanticize Deck. Over six foot, with dark eyes and tatted-up, muscular arms—hard and untouchable. Actually, you'd be stupid to touch Deck, but I was good at stupid and often teased him by purposely touching him.

Right now, though, with him looking down at me with his eyes narrowed and his body tense as a metal post … yeah, even I knew when to shut it with Deck. He had thrown me over his shoulder and carried my ass out of bars numerous times and every time he did it, I felt the guilt wash over me.

"Listen, man, I didn't know she was yours. I was—"

That got my attention. "His? You think I belong to him? Like a fucking hamster? Listen here, cheesecake." Because he really was cheesecake, smooth with no hardness about him. Shit, he was even missing the best part … the crunchy granola. I started toward Lionel, my eyes blazing and my fists ready to smack him a good one. I was sick of men who were pissants. "I'm not a pet. I have—" I screeched as I felt my body fly into the air and land hard on my stomach over Deck's shoulder.

"Shut it."

I did because I had the wind knocked out of me and couldn't breathe. Plus, I felt kind of sick as my stomach sloshed with the five shots I'd consumed. So, I was a little tipsy tonight, nothing wrong with that.

Shit, I was going to throw up and it wouldn't be pretty all down Deck's back. I cupped my hand over my mouth and swallowed several times.

"She's mine. That means you touch her again and you'll be in a body bag." He abruptly turned on his heel, which did nothing for my uneasy stomach.

I caught a glimpse of Lionel, pale and cringing in the corner of the room. "Pussy," I blurted then clamped my hand over my mouth again as Deck strode out of the room. Tonight was a total fail, and I was so going to hear about it.

I WOKE UP to the familiar grey, sterile walls and the cold, smooth, black furniture, which was Deck's bedroom. I swung my legs over the side of the bed and saw the bottle of water on the nightstand half-gone. He'd forced me to take two pills and drink water before he put me in bed and tucked the covers in around me. Whenever he thought I was too drunk, he brought me back to his place. That was, whenever he was around.

I grabbed the bottle, cracked it open and tossed the lid on the floor as I tilted the liquid back until the plastic bottle was sucked dry. No matter how much I was immune to the drinks, I still felt like shit in the morning after having tossed back a few.

I set the empty bottle on the nightstand and it fell over then rolled to the floor. A little mess would do Deck some good. Besides, he was probably gone by now, considering it had to be … I looked out the window and saw the sun beaming high in the sky … noon. I'd woken up in Deck's bed—minus Deck, of course—enough times to know he was rarely around in the morning.

I shuffled to the bathroom, leaned my palms against the counter and looked at myself in the mirror. Makeup smudged, the dark black eyeliner in the corner of my eyes was exaggerated even more than usual with bright blue and gold now faded on my eyelids. A few sparkles were on my cheeks from the eye shadow. I tried to run my fingers through my blue streaked mass of hair, but they got caught in the mess and I groaned as I tried to disentangle them.

I didn't recognize who stared back at me, and I really didn't care. No expectations. That was the best way to live. I'd done it for so long now it was second nature.

I looked away and snagged Deck's blue toothbrush hanging in the metal holder on the wall. I opened the drawer, piled a ton of toothpaste on the tip and stuck it in my mouth.

I wonder if he knew I used his toothbrush every time I stayed here. Ha … Deck knew everything. He was the sniper of knowing everything, except what was right in front of him—me. He didn't know me. Although, it wasn't his fault. I did everything I could to make certain he didn't.

I spit into the sink then brushed some more, trying to get rid of the sandpaper feeling on my tongue and down my throat. I spit again, stuck my mouth under the running water and swooshed.

"What were you thinking?"

I spit my mouthful of water into the sink. "Jesus, Deck. Make some noise when you enter a room, would ya?"

I held up his toothbrush and smiled. His brows rose, but he said nothing. I put it back then turned off the taps.

"I asked you a question."

I grabbed a facecloth from the metal basket on the counter. "Heard you, too. Just not feeling up to answering your sexy ass right now." I turned on the water again, wet the cloth then looked in the mirror while I wiped away the makeup smudges under my eyes.

I was paying attention to the big, black mascara mark under my left eye when I should've been paying attention to Deck, because you should always pay attention to Deck. He was quick, agile and reminded me of a panther. He had those penetrating eyes too that knew which way you were going to run before you knew yourself.

He was behind me before I had the chance to stand up straight.

"In my personal space, sexy. Want to back off?" Before my body betrayed me and I was panting for him to grab me and kiss me like in one of my fantasies.

Deck had never kissed me and it pissed me off that my body reacted that way around him. He was my grim reaper when it came to having a love life of any kind, but I couldn't help my body's reaction to him; it had always been that way. Love can't be stopped. I should know. I'd been living with him wrapped around my heart since I was sixteen. Even when my life changed into something that wasn't real, my feelings for Deck never faltered.

He didn't back off. Instead, the heat from his body seeped into me and I wanted to dunk my head in the toilet and flush. But that would mean moving and if I did, my butt would be against his cock ... no, he was tall ... his cock against the small of my back. Whichever, it was so not a good idea.

"What you did was reckless."

I sighed and tossed the facecloth down on the edge of the sink. Reckless—no. Stupid to get caught by Deck—yes. A blob of toothpaste sat in the bottom of the stark-white sink and the urge to clean it away hit me, but I couldn't. That wasn't who I was now.

"He could've raped you."

Hardly. I had my knife with me just in case shit went bad. "Oh, come on, Deck. Luther's a pussy."

"Rapists and murderers excel at luring women. They pretend they're pussies then tie you up in five seconds flat and are no longer pussies."

I blew air through my lips, making them vibrate, and rolled my eyes. I placed my palms on the lip of the counter and looked up into the mirror. Big mistake. Deck's eyes met mine and they were steady. Yet, in the depths swirled a heat so hot I was fusing into them.

"Lionel," he said.

"What?"

"His name. Lionel Harrington. Twenty-eight. Programmer. Never been married and has connections with men you don't want anywhere near you." Obviously, Matt had known about Lionel's connections, too, and that was why he'd called Deck. The plan would've worked out fine if Avalanche hadn't been Lionel's latest hangout.

Deck's hands did something they'd never done before. They lowered onto my hips and he was looking like he was going to fuck me from behind right here in his bathroom. Was I awake? I had to be still passed out and having one hell of a wet dream.

Deck kept his emotions in check and it was rare I caught anything but his steady resolve of control. But Tuesday, he'd punched Tyler and the espresso machine in my shop.

Should've known Deck would've checked into the guy. Probably did it on the plane back here last night after Matt tattle-taled on me. Shit, Deck was getting too close. Over the last few months, his men had been on my ass every second. Pretending was getting harder and harder.

"The babysitting is over, Deck. Well done. My brother would be proud. Time to move on." I needed him to back off for a number of reasons. One of them being it was the anniversary of Connor's death soon and I couldn't have him around. "And I have to go. Rylie will need my help." I needed to breathe and put my heart back in place because it had leapt through my rib cage and was free-dancing something fierce across my skin.

I shoved him with my shoulder, but the stone statue didn't move. Instead, his fingers tightened on my hips and a current of electricity went shooting across my body.

"Not this time."

"Excuse me?" Red alert. Red alert! Something was off and it was standing pressed against me. Deck had never touched me, kissed me, done anything sexual, and suddenly this was everything sexual.

But being with Deck ... that would be the deliverance of my world collapsing. And if mine collapsed, so would his.

"You going to kiss me, Deck? Or just stand there and get my panties wet then walk away."

He swung me around so fast, the counter banged my hip. "What you did was stupid and foolish."

"Yeah, you said that."

"No, I said reckless."

Hmm, so he did. "Well, I think you said it last night. While you were forcing pills down my throat." Actually, I think it was while I was puking—my choice and it hadn't been fun.

His brows rose. "No. It was while I was holding your hair back while you puked in my toilet." What a lovely image; kind of destroyed the sexual tension. Okay, maybe not. I was pulsating with sexual tension and nothing was going to kill it. "Were you going to fuck him, Georgie?"

That was Deck, straight-up and to the point. "Not your business."

"It's always my business." His hands slipped up onto my waist, and then I felt his thumbs slowly stroke back and forth on my rib cage.

Holy shit. Deck—who had been around me for ten years, minus the two he went back to his team—had never touched me intimately and now he was. This wasn't trivial baby sparks; this was a horde of emergency flares going off.

"Care to try me out?" It was a rash remark, but I was on a roll and I had nothing to lose.

CHAPTER THREE

"YOU KNOW THAT'S not going to happen, Georgie."

Yeah, I did. I may have fantasized about Deck, but he always kept a spreader bar between us. Ha … now, wouldn't *that* be a sweet sight between my legs. Deck and a spreader bar.

I was completely screwed up thinking shit like that, but I wasn't hurting anyone but myself and even that was debatable. "Ever thought about tasting my pussy, Deck?" I decided my best course of action here was to make him be the one to run. His hands dropped from my waist and I huffed. Mission accomplished in seven words.

Disappointment settled deep in my stomach. I didn't know why. I was so used to it; I should have been immune. I was to everything else. I pushed a little more, putting my hand on his rock-hard chest as I slowly trickled my finger down between his pecs. He remained stone cold and unmoving—typical Deck, not giving anything away. Pissed me off when I was an open book with pages being ripped out—and he was reading them. At least when it came to my sexual attraction to him. He read nothing else of what I'd become. Deck skipped the most important pages when he'd disappeared for those two years.

I pushed him a little more because … well, it was what I did. "You ever think of what it would feel like to have your cock inside me? Easily sliding in and out. No, it wouldn't be easy, would it? It would be crass, rough and pounding." I looked up at him and froze. Jesus, his eyes were blazing and not with anger; they were smoldering with desire.

Maybe—

"What I need in bed is not you, Georgie."

Talk about having water thrown in your face. The heat I felt in my cheeks must have said it all. Such a bastard. I wanted to slap that confident, cold face so badly just to get some reaction out of him. To have him do something … anything. Grab me. Hurt me. Stop his detachment from growing like a weed.

Instead, I smiled and winked. It was a little awkward and killed me to do it, but I couldn't let him see how much his words hurt me.

"Oh, sweetpea, I didn't say I wanted you in bed." No, it would be against the wall, on a table, in the shower. "Unless, of course, you were tying me up. Then we could do the bed." Shit, that pushed something in him, because Deck's eyes narrowed and he grabbed my arm, his fingers bruising.

"Never going to happen. You need to stop this."

"Stop what?"

"This bullshit. The drinking. The attitude. The pretending to be someone you're not."

The thing was … he was so close to the truth it scared me. I couldn't imagine what Deck would do if he ever figured it out. But I was careful and there were only two people who knew about me. I had to keep it that way. I had no choice. I'd made that decision a long time ago and there was no escape. Besides, I didn't know how to be anything else anymore.

Deck believed I drank because of my brother's death and he was partially right. I was this way because of what happened after my brother died, but it wasn't the only reason.

This was me. It was rather contradictive because I hid behind a curtain of falsity pretending to be someone I wasn't and making Deck pity me. Yet, if he knew the truth, he'd probably hate me. Either way I lost.

I looked away from him. I couldn't help but think about the risks Deck took, what he did for a living. Every time he left, I wondered if it was the last time I would see him. Sometimes, I wondered if it would be better if I didn't see Deck anymore, so I didn't have to go through this. Not like he'd allow that anyway.

"Oh, sexy, I'm not pretending shit." Lies. It made my stomach lurch. I flattened my palm on his chest and felt the steady beat of his heart. Did it ever speed up, or was it always as calm and collected as he was? He put his hand over top of mine, and for a flash, I thought he was going to caress it, hold it, and drag me closer. That flash lasted half a second as he pulled my hand off him.

"Take a shower." He turned and walked to the door then stopped, looking over his shoulder. "And Georgie … you ever pull shit like that again, I'll lock you up."

The door shut and I grabbed his toothbrush and threw it in the toilet.

I WALKED OUT of Deck's bedroom, my hair wet and dripping down my back. I was wearing one of his dress shirts, which reached my mid-thigh. *Who knew he had a dress shirt?* And in white. Raiding his closet had been fun considering I'd never seen him in anything but t-shirts and cargo pants or jeans. He didn't have much, but he owned a wicked loft penthouse with a terrace and plunge pool.

I stopped.

Josh, Tyler and Vic sat on the bar stools at the island with Deck. They were talking quietly until they noticed me, and then they all turned and stared. Their eyes took in my naked thighs and Deck's shirt I'd only buttoned partially up my body. It wasn't like Deck took notice of me anyway.

Deck moved and his chair scraped the hardwood floors. The men lowered their heads and avoided looking at me. He stood and now I was wondering why I hadn't gotten myself off in the shower. It would've eased some of the sexual tension I had bundled inside me.

Deck was hot, no question, but that wasn't what wrapped me up so tight with him. It was *him*. The way his eyes looked at me as if he could read every thought tap dancing in my head. How he strode toward me, not a flicker of unease—ever. How he made me feel … okay, nix the getting all wet and bothered … it was more than that. He made me feel taken. Protected. Wanted. His.

Yeah, I was fucked. Not only did Deck not see me that way, but it was the last thing I needed.

I cocked my hip and put my hand on it, knowing full well when I did, it pushed up the shirt a little further on my leg. "Looks like a cupcake meeting. Hey, Tyler, Josh, Vic." The boys nodded but still didn't look at me. Well, Tyler did, winked, and then got up and poured himself another coffee.

"I thought you guys were overseas?"

"We were. Met Deck and Tyler in New York then flew back here," Josh said. "We're headed back overseas."

"What was in New York for all the boys?" I already knew, but I was better off asking. What I didn't know was what was overseas. They'd been going over there a lot.

"A strip bar with hot women," Tyler offered. Of course, they'd never tell me.

I walked over to the kitchen and pulled a mug down then slid it in front of Tyler. "Fuel me up, hot-stuff."

Tyler poured coffee into my mug then leaned back against the counter, cradling his coffee in his hands at chest level. He had this devilish look about him, handsome with a dash of hot sauce. Early thirties, never been married, had wealthy parents he was estranged from. Tyler's left arm was inked up and he had piercing green eyes, which contradicted his dark walnut curls, lazily falling in every direction.

Deck nodded to the men and Josh and Vic got up, each making excuses and going into Deck's office. There was a moment's hesitation before Tyler decided he better follow suit, but not before he gave me his crooked grin.

I sipped my coffee, brows raised while waiting for the hammer to come down.

"Vic will stay at your place with you."

"What?" Now, this was a new one. His men never stayed with me—ever. Shit, this was so not good. Total bad timing. Plus, I wasn't sure about Vic. He wasn't ex-military, but I'd heard he had skills with torture tactics. He was friggin' scary; a real dark scary, as if he had a closet full of dead bodies and liked to look at them before bed just so he could sleep. "So, not happening, Deck. Vic is creepy and I like my space." I licked my upper lip to get the remnants of coffee, although it was more for Deck's sake. It caught his attention and he watched, but I was disappointed as usual that there was no reaction out of him.

Unbreakable. Didn't I have any effect on him?

"Either that or you stay with your parents for the week and Vic's your bodyguard. After that shit you pulled last night …" Deck approached and I hopped on the counter, his shirt crept up on my thighs so a hint of my panties showed. He kept coming and my breath hitched when he stopped inches away from me. He grabbed my arm and pulled me down. "And you dress like that in front of my men again, I'll spank your ass."

I swallowed. I didn't even want to begin to imagine what Deck would think if he knew how turned on I was. I remained quiet because the image of Deck spanking me was getting way out of hand and I was a little flustered.

"I don't know how long I'll be gone this time."

I shrugged, but it was stiff. "Don't need to tell me. I'm not your wife or girlfriend. I'm merely a promise to my dead brother. And I'm not staying at my parents'." Heck no. I loved them dearly, but with their concern over my drinking … it was the last place I needed to be.

Deck was looking pretty damn firm with his rock-solid stance and unflinching eyes. Okay, I'd need to give on this one; otherwise, he might do something drastic like lock me up.

"Fine. Vic can stay with me." Shit, Vic hated me. I saw it in the way he looked at me with those dark-grey eyes filled with contempt. "Who knows, maybe we'll hit it off and I'll get to taste a yummy chocolate—did you know black men have bigger cocks? I read—"

"He'll take you to the cemetery."

Fuck. I always disappeared on the day of Connor's death and it was a week away. No one knew where I went. I always took a bottle of scotch for pretense and then I went dark. It was the only day of the year that no one, not even Deck, could find me. Looked like he was trying to end that. Well, I was pretty good at what I did and Vic wasn't going to stop me.

"Stay and come with me." I asked him this every year, kind of a ritual, and I already knew his answer. Each time, I breathed a sigh of relief when he refused. I'd be fucked if he said okay.

43

For the first year after Connor's death, I hated Deck. Then I learned to harness that hate. I found my outlet, and the hate I thought I had for Deck wasn't for him at all. It was for me. I hated myself. For who I was. For being scared all the time. I used to feel as if I was falling and the only way I'd survive was if Deck caught me. The thing was I knew if he'd been around back then he'd have caught me, saved me then tossed me aside like some annoying pebble he'd found in his combat boot.

So, I did something about it. I found a way to survive. Or rather, it found me.

"I don't need a tombstone to remember him." He always said that. "Leave the scotch at home this year." Deck looked over his shoulder toward the office. "Vic."

And that was that.

DECK

I WATCHED GEORGIE go back into my room, my shirt just covering the cusp of her ass. Fuck. My cock nearly burst through my jeans at the sight of her coming out of my bedroom, hair wet, skin glistening from the heat of the shower and that sassy smile on her mouth. A mouth I'd dreamed about having around my cock as she knelt on the floor in front of me.

Then it blew up in my face as I realized what I was looking at, my men were seeing, as well. I couldn't blame them. Georgie was hot. She had hips to grab, an ass to match and the attitude to make a guy bend to her will, and that was what fucked with my head. I wanted her to bend to my will and yet, that had never been a possibility. Not with my promise to Connor. Besides, I didn't want her like this. I also didn't want another guy fuckin' touching her, but that wasn't possible or fair, either. My word was to protect her and that included making sure the men she dated were good enough for her.

Who was I kidding? No fuckin' guy would be good enough for Georgie.

"Boss?"

Tyler slapped me on the shoulder. "When are you going to give her what she wants? Man, your control is fuckin' epic. That hot piece …" His voice trailed off when I glared at him. "Yeah, I'll get the car."

"Do that." I was still looking in the direction Georgie had disappeared. I was worried. Emily and Kat were away with Tear Asunder, and after last night, I didn't like the idea of leaving her.

Seeing her in some guy's bedroom with her shirt off and her bra all fucked up—yeah, I was still reeling. Georgie had never pulled a stunt like that, at least that I knew of. But Matt's call last night saying she showed up at Avalanche when I specifically asked her not to … that had me on a plane coming back. Shit got worse when Matt called back before we landed saying she was heading out with some guy named Lionel Harrington who frequented the bar and was often seen with some seedy guys. I was able to dig up info on him and found out the smart as hell programmer might not be trouble, but his 'business' acquaintances certainly were.

Yeah, I was careful. I was alive because I was fuckin' careful, and Georgie was my responsibility. I promised Connor if anything ever happened to him I'd watch out for his sister. And right now things were delicate as hell. Fuck, I had to get her drinking under wraps.

I ran my hand over the top of my head. If Matt hadn't called me, she'd have fucked some pussy who nearly pissed himself the second I walked in the door. More like burst through the door. Georgie didn't need a guy who she could walk all over. Because she would. The guy would survive one day under her sass and then he'd be crawling around on his knees doing anything she asked of him. He'd hate it, but more so, she'd fuckin' hate it.

"Pilot called. Ready when you are," Josh said then followed Tyler out the door.

I turned to Vic who was leaning against the sliding glass door out to the terrace, his arms crossed. Yeah, he was pissed he was on babysitting duty instead of coming with us. But Vic was the only guy I trusted not to fall for any of Georgie's bullshit.

"Keep her contained. I don't want her disappearing. She's been drinking far more than usual and …" I stopped. I couldn't put my finger on what was happening with her. She drank, partied hard, stayed out late and yet—something didn't sit right. Hadn't in a really long time. I felt like the real Georgie was hidden behind all the bullshit with her drinking. I wanted the fuckin' Georgie I knew who was smart as hell, determined, strong and even vulnerable and soft.

Vic shook his head and huffed. "Told you what should happen here."

Yeah, Vic thought I should lock her up. "Can't do it. Not going to."

"So, you'd rather see her kill herself slowly? Or better yet, get killed or raped or found in the street dead because she tripped and fell, so drunk she couldn't even pull her head out of a puddle of water?"

"Fuck you, Vic." This was a sore spot between us. Vic thought I should have Georgie forced into rehab. Of course, it wouldn't be legal because she was over eighteen, but that wasn't the issue. The issue was I wasn't going to do it. Flat out. Not a chance. I'd protect her, help her any way I could, but I wasn't locking her away with people I didn't know while I was across the ocean, not knowing if I was coming back.

Georgie came out of the room wearing the tight black skirt she had on last night and my shirt—no fuckin' bra. I could see her erect nipples through the material, and I silently cursed. "Going to borrow the shirt," she said. She pulled it up to her nose and breathed in. Jesus, if that didn't turn me on and make my cock hard. "Might even get myself off while wearing it."

I took a deep breath and controlled the grin threatening to emerge. The girl lived on turning me on. All I could think about was how she would look naked laying over my lap while I spanked her until she begged me to stop.

I had to get the fuck out of here. "Be good, Georgie." I started for the door.

"Definition of good: to be desired," she called out.

My hand stiffened around the doorknob. "It also means to be approved of. Don't disappoint me."

I heard her sharp intake of breath and knew I reached her, somewhere in that numb oasis she was drowning in. Could I save her? I didn't know any longer.

CHAPTER FOUR

Georgie

VIC WAS A pain in my ass, and I was beginning to think he enjoyed pissing me off. Normally, I could schmooze Deck's men—actually, any man—but Vic was like a beetle with a hard outer shell that refused to crack under pressure. I realised why Deck had chosen him to stay with me this week.

My parents had called wanting to go to the cemetery together, but really I couldn't deal with Mom coddling and Dad pitying me. This was one day of the year I let the demons in and became who I hated, who I hid from.

I needed to be on my game because what I had to do was not something Deck could ever find out about, and pit-bull Vic was making that really difficult.

He'd slept on the couch all week which left no option for the front door escape last night. I'd already tried the pathetic excuse 'going to the store for some milk' early this morning. Vic actually rolled his eyes, which looked real funny for a six-foot guy built like a friggin' Mack truck. It even got a smirk out of him. I wasn't sure if it was because he thought it was funny or because he was getting ready to lock me in the closet.

I poured myself an orange juice, which I deliberately left on the counter, then went to the cupboard and took out the Froot Loops. I stuck my hand in the box, pulled out a handful of colorful rings and shoved them in my mouth. "Want some?" I held out the box.

Vic didn't look up from his iPad. I approached, peering over his shoulder, seeing emails from— He flipped it over, set it down on the kitchen table then got up and went over to the blender he'd been using every morning to make a shake with God knows what mixed in. All I knew was it was green and looked like vomit.

He poured himself another one then grabbed my orange juice, dumped it in the sink and filled my cup with his concoction.

God, so predictable. "Hey. What the fuck?"

"You want to tell me that orange juice doesn't have vodka in it?"

It did. I'd made sure of it since the first day he came to stay. "What's a little pick-me-up in the morning? And they say alcohol's a downer … I totally disagree."

He slid the cup of green goop along the marble counter toward me. "Drink it. Then have a shower. We're meeting your parents at the cemetery in an hour."

I ignored the green stuff and put my hands on my hips. "How about we skip the vomit? Forget the cemetery and my parents and you take off your clothes and join me in the shower."

I expected shock. Maybe if I was lucky, a mild smirk. I got neither. Actually, I got scary badass with bodies in his closet. I wasn't brave enough to laugh it off; instead, I faltered and Vic plowed me right over.

"Deck may put up with your crap, but I sure as hell won't." Vic approached until he was right in my face and I was backed into the wall. His palms slapped the wall above my head. "You want to fuck, *cupcake?*" He was quick, grabbing my throat, his fingers bruising. "A quick fuck in the shower? I won't tell Deck. Shit, he's too busy getting his ass shot at anyway."

I reached up and put my hands on top of his, trying to pry his fingers back. I really didn't want to have to use the knee in the crotch, but I would if he didn't get his hands off me in two-point-two seconds. "Vic, hands off."

It took him a second before he abruptly let me go. "Better learn to bite that tongue before some guy doesn't take his hands off you when you ask." He pushed away, turned his back then walked back to the kitchen. "Take a fuckin' shower then we're going to the cemetery."

I didn't say anything. What was there to say really? Except I knew I wouldn't be taking a shower and we certainly wouldn't be going anywhere together.

CLIMBING OUT A second-story window should have been easy except when there's only a spindly tree branch to grab hold of and it ends up breaking. I'd never had to escape my own house before. I just hoped Vic would hear the shower running and not get suspicious for at least ten minutes. After that … well, no one would find me until I wanted to be found.

Just me and my pain.

I stopped at Perk Avenue and grabbed the bottle of scotch I kept there for this particular day every year, and then had the cabby drop me off a couple miles from where I was going.

I swear Deck's men had GPS tracking devices in their heads with the way they could locate people. I had no doubt Vic would be calling every taxi service in the city to see if anyone matched my description.

Of course, I paid off the driver, but that would only go so far. Deck had loads of money. Shit, I couldn't even begin to guess how much he raked in for locating, killing and torturing the scum of the Earth.

"You sure, lady?" the driver said as he pulled onto the shoulder. "There's nothing around here."

I leaned over the seat and passed him a wad of cash. "Yeah. Thanks." I opened the door. "Good luck with the party." He and his wife were having twenty kids over this afternoon for his daughter's fifth birthday.

He laughed. "Good luck to you, too, Goldie."

I waited until he pulled a U-turn and was out of sight before I crossed the road and went into the bush. It took fifteen minutes before the car pulled up on the side road where I waited. The passenger door flung open and I hopped in.

"Have any trouble?

I shrugged, looking over at the young good-looking guy with tatts inked up his left arm and a piercing in his right brow. Sharp, dark features with greyish-green eyes that drooped in the corners, which made him look sad … or seductive. Both worked.

I was fourteen when Tanner and I first met. Connor had given his dirt bike to this lanky kid who couldn't even afford a new pair of jeans. The joy on his face had me tearing up and Connor laughing at me, especially because I was a prissy girl who wore a dress to the motocross track filled with boys. I'd been so out of my element, but I was with my brother and he loved it, so it kinda became our thing to do when he was around.

Tanner was a couple years younger than me and yet he'd always acted so much older. It was after Connor died and I'd been driven down into a black hole of despair that I found out why Tanner was so mature for his age.

He reached over and ruffled my hair. "Blue? A reason for that?"

There was always a reason for my actions. "Tristan likes blue."

"Ah, the coffee shop guy. I assume he is one of your … tasks?" I nodded. "You get a date yet? Looked like something was happening … before Deck came in."

The way he ground out Deck's name made my back stiffen as my protectiveness over Deck came surging to the surface. I didn't react, though. Drunk Georgie would've, but I wasn't her right now. I had learned to control my emotions and my tongue when need be. "Got his number. Date pending."

"Better be careful with that one. Something odd about him, the way he watches you. Don't think the alcohol thing will work."

Yeah, I was thinking the same thing. Tristan had smarts, wealth and when he looked at me, it was like he knew exactly what I did. Of course, he didn't, but I knew he wasn't a pussy like Lionel. He radiated prowess and that had me handling him a little differently.

Tanner reached over and took my hand. "I know today is tough for you, but you need to do this, Georgie."

I slipped my hand from his and looked out the side window, watching as the pine trees zipped by. Yes, I did know. If I didn't, the emotions would slowly creep back in. "Don't call me that."

I was tense and uncertain. I almost didn't come here last year, but Tanner showed up to bring me and my indecision was quickly expunged. This was the only thing that helped release all the pent-up emotions I kept hidden about my past, about my secrets.

The leather on the steering wheel cracked under his hands. "I fuckin' hate this. It's like delivering the lamb to slaughter."

I huffed. "I'm not a lamb, Tanner. Far from it."

"Yeah, well, you are today."

Yes. Vulnerable and alone with my pain. But, it could never end. I needed this reminder of what was done to me. I wanted to feel the pain today so I could walk away and live tomorrow without those emotions. It was dangerous and risky for all of us if I couldn't keep what I was doing a secret.

"If he ever found out ..."

I knew exactly who he was talking about—Deck. "I told you before. I'll never tell him, and he won't find out." Tanner was always worried Deck would find out and then ... well, I wasn't really sure what would happen, but I was warned by *him* that Deck's life was 'fragile'. Kind of contradictory to who Deck was, but I knew that wasn't an idle threat. That made me really careful as to how I lived each day. The thing was, this year would be a little trickier with Vic on my ass.

"We'll need a cover."

Tanner nodded. "Yeah. He has an idea that fits with your ... drinking. Shouldn't be an issue."

I tapped my fingers on my thighs, not saying anything.

"I don't like him."

"I know." Tanner had issues with Deck and wanted me to break away from him. Considering Deck and I had the same friends, it wasn't so simple. Besides, letting go of Deck was like chopping off a limb; I could do it, and I sure as hell didn't want to. Tanner didn't understand, so I tried to keep Deck-talk to a minimum with him.

Tanner nodded, but I could see the flicker of irritation on his face. He was good at what he did, but I'd known Tanner practically my whole life, and he gave away his emotions with his breathing patterns. If he was pissed off, it slowed. Worried, it became arrhythmic. Calm, it was regular, but deep.

The tires hit gravel and Tanner turned into a long, narrow pathway, which didn't look like much except a deer trail. My heart pounded and I felt the tremors in my body. It knew what was coming; the thing was I wasn't sure if it came from fear or relief. I never did.

He stopped the car in front of a barbed-wire gate and jumped out, unlocked it and pushed it open. Tanner got back in and looked over at me then down at my hands that were wrung together.

Fuck. I quickly laid them flat on my thighs, feeling the heat leaking into my skin through my jeans.

Silence.

He reached toward me and tucked my hair behind my ear, his fingers lingering there a few seconds longer than what a friend might do. Then he sighed, threw the car in gear and drove up to the old, metal shack with the leaky roof. When it rained on the day I came here, it sucked because the pain was unbearable with my skin wet and cold.

"Georgie—" He stopped abruptly when I glared at him. He couldn't call me that ... not here. "Chaos, maybe if you let me do it again then—"

"No." My voice trembled and it pissed me off because Tanner heard it. The first time I came here, Tanner had been the one to do this to me.

He bowed his head. "Shit. If your brother were—"

"Shut up," I shouted. "He's not. He'll never be."

Every single day, I lived a lie. I pretended to be someone I wasn't. I broke the bond of trust with the one man who protected me no matter how much bullshit I threw at him. If he knew, he'd never understand why I did it. We were all broken in some way. It was how we lived with our broken pieces, which made us who we were. And I just had more broken pieces than most.

"I'll be here when you're done."

I nodded and walked toward the shack, the squeak of my sneakers on the gravel sounding like walnuts being cracked. I stopped outside the door, looked up at the sky and took a deep breath, closing my eyes. A ritual I did every year before I walked into the darkness of unbearable pain where past met present.

Soon, my haunted dreams would wash away with the blood that trickled down my back. I'd be free. At least until the pain built up and I needed this again. I didn't know how to stop it, and sometimes I wished I could just stay here. Stop pretending and drown in the darkness that lingered in my mind. I lived with the dirty black rag he used to keep me silent still choking me.

The smell of the nearby creek and the sound of the chirping of birds surrendered me to its hold. The trembles eased and my heart slowed.

Peace.

I opened the door.

"Hello, Chaos."

CHAPTER
FIVE

I STRAIGHTENED MY shoulders and embraced the cold shiver that ran down my spine as I met his eyes. Direct and without mercy, no pity or sympathy as to what was going to happen. And this was why he was the one who did it to me. Ironic that he saved me from the very thing he did to me every year.

He wore a black suit, perfectly cut to his sculpted body. He was the same height as Deck and dark like him, but that was where it ended. When he smiled, it was charming with a cocky twitch, but there was a touch of sinister which could make a girl think twice before approaching him.

I'd stepped into his domain at sixteen and he gave me back what I'd lost. There was no coddling, no sympathy for what had happened to me. Deck was always an issue between us as *he* told me Deck was my biggest weakness, but he was also the part of me, which kept me from breaking completely. My solid.

He leaned against the rusted metal wall, ankles crossed, arms matching, oblivious to the smothering heat in what felt like a sardine can. It was where this had to happen, mimicking before.

It was months after Connor's funeral when *he* picked me up walking home from Robbie's house. That was the day the abuse stopped but for me it never really ended. The pain … I needed the reminder. Pain set me free from the memory.

There was no need for idle conversation and I walked to the center of the shack, the wood floor creaking with each step. It hadn't rained in a while and the place had a film of dust everywhere.

This would put me out of commission for a few days. Deck was observant, but fortunately, every year at this time, he made certain he was on a job. It made it easier to keep my pain hidden. I knew Deck felt responsible for Connor; he'd been his team leader, and Deck felt accountable for everyone.

I knelt on the ground and lowered my head.

Deep breaths.

Slow and rhythmic.

I knew how to take my mind elsewhere. It was one of the first things I'd learned when the pain became unbearable. I used to cry and beg and fight, but none of that worked. Separate myself from my body and live within the stillness.

But this was different. Now, I sought the pain. I wanted to feel every muscle strain. My flesh tearing apart then burning. To hear my own screams. With each one, it was the release of the past. It was regret. It was for the lies. And when it was over, it brought me back from the hatred and gave me the numbness. But nothing … no amount of pain could make me numb to Deck. My solid was also my greatest flaw.

I pulled my shirt over my head, folded it neatly and placed it in front of me. I felt the subtle change in air, heard his quiet steps as he moved toward me.

He never asked if I wanted to change my mind.

He never asked if I was sure.

He did what I asked him.

I didn't know his past, but I saw it lingering in the depths of his eyes—the bleak darkness.

He found me when I was lost. Brought me back from the pit of fear and desolation.

He showed me how to survive. To bury the fear and replace it with strength. The only thing he could never get me to let go of was Deck.

Deck was embedded, carved into my bones. One part of me that wouldn't be repressed.

A tear slipped from the safety of my eye and trailed down my cheek. I wasn't embarrassed or tried to hide it. This was why I came here.

He stepped closer.

I closed my eyes and more tears fell.

He crouched behind me. I swallowed and kept my hands perfectly still on my lap. It was the familiar clang of his belt being unbuckled that caused the bile to rise in the back of my throat. I took several deep breaths.

I felt him hesitate as if giving me a moment then his unforgiving grip grabbed my wrist and yanked it behind my back. Then he grabbed the other one. I sucked in air at the strain on my arms then relaxed again as he tightened the belt around my wrists. I fell forward, my cheek pressed into the rough planks, exactly like it had been before. It didn't take long before the memory flooded into me.

The first cut always hurt the most and he made it the deepest and the longest; a slow drag of his dull knife from my hip at my lower back, curving across to just below my armpit. He kept the flat of his palm on my neck, pressing me forward, keeping my cheek pressed into the floor. I felt the rain of blood slide down my heated skin. He wiped it away with a piece of coarse material as if he was cleaning the drips of paint off a canvas.

He cursed. I jerked. His palm pressed harder on my neck and I could feel the ache in my joints as I curled over, further exposing my naked back to him.

I held onto my sobs. It only made it worse when I moved and I had to stay as still as possible. He'd get mad if I ruined his work.

I knew what was next. My body knew and I couldn't control the trembling. He punched me in the side and I gasped, falling over then quickly righting myself in position again.

"Stupid bitch. Stay fucking still."

I felt the slap of the wet material hit the fresh wound. I couldn't control the cry from escaping. I always cried when he did that. I never could block out the pain.

He laughed, the sound like the screech from a badly played banjo.

Then a filthy, black rag, which tasted like oil was shoved in my mouth so forcefully I gagged.

"Not a sound. I told you. No crying. No moving." He leaned over me so I could see the evil glare in his light-brown eyes. "Your big brother isn't around to protect you now, is he? I heard he burned to death." He shook his head, clucking his tongue. "Real painful way to die."

I silently cried, trying to block out his voice, yet his words cut into me just as painfully as his knife.

He lowered his voice, his peppered breath sweeping across my face. "A blank canvas. That's what you were. Not anymore. Now, you're stained."

His knife drew some kind of design on my back and then pinpricks as if he was making snowflakes. "The perfect little princess isn't perfect anymore." My eyes squeezed shut so hard the tears couldn't escape. The pungent smell of alcohol hit my flesh and slid into my cuts again. Scotch. It was always scotch. I'd never forget that smell.

His breath hit the side of my neck and I gasped, shivering from the pain and fear that coursed through me. "Did you know I got an A in art? The teacher said I had a unique imagination."

He suddenly yanked me upward by my hair. "Do you know why you were picked, Georgie?"

I shook my head. He was a senior, and I'd never seen him before last month when he first dragged me into the school's maintenance shed.

"Didn't think so. Just consider yourself lucky I didn't pick you myself." He ran his finger down between my breasts then chuckled when I squirmed to escape his touch. I heard a bang outside the window at the back of the shed and he stiffened and looked up then laughed. "Stupid boy." He grabbed my chin, tilting my head at an awkward angle so I was looking right at him. "No telling anyone about our little art session, right? You don't want to lose another ... family member, do you?"

I sobbed, squeezing my eyes shut as I silently prayed for him to let me go.

The sudden splash of scotch hit the fresh wounds. I writhed and jerked and screamed, but it was useless as he held me down. "Do you?"

I shook my head.

He shoved me hard in the back and I fell forward. He untied the belt around my wrists and I heard him slipping the leather back through his belt loops. I waited for the creak of the door to open and close before

I yanked the rag out of my mouth and vomited until my sides cramped and I had nothing left.

"Chaos? Come back, love."

Deck? No, Deck didn't know Chaos. He'd never know Chaos. I kept that from him. I had to for both our sakes.

But there was a small part of me that wanted him to see me. Instead, he believed in the lie I'd become. How could he think I was that drunk girl who wasted her life away? Because I'd made sure he did. I did everything in my power to hide my lies.

I jerked away from the hands slowly helping me up from lying on the floor. He gently undid the belt then removed the rag and I licked the saliva accumulated around my mouth. I kept my eyes squeezed shut, needing time to pull myself back from the memory. Contain the pain that revisited.

I heard him walk to the far side of the shack, the creak of the metal wall as he leaned against it. He'd stay and watch me like he always did. I didn't know if he did it to make certain I was okay or because he enjoyed watching me curl in a ball and cry until I had nothing left in me.

Tears for Connor. The brother I'd lost and missed with every breath. Tears for the other girls Robbie had hurt. Tears for Deck. Yeah, I cried for him because I knew behind the unyielding man was pain for what he'd seen in his life.

Emotions drove through me—Guilt. Pain. Rage.

Then finally acceptance.

That was why I needed the purging, to prove I was strong. To let go of the weakness I hated so much. To remember who I was now.

It was a long time before the raw emotions became controlled again and I was able to take a deep breath without the catch in my throat. I felt the release, like a balloon being set free in the wind—freedom. It was euphoric and completely fucked up, but it was my fucked up and what happened here worked for me. I could walk away strong and immune to the nightmare that destroyed who I'd been.

It was my way to tuck my past away in the far corners of my mind, not to be released again until I came here.

I sat up on my heels, hearing the soft tread of his approach before he was carefully applying bandages over the cuts. They weren't deep, and most likely wouldn't ever scar me. Robbie had made certain of that, too. Wounds that healed so my back could become a blank canvas again, but my memory would never heal.

I patiently waited for him to finish and then picked up my shirt and slid it over my head. I could smell the scotch. It must have splashed onto the material. I watched his long fingers do up the two buttons at the top and then his thumb came under my chin and raised my head so I'd look at him.

He always did that. Looked me in the eyes as if reading whatever was going on in my head. He never said anything, and I suspected it was to make certain I was okay.

He took my hand and helped me to my feet then we walked outside. The sun beamed down on my face so brightly I couldn't see for a few seconds while my vision adjusted. Every step I took, the cuts on my back rubbed under the bandages. I learned to wear loose clothing when I came here. This time ... I'd worn Deck's shirt. It smelled like him despite the scotch that now splattered the material. Still, if I tilted my chin down, I could breathe Deck in and feel ... solid again.

"Faster than usual." I heard Tanner say as we approached the car.

He snorted and when I looked up at him through parted blue streaks of hair, I caught the fierce glare he sent Tanner. I had the impression *he* didn't like him very much, but Tanner had been with us since the beginning. It was odd. If *he* didn't like him, why was Tanner still part of this? "Get your head on the job, Chaos," *he* said.

I opened the passenger door and slid in, careful to keep my back from touching the leather seat. Like always, my mind was a fog of emotions attempting to block out the memories and bring me back to the numbness of surviving.

"You have the cover story?"

I nodded.

"Better be convincing. Vic isn't stupid." He looked at Tanner then back at me. "You need to find a balance to what you're doing."

I knew what that meant. Cut the drinking back.

He placed the bottle in my hand and shut my door. Fuck. I hated the taste of scotch. I hated the smell and I hated everything about it. I unscrewed the lid and chugged it back, ignoring the scorching pain in my throat and drinking as much as I could.

"Whoa, Chaos. Take it easy. Didn't you hear what he just said? You need to be drunk not comatose." Tanner's door shut and he started the car.

It was only a half-hour back to the city, and I needed to be pretty smashed by the time we arrived. It was the one day of the year that I really did get drunk. All the other times … yeah, it was a façade, a cover-up, but today wasn't by choice. Getting drunk at Connor's tombstone then cabbing it home was our cover. I would hide in my bedroom and no one would bother me for days.

Another year gone. Another year filled with lies.

This was who I needed to be.

The perfect chaos.

DECK

I HAD TO consciously relax my grip on my cell phone before it crushed under the pressure. Fuckin' Georgie. I should've known she'd do something stupid like this. Shit, I *had* known. That was why I left Vic with her. Every year, she got drunk at Connor's grave and every year, I fucked off not wanting to be around to see her destroyed. I had no way to stop her pain, and it cut through me so deeply I couldn't breathe thinking about it.

I knew exactly what would happen if I saw her upset—I'd take from her what I'd always wanted and that could never happen.

Tyler, Josh and Sam leaned against the crumbling wall of the beaten-down house and watched as I calmly took the news Vic laid out for me. They knew me well enough I may be calm on the outer edges, but past that I was fuckin' furious.

"How long?" I asked Vic.

"Couple hours. She went by her coffee shop, grabbed a bottle of scotch, and then got in a cab. Located the company, driver was at his kid's birthday party. Fits her description, but her name was Goldie. Not sure why she'd go way the fuck out there."

Goldie. "Jesus." The name of her fuckin' goldfish Connor had buried in the backyard. "Follow the lead. That's her."

"Got it."

I heard the tires squeal as if Vic was making a quick turnaround. "And Vic?"

"Yeah, Boss."

"You find her. Lock her down." It was escalating. It was as if she didn't give a shit about herself. That wasn't her and yet … Georgie had become a different person when I came back two years after her brother died. Harder. And the sweetness I used to see in her eyes—vanished.

"Got it."

I pressed 'End' then tossed my phone on the makeshift table. An uneasy feeling crept down my spine and made my stomach churn and my heart pound. Why couldn't I fuckin' get through to her? This wasn't just about her brother. Something else was fucking with her mind to make her want to numb it out with alcohol. It didn't fit. She didn't fit.

She was stronger than this. Where was the girl I used to know? It was like she was drifting further and further away from me year after year. She was hiding; I'd known it for years. But what I didn't know was from what.

What the fuck was I going to do with her? This shit had gone on too long. Maybe it was time to cut her loose like Vic said. Was I enabling her by protecting her? Probably, but the thought of losing Georgie was like having to cut off my leg. I couldn't do it slow and easy; it'd have to be brutal.

"Fuck." This mission was too important to not have every man I had available, and here I had one of my best men watching Georgie.

I ran my hand down my face and then got my shit together. I was not fucking this up.

"All good, Boss?" Tyler asked.

I met his eyes then looked to Josh. "Failure is unacceptable. We bring our boy home."

But it was only two hours later that all went to shit. The snitch turned up, bloody and tortured. Eyes wide open, staring and lifeless. There was a note pinned to his shirt, written in blood.

TEN YEARS.
I'M A KILLER.
THIS IS MY HOME.
STOP LOOKING FOR
ME
OR CHAOS IS NEXT.

"Jesus Christ," Tyler said, crouching down beside the mangled body. "Boss, do you really think it's Connor? And who the fuck is Chaos?"

Did I think that was him? Fuck, yeah, I did. Only I knew who Chaos was because Connor had called her that and Georgie Girl. "Yeah, it's him."

I knew torture. I knew the shit it did to your head. But ten years of it? Even Connor could break under that. Any man would.

This wasn't bullshit.

Fuck this all to hell. Damn it! I punched the rock wall and blood instantly rose on my knuckles. I did it again and again until Josh pulled me back with an arm around my waist and shoved me.

It didn't stop me. Nothing would as I picked up the table, laptop crashing to the floor, our map billowing in the air a second before settling on the floor. I threw the table at the wall and the loud cracking of wood splintering felt like me. I was splintering. Parts of me were being ripped off and burned as my anger tore through me.

But it wasn't just anger. It was fear, an emotion I kept locked down all my life, but seeing that word in blood broke the dam and I couldn't control it.

I destroyed chairs, ripped up plans, crushed the laptop with my fists. I sensed the men watching and I didn't give a fuck. This was bad.

All my hope for bringing him home detonated in my face. No wonder it took us so long to locate him.

He fuckin' didn't want to be found.

"Boss."

I heard the voices, but they were drowned out by my madness of destruction. This was my fault. I should've found him sooner, but fuck, how could I? I thought for years he was dead. Christ, I'd seen the truck blow up. The memory. The anguish was still vivid in my mind even knowing he lived.

"Boss."

Now, he was threatening Georgie? Fuckin' Georgie? His sister? How was that even fathomable? The one person he loved more than anyone.

Because he knew me too well. That was my failure. He knew I wouldn't give a shit if he threatened me or my men, but Georgie … he knew I'd walk if Georgie's life was in any way threatened.

"Deck!"

Tyler held his phone out. "You need to take this."

I really didn't need to hear what bullshit Georgie had managed to get herself into this time. My patience with her was thinner than a moth's wing. One more fuck-up and I was tearing free of her. Fuck my word. Fuck Connor.

I took the phone. "What?"

"There's been an accident."

It was as if all those words I just thought were blown up with a grenade. My heart pounded and I had trouble swallowing.

Keep your shit together.

I'd been trained by the best to withstand torture, the worst circumstances possible, pain, agony, and yet this tested all that.

I turned away from the guys so they couldn't read my expression. I needed a fuckin' second to pull my head from my ass and gain some control.

"She's in the hospital. Some guy found her unconscious and convulsing at the cemetery."

I didn't know what to say.

"Deck." Vic never called me Deck. "It's bottom."

Yeah, it was. I slapped my palm against the wall above my head and closed my eyes. "I'll meet you there. Ten hours."

"What about Connor?"

"Mission is dead." I pressed 'End' before he could respond. Talking was pissing me off and I had to reel my shit in—fast.

"Boss? She okay?" Tyler questioned.

"No, but she will be." Because this shit was ending.

CHAPTER SIX

Georgie

I HEARD VOICES calling my name.

Stop it.

It was like I was in a boiler and the sounds echoed, drilling into my head. I wanted to put my hands over my ears, but I couldn't move. Why couldn't I move?

I was cold.

Shivering and yet I didn't feel my body shaking. No, it was jerking—hard. I tried to open my eyes but I couldn't see anything.

"She's convulsing again."

Convulsing? Were they talking about me? The last I remembered was being at the shed—in pain. Hurt. Then numbness.

A loud screeching sounded over and over again. I tried to moan, and I think I opened my mouth, but nothing came out. Why couldn't I move? It was like being immersed in quicksand, limbs so heavy.

"You're going to be okay, miss."

Miss? Why would he call me miss? I recognized the voice and yet couldn't put my finger on who it was. Where was Deck? Was he here with me? He was always with me when I fucked up.

Fear swarmed me like a horde of wasps. What did I do? Why couldn't I move?

"Sir, do you know what happened to her?"

I felt hands on me and wanted to swat them away but couldn't.

"No. I found her like this." His voice trailed off and all I heard were a mumbling of sounds blurred together.

I felt a sudden, sharp pain shoot through me and then it was like I was falling through a black hole. My arms strapped to my sides, unable to reach out and stop myself.

It was getting darker and colder.

I screamed and screamed.

But I kept falling, sliding down the dark tunnel until I hit bottom—then nothing.

I BLINKED, ADJUSTING my eyes to the bright fluorescent lights and the sun beaming through the window. Last night, my parents had been the first ones to see me, but my throat was so sore from the stomach tube pushed down my throat I could barely talk. They sat with me a while until the nurse came in and told them visiting hours were over. My dad smoothed my hair back like he used to do when I was home sick from school and then said they'd see me tomorrow.

As I sat up and reached for the glass on the table beside the hospital bed, I heard the slight movement on the other side of the room.

I glanced over, assuming it was a nurse, and my eyes widened and my heart started pounding, which made the stupid machine I was hooked up to beep faster. Fuck. Deck was leaning against the wall, arms crossed and looking sexy in his black cargo pants and … he was furious.

I had to get my shit together—fast.

I saw the twitch in Deck's jaw. "Not liking getting that call, Georgie."

"Yeah, well, it wasn't pixies and sunflowers for me, either. And Vic didn't have to call you. And you didn't have to come." But of course he would. Unpredictable Deck was predictable when it came to keeping his word. And no matter how much more difficult it made my life … I loved him for it.

He frowned and approached the bed. "Shit is changing."

I avoided his eyes, which I rarely did, but right now I felt like crap and was a little nervous about what Deck knew. A lie. I was a lot nervous. "Do you know if my parents are here?" They could be my buffer with Deck.

"Your parents aren't coming by today. They agree with me. Shit changes." Oh, God, he talked to my parents and they liked Deck. Respected him. My dad even laughed when Deck threw me over his shoulder and threatened to spank my ass when I was drunk at Emily and Logan's dinner at the farm. "Today."

"I can look after myself." Stupid ass thing to say, but my head was fogged up something good and I was floundering.

"You're living in *pixie* land if you think you can." Yeah, this was a little more than Deck being pissed. This was Deck taking control of a situation he didn't like—*my* situation.

Deck sighed and it was a strange sound coming from him. Actually, it didn't suit him at all. "Georgie, I've been watching and doing nothing about this for a long time. Now, I'm doing something. Don't have a choice here."

My breath stopped. A part of me knew exactly what he was talking about. I pushed it too far. *He* warned me yesterday to find a balance. I went right off the scale. Shit. I drank so much I poisoned myself. What had I been thinking chugging it back like it was grape juice? I *hadn't* been thinking. I knew I had to be drunk to fit the cover story and I'd gone overboard because … well, because after the purge I wanted to drown in darkness.

Vic was supposed to find me drunk at the cemetery, take me back to my place and then I would crash for a few days.

"You drink that entire bottle of scotch?"

Oh, fuck. I didn't remember, but I sure as hell felt like I had. I chugged it back in the car before Tanner got to the cemetery. I remember Tanner taking it from me at some point. "Deck—"

"Jesus, Georgie." Deck turned away and I again tried to get up, but he heard me and said, "Don't move."

I halted, plopping back down, which made me wince because of the cuts on my back. He noticed it and looked at me over his shoulder then scowled. "Deck, it was Connor's—" He walked over and grabbed the doctor's chart off the door. Shit.

"I don't give a fuck what crap was fucking with your head. I should've seen this coming. I *did* see this coming." He flipped the page, read, then looked up at me. "You should be dead."

"I'm not." It was a sass reply, and I should've been keeping the sass toned down right about now. What I had to do was get him away from the chart. "Hey sweetpea, can you get me some ice-cream? My throat is so friggin' raw and I'd love—" I knew the second he read the doctor's notes concerning the cuts on my back.

He froze. I saw the tightening of his muscles, the way his hands squeezed the clipboard. Then he tossed it on the plastic chair and without a word, strode toward the bed. I grabbed the edges of the sheet and pulled it up to my chin.

With one yank, he had it out of my grip and at the foot of the bed. "Deck—"

"Turn over or I'll turn you over."

I'd never seen him so mad as he leaned over, his fists pressed into the mattress on either side of me. I may live this life of lies, but Deck was real. Unlike me, every word out of his mouth was the truth. If I didn't turn over myself, he'd make me.

The second I did, he untied the thin tie, which did a shit job of keeping my gown from showing my ass and yanked it open. Then I felt one of the bandages being lifted and it was as if I could feel his shock vibrating through the mattress into me. "Deck, it's not what you think." Shit, how was I supposed to explain the cuts? I had to play the part, yet all I wanted to do was scream the truth.

But I couldn't. There were rules and severe consequences for breaking those rules.

He was quiet, and I lay completely still. There was nothing to fight or lie about or pretend. He knew it was impossible for me to put the cuts on myself. Holy fail.

"Who did it?"

I pulled at the numbness, desperate to hide behind the safety of its shield, but with Deck, it was as if I was trying to pull down a steel blind that weighed a thousand pounds. My only escape was my sassy mouth.

"His name is Pine and he smells delicious, but he's a little sticky around his core." He scowled and I quickly tried to explain. "Sexy, I jumped out of the second floor window of my bedroom onto a pine tree. You want to go chop him down for cutting me up, because I'm thinking it wasn't his fault and the tree police will be after you."

His eyes narrowed. "You're lying." I knew it was a long shot. Tyler or Josh might have let it slide, but Deck … not a chance. He didn't skim the doc's report; he'd have read word for word and no doubt it suggested the wounds were made with a knife. "Who the fuck did this to you?"

My best defense right now was silence. I had no choice. I hated it. The lying to him. Seeing the rage in his eyes. But I'd never risk losing him—ever. I'd do whatever it took.

"You're getting help." Deck's words hit me like a punch to the stomach and my eyes widened with panic.

"What?" His expression remained still. Shit, he was serious. He was going to lock me up. "It's illegal. I'm over eighteen and—"

"Do you think laws matter to me, Georgie? I kill for a fuckin' living."

Shit, there was no doubt he could lock me up and throw away the key. But this was why *he'd* given me this cover story when Deck came back when I was eighteen … because he couldn't lock me up. "Deck, please. Don't do that to me." The webs began encasing me in their sticky substance as fear gripped me. Everything was unravelling and it was happening fast. Too fast. I was losing control here.

"You drank until that shit poisoned you." His tone hardened. "You have fuckin' cuts on your back. *From a knife.* How did you get them, Georgie?"

I'd never tell him. "I don't know." He knew I was lying. It was the first time I think he suspected something. Shit, I totally screwed up. "I drank too much yesterday and I was—"

"How?" he shouted.

I looked at my hands.

"Look at me." When I didn't, he punctuated each word. "Look. At. Me."

I couldn't.

"Fuck this." Deck strode over to the window and looked out into the street. "And it's every fuckin' day."

69

"I'll sober up." Damn it, I went too far.

"It's too late."

I yanked off the heart monitor and then the intravenous, scrambled out of the bed, and darted for the door, making it into the hallway. I had no idea where I was going except the word *run* kept pounding into me like I was that sixteen-year-old girl again.

I heard Deck swear and I was grabbed from behind. I kicked and struggled, but to Deck, I was a flimsy piece of foil. No chance was I going to rehab. The second that happened, he'd find out the truth and then ...

I panicked at the thought and reacted by dropping my weight then jerking my elbow back to hit him in the head. He let me go as he staggered back a step, his hand going to his cheek where my elbow hit. It must have throbbed because my elbow sure hurt like hell. It was a classic defense move when someone grabbed you from behind, one of the several I'd been taught. Except he wasn't supposed to know that.

We both froze.

I saw his face, showing the surprise at what I'd just done and then the suspicion. I shouldn't know how to do that move. I surprised myself that I managed it with Deck, of all people. But it didn't last long. He launched for me, and my breath hitched as his arms locked me down and held my back to his chest. This time, I didn't attempt to move.

His voice was a low whisper as he growled into my ear. "Where the fuck did you learn to do that?"

I had to calm down, get myself back in control here. Deck was my biggest challenge over the years, because he knew me. Hiding who I was took talent, and I think the only way I got away with it was because he was gone most of the time. But Deck knew damn well I'd never taken self-defense, never been a fighter and never been able to get off a punch on him.

"Answer me."

I didn't have an answer. For once, there was no sassy comeback.

"Answer me. Damn it."

I was slipping. I knew how to keep my mouth shut. And this was one of those times, but feeling Deck's pulsating fury and hearing the confusion in his voice ... it made everything I was doing worthless.

"I don't know what the fuck is going on with you, but I'm finding out. In the meantime, you're being locked down. Bullshit has ended."

"Deck!"

"No, Georgie. I'm done."

Oh, God. I need my phone. I had to call *him*. "Don't do this."

"Everything okay here?" A nurse came running over and looked from me to Deck and back again.

"Deck. Please." I resorted to begging. I'd have no access to a phone, no way to contact Tanner to get me out. Shit, would he even know where Deck was taking me? Well, he would, but the question was how long would it take and by then …

"Sir, she should be in bed—"

Deck ignored the nurse. "You drank so much you nearly died. You have cuts on you that you say came from a tree but a doctor says are likely caused by a knife. You snuck out on Vic and disappeared for hours only to be found convulsing in front of Connor's grave. And you executed a defense move when you've never been to a single class. What the fuck do you want me to do, Georgie?" His voice was that of a drum, pounding through the room so loud it made my head vibrate.

Then Tyler was there. "All okay, Boss?"

The nurse touched my arm. "Miss. I've alerted the doctor. Come back to your room and lie down."

I shrugged her off. "How can you throw me away like this?"

Deck held me by both shoulders. "Damn it, Georgie, I'm not throwing you away. I'm bringing you back to me."

But there was no going back, was there?

If he put me in rehab, he'd find out damn fast I never had an addiction. There would be no withdrawals, no shakes, and no friggin' nothing. I couldn't fake through that. Shit. Shit. Shit. I'd played it too good. Deck thought I was a pathetic alcoholic who nearly killed herself.

Deck's cell rang and he passed me off to Tyler. Smart, both of them knew I'd make a run for it. The nurse stood there a little stunned and then she slipped past both of us, ran to the nurses' station and picked up the phone.

"Why are you calling, Kai?"

My breath hitched, and I quickly smothered it by pretending the wound on my back hurt as I put my hand to it and winced.

Deck locked eyes with me and then walked away a few steps. Holy

71

shit. Panic gripped my lungs with each breath. I was still fucked up from my annual purge, waking up in the hospital and then having Deck question me about things I had no way to answer unless I told him the truth.

"You could've died, sweetie," Tyler said. I yanked away from Tyler's grip and propped myself against the wall, but he stayed within inches of me. "You didn't see him." He kept his voice low as he leaned into me, arms on either side, palms against the pale-blue walls. "He was scared, Georgie. Getting that call from Vic and he was ten hours away …" Tyler lowered his head, shaking it slowly back and forth. "What if we'd been on a mission? What if he couldn't get here? Sweets, if anything ever happened to you … Jesus, I don't know what he'd do." I looked to the side, avoiding his eyes. He wouldn't let me and cupped my head with both hands. "Don't know what's going on with you, but you need to get better."

This *was* me better. I had no better. No overhaul, renovation or restoration job was going to fix me. But I learned to accept it and live with pieces of me undecipherable and stained.

DECK

I LOOKED OVER my shoulder and saw Tyler standing far closer to Georgie than I liked. "Why are you calling?"

"I heard Georgie got herself into some trouble."

"I'm not going to ask how you know about that. But I *do* want to know why she cares if I'm talking to you." I saw the look on her face when I said his name. She'd met Kai when he'd helped kill the sex trafficker. Was Georgie nervous of Kai? She must have known I'd never let him near her again.

"She okay?"

"I don't have time for idle conversation with a guy I don't like. So, why the fuck are you calling?"

"Ah, so Georgie is idle conversation?"

"Georgie and anything to do with Georgie is off-limits to you." The

72

bastard had the gall to chuckle and I clenched the phone harder. "I told you never to call unless it was an emergency."

"It is." I waited. "I need the girl found."

"Jesus. Like I told you in New York, it's not happening. I don't have time for that shit." London, the girl I rescued from the sex-trafficking auction a number of years ago. She'd stayed at Georgie's place until I found out who she was and where she came from. Found out she's from a very wealthy family. She has been a constant runaway ever since she came back. Last I heard, she'd been missing for nearly a year … longest yet. Kai was interested in finding her. Wealthy family probably was paying him a shitload to bring her home. Thing was, it didn't fit with the type of work Kai did. According to what little I could dig up on Kai when I'd first met him, he stayed low. Meaning no high-profile shit. London was high profile.

"It's a time issue."

I coughed on my half-laugh. "Why? The parents paying you extra if you find her before a year is up?" When he dragged my men and me to New York, I was under the impression it was something big—it wasn't. But I owed him a favor, so we went and checked out the area London had last been seen. Then the call came in about Georgie from Matt and we flew back.

"The favor was for two days."

"Yeah, well you got one." I had enough problems with wondering what to do about Georgie. Vic knew a place she could go to sober up, get help, but no matter what I said two minutes ago, I was following my instinct and backing down. Something wasn't right. It was like a tickle in the back of my throat constantly niggling me. Her cuts. Her disappearing act. That self-defense move she pulled. Shit, the bottle of Scotch she drank somewhere other than Connor's grave, because Vic had sworn she wasn't there all day. But suddenly she shows up there, passed out with some guy calling an ambulance.

Who the hell was the guy? A coincidence that he finds her lying unconscious and convulsing at Connor's grave. I didn't believe in co-incidences.

I looked over the moment Tyler put his hands on either side of her head as if he was going to kiss her. I knew he wouldn't, but still, I didn't like it. I had to end this conversation fast. I kicked at the orange plastic chair in front of me and it toppled over. Both Georgie and Tyler looked at me, he dropped his hands from her and a nurse behind the desk scowled at me.

I felt like a fuse had been lit inside me and was slowly burning. Soon I was going to lose it, and losing it in front of strangers didn't happen. But my thread was pulled so tight right now it was going to snap any minute. I couldn't get out of my head the look in her eyes after she drove her elbow back into my cheek. It was an expert's move. When the hell did she ever take a class to learn that shit? Georgie was too busy partying to take a class. It didn't make sense.

I heard the ding of the elevator, then watched two burly men wearing security uniforms walk out, a doctor with them. Kai was saying something about the fuckin' favor, but I was focused on what was about to go down. My eyes shot to the nurse behind the desk who was looking at me and talking on the phone. The men coming our way had eyes locked on Georgie and Tyler.

"Tyler." I snapped my phone shut, hanging up on Kai.

He was instantly alert, turning and standing in front of Georgie like armour. I strode toward the doctor and the two buffoons to intercept. The nurse called out to me, but I knew enough about hospital policies to know what was going down.

The doctor stopped in front of me, cocky little bastard wearing a fuckin' sneer on his narrow face. I was blocking him from getting anywhere near Georgie, although I suspected from his expression, and Rick and Mick at his side, that he thought differently. "Sir, only family members are allowed to visit."

"I'm not visiting."

He cleared his throat and shifted uneasily while adjusting his glasses, which didn't need adjusting. "We're going to have to ask you and your friend to leave. The nurse will help the patient back to her room." From the corner of my eyes, I saw the nurse——name tag, Belinda—come out from behind the desk.

"Deck," Tyler warned. And it *was* a warning because I had my hand on the gun beneath my jacket. "Not here, Boss."

"We'll look after her. She can leave after a psych evaluation scheduled for tomorrow and after the police have been to question her about the wounds on her back. It's mandatory after something like this.

We'd also like to re-run her blood for precaution."

I stared at him for several seconds then I glanced over at Georgie, who stood quietly behind Tyler. I didn't like it. And I sure as hell didn't like the doctor, but starting a fight in the hospital would cause us problems. Besides, Georgie was better off here for one more night and I *did* want to hear what she told the police about the fuckin' cuts on her back.

I nodded to Tyler. Fine, one night.

"When can we pick her up?" Tyler asked.

The nurse gave instructions about discharge to Tyler and I approached Georgie. She was still up against the wall, having not said a word during the whole exchange.

"Tomorrow, you're coming with me. We need to sort this shit out. Okay?" She nodded and I felt her tremble as I ran my hands down her arms. There it was … in her eyes. The vulnerability and softness that had been hidden for years. Fuck, I wanted to wrap her up in my arms and kiss her so fuckin' badly. I cleared my throat. "Pass the psych exam, would you?"

She smiled and it was the first time in over ten hours I felt like I could breathe. She grabbed my sleeve before I walked away.

"Deck. I need to tell you …" She stopped, straightened her shoulders and looked around as if searching for someone. Then her eyes dropped to the floor and she looked … scared. Georgie rarely looked scared, and it reminded me of the moment I told her about Connor. "Please, don't put me in rehab."

Jesus. Then she said shit like that.

I paused. Blue streaks hung down the side of her face, no makeup, standing against the wall in the light blue hospital gown. Innocent. She was innocent and yet, I knew Georgie. She was a lot more than that. She was stubborn and determined, had an attitude, which was part of her, but for some reason, it was more exaggerated than I thought suited her.

But her looking at me, uncertain, exposed and yet still with confidence … this was the Georgie I knew.

This was who I'd fight to bring back. "I won't." I nodded to the right where the doc stood watching me. "Don't let that guy touch you." She smiled at that and I tucked her hair away from her face. "We'll talk tomorrow. Get some rest, baby."

The nurse put her hand on Georgie's arm and guided her back to her room.

CHAPTER SEVEN

Georgie

I MOANED, MY head rolling side to side as I repeated over and over in my head the word—No. A spider crawled over my skin, but it wasn't a spider—it was blood droplets. I couldn't move to push it away as the fear felt as if an oil drum sat on my chest. Oil. The rag. It was choking me.

I couldn't breathe.

I couldn't spit it out. The material scratching at the back of my throat making me gag.

My stomach rolled and swirled as the breeze swept across my face—his breath—Scotch. It was him. I had to run, but it was foggy. The shed was a long, narrow hallway now and I ran and ran but never moved.

No.

Stop. No more.

The words were in my head and I tried to form them, but the sounds were trapped in my throat. Moans. Strangled moans. Were they from me?

I fell to my knees and sobbed.

The shadow hovered over me. The glint of the knife.

I froze. Terror grabbed hold as I waited for the pain. The fear. The taste of my blood in the air.

I scraped my knees when he knocked me down then dragged me into the maintenance shed with the school's lawnmower and gardening tools. The door clanged shut, making some of the metal tools hanging on the wall hit one another at the vibration.

I completely lost it.

Struggling against his hold like a shark caught in a net above water, I flailed, hitting him in the teeth with my fist. I even managed to escape and get a few feet from the door before he dove on me and we landed hard on the plank floor, the wind knocked out of me. "I didn't expect such a fighter."

He flipped me over and held my hands down above my head, but I still tried to get away. Desperate. Hoping someone would hear my screams, but the shed was far enough away from the main school that few people would ever walk by it.

I didn't know who he was except that he was a senior. He had sandy-blond hair and a big, crooked nose as if he'd had it broken a few times. Wide features contained a stern, hard look in his eyes as if whatever cries I made would do nothing to change that unsympathetic gaze.

He raised my dress above my thigh and I freaked, screaming and kicking and crying. He pressed his hand over my mouth and then used his weight on top of me to keep me from squirming away. The cold edge of the blade pricked my throat and I shrunk away tilting my head to the side, kicking my feet but unable to move anything else.

"Stay still, damn it. I don't want to hurt you—not much, anyway." *He ran the blade down my skin until it rested in the hollow of my throat. "Not allowed to. I could get into trouble." I whimpered. He pressed the tip of the knife into my flesh and I tried to move away. He scowled and I stopped. "You know what happens if you don't behave?"*

No, I didn't. I had no idea what this guy wanted from me, but I suspected and it made my blood run cold.

He laughed then clucked his tongue as he sat up, straddling me. I went to move and he sliced the knife across my arm. I screamed and he shut me up with a rag from the ground beside the lawnmower.

He slowly undid the buckle on his belt, and I started crying and sobbing beneath the oil soaked rag. He pulled the belt from the loops of his jeans.

I swallowed the bile, knowing if I threw up I'd choke.

"Maybe next time you won't try to run." He got off me, yanked me up so hard my neck cracked, and then I was on my knees with my back to him. He pulled my dress over my head and threw it aside, then pulled my arms behind my back and wrapped the belt around my wrists so tightly I lost feeling in my fingers within seconds.

"That's a good girl. Relax and it won't hurt."

He ran his hand down my back, gentle and soft like he was caressing my skin. "A blank canvas. I watched you. So perfect and sweet, quiet. And then ... " He sighed. "And then the perfect opportunity came, and I was given the chance to fix you." His hand on my back became rough.

Then I felt the sharp prick of the knife on my spine. I arched and tried to move away, but he shoved me hard in the back with the heel of his hand and I fell forward so my cheek was pressed into the wood floor.

"Now, don't move, princess."

Then the cutting began.

I sobbed quietly the entire time. It was as if he was drawing on me with his knife. He hummed as he did it, a joyful tune he repeated over and over again. It didn't feel deep, as if he wanted to mark me, but not scar me.

Suddenly, it all changed and Deck was there. So was Connor. They were fighting him, trying to get to me. I was screaming and crying, but I couldn't get free.

I couldn't get free.

I couldn't get away.

"Deck!" I flailed, kicked and sobbed.

"Hold her."

Hands held my wrists. No. No, it was the belt. The belt was being tied around my wrists.

I couldn't distinguish what was real. "Let me go. Let me go!" I yelled as loud as I could.

Everything meshed together. The voices. Images.

"Damn it, sedate her."

I screamed again and again as the images roared through my head.

He was running after Deck, knife in his hand, his eyes laughing. Deck was just standing there looking at me. He was shaking his head—disappointed. He was disappointed with me.

Why wasn't he looking at the boy who was going to kill him?

"Deck. Deck."

Heaviness gripped me and I was running in slow motion toward them. I wasn't going to get there in time. *No, don't take him from me, too.* "Please. No."

The knife came toward Deck's chest in slow motion. I sobbed hysterically, but Deck just stood there watching as the knife kept coming.

"Nooo." I couldn't lose him.

"Sir. Sir. You can't go in there—"

"Out of my way before I throw you out of my way."

Deck?

I moaned.

What was happening? I couldn't see him anymore. It was dark and … I struggled again. Tossing and turning trying to find him.

"Shh. Calm down." I didn't recognize the voice. I heard the shuffling of feet. Who was here? "What the hell is going on out there?"

"You need to move. Now."

My eyes flew open when I heard his voice. Deck. He was alive. Robbie didn't kill him. I tried to sit up, but I couldn't. I pulled upward again, my brain foggy, limbs weak and … I looked down and saw the straps around my wrists.

I jerked violently on them as the nightmare of the belt became real.

"Just relax. We'll let you go once you settle down."

I choked on the sob screeching from my throat as the doctor's words hit me. "No," I cried and yanked on the straps, but everything was so heavy and slow. I couldn't focus as the room blurred and the man standing beside the bed became what my mind was fighting to make him.

I heard something hard hit a wall outside the door and then the crash of what sounded like a metal tray with dishes hitting the floor.

A woman's voice, "Oh, my God. Please. Don't shoot me."

"Then move out of my fuckin' way." The door burst open and the glare of the hallway lights blinded me for a few seconds. All I saw was a large shadow standing in the doorway.

I let the sobs take hold and tears streamed down my face.

His long strides reached me in seconds and I kept my eyes on him, afraid if I closed them, he'd disappear.

"Sir, she was violent and we—"

"What the fuck did you give her?" Deck put his hand on my arm, and with one pull, he ripped off the tape holding the catheter and tossed it aside. He leaned over and I heard the sleek sound of the knife pulled from its leather case.

"It was a mild sedative, but you can't—"

He interrupted the nurse by saying nothing, merely giving her a hard glare. There was no fear with Deck. He didn't think about the consequences; instead, he reacted to his instinct and didn't back down from doing what he thought was best. It was one of the things I loved about him.

"Deck," I cried.

"Yeah, baby." He cut the straps on my wrists with one quick movement.

"I'm sorry." I didn't know what else to say, because it was all I had.

Deck never said a word as he lifted me into his arms. My head fell against his shoulder, too weak to hold upright as the sedation took effect. Arms tight around me, a rag doll hanging limp in his hard, familiar arms.

I noticed he never looked at me.

He strode from the room, but I could hear running footsteps coming toward us.

"Mr. Ryan." Deck's arms tightened, but his stride never faltered as the doctor's voice cut through the air following us.

"Mr. Ryan, she can't leave. It's the middle of the night. We haven't discharged her—"

"Georgie, can you sit?" I sighed as a wave of comfort settled over me at the familiar sound of his voice.

I nodded.

He set me in one of the orange plastic chairs against the wall, his hands lingering on my hips as if making sure I was steady. Then he let me go and faced the doctor.

I saw the cold, piercing stare as he slowly pulled his gun from the holster. I could hear the click of the hammer and then the doc's fumbling words as he put his hands up and stepped back. I also heard several gasps from the nurses.

"Whoa. You can't do that."

"I can do whatever the hell I want. I'm the one with the gun."

"The police have been called …" I heard the shakiness in his voice and his eyes never left the barrel of the gun.

Deck took out his phone, pressed a few numbers and put it to his ear while he kept his gun on the doctor. "Call our guy. Tell him the incident at the hospital is me taking my girl home." He paused. "Tell him I'm her emergency contact and she wants to leave. He can call me and verify if he needs to." He shoved the phone back in his pocket, taking two steps to reach the doctor who still had his hands up with his back to the wall. Deck slid his gun back in his holster then got right in his face.

I couldn't see Deck's face, but just the way he held himself was intimidating. The doc's eyes were like dinner plates and his skin was solid white.

"If she tells me anything else happened here that I don't like, I'm coming back for you."

Deck walked to me, picked me up, cradled me in his arms then strode down the hall to the elevator and pressed the button.

I SAW TYLER—well, a blurred form of Tyler—waiting by the car, arms crossed, leaning back against it, his face pensive. "Jesus. What the fuck?" Tyler opened the car door and Deck gently lowered me onto the leather front seat. "Drugged?"

"Sedated," Deck said.

"What the fuck? Why?"

"Tyler, leave it." It was an abrupt order, and I could tell from his lowered brows and pursed lips he was barely holding control. By Tyler's nod and his glance at me, he got that.

He grabbed the seat belt and began to pull it across my lap. I shook my head. "No."

Deck's eyes closed for a brief moment then he let the seatbelt go, straightened and shut the door. He turned and spoke to Tyler, although I couldn't hear him. Tyler nodded, looked at me then hopped in the back seat, the phone to his ear.

I watched Deck's tall, lean form walk around the front of the car. Every muscle flexed, fury pulsating off him. He was like a time bomb, quiet and patient, but the tick, tick, and tick was a reminder that eventually there would be an explosion.

The car door slammed and he started the engine. Stray pebbles scattered beneath the tires as he drove. The radio was off. Tyler was silent and even the subtle sound of breathing seemed offensive to the tension in the car. I crossed my arms over my chest and stared out the side window at the whoosh of cars speeding by in the opposite direction.

I felt like a guppy floundering in a sea of sharks, always trying to escape from something. I didn't know what I was doing anymore. The path I'd drawn for myself always seemed so clear, but suddenly … suddenly, it was all fucked up.

"What happened?"

I jerked at the sound of Deck's harsh voice breaking the silence and then a rush of comfort settled over me. He always had that effect, as if I was cocooned in his protective warmth. In the beginning when he came back, I tried to escape it, fighting him, but I was only fighting myself. Deck was part of me whether it was right or wrong, good or bad. He lived in me, and I'd do anything to keep that part of me alive.

His voice cut through my thoughts. "What happened?"

"I … I had a bad dream."

"It was more than that." A statement.

I nodded. It was my past coming back to find me. After the purging, the memories flooded me, but normally, I was home alone for a few days where no one could see me as my mind and body healed.

"The cuts. The drinking. The 'bad dream'. I want it all."

My eyes shot to his.

"You have one day to get your story straight." He briefly glanced at me. "And Georgie, the story will be the truth." He was still pulsating with fury, lips tight, brows drawn over his dark eyes, but he was no longer clenching his jaw. He glanced in the rear view mirror. "Tyler?"

"All good, Boss."

I looked over my shoulder at Tyler and he was typing on his phone. He looked up at me as if he sensed eyes on him and there wasn't the usual wink or grin, it was his mouth drawn downwards. He went back to typing and I faced forward.

"The police—" I started.

"Are dealt with."

I nodded. Deck knew people, but breaking me out of a hospital at gunpoint …

"Where are we going?" *Please don't say rehab. Please don't say rehab.*

"My place."

I took a deep breath then leaned my head against the window. I didn't want to close my eyes again. I was scared the nightmare would come back, but the drugs weren't giving me a choice. "Don't let me fall asleep," I whispered.

"It's safe to sleep, Georgie. You're always safe with me."

I nodded. Yeah, I was. Deck made sure of it; he always did. "I was scared." I think it was the first time I ever admitted that.

Deck would naturally think I was talking about the hospital, but I wasn't. I was talking about my past. The days I walked home from school looking over my shoulder, afraid he'd catch me. My heart slamming into my chest, so scared I'd vomit. I never knew when he'd take me to the shed. It could be weeks or days before he'd grab me.

My parents became concerned because I'd lost weight, but they assumed it had to do with Connor's death. I thought of telling them what was happening. So many times, I'd opened my mouth to blurt it out then I'd slam it shut, terrified of losing someone else in my life. Robbie was sick. He'd do it. He'd kill my parents if I told anyone.

"I know." Deck looked at me as his eyes said everything. There was no shield blocking that look. It was him telling me he'd always be there. Him telling me he cared. Then the shield slammed down again and he looked away.

This man … I would never have him, but I also knew I'd never deserve him. Deck was everything I wasn't and more.

Deck was selfless.

And I knew he protected me because Connor asked him to, but Connor had been dead a long time. Deck put up with my shit, and it was a lot of shit. I knew soon it would blow up and I wouldn't be able to stop it. I'd tried for most of my life to protect Deck from my lies. It wasn't for my sake—it was for his. If anything happened to him...

The car went dark as we pulled into the underground parking lot and lurched to a halt. Deck got out, walked around and opened my door. He lifted me in his arms and I curled into him. I inhaled and my body sagged with relief as his scent swirled into my lungs. There was no question, drugged or not, my every molecule knew Deck. I'd recognize him buried beneath the ground.

"Later, Georgie girl." Tyler headed to the driver's door. Without waiting for a response, he jumped in the driver's seat and peeled away.

I looked up at Deck. Our eyes locked and my lips parted about to say something, I just didn't know what.

DECK

I'D NEVER FELT so fucked up in my life. I was on the edge of losing it. Who was I kidding; I'd already lost it, pulling a fuckin' gun on a nurse and then a doctor. Shit, I could imagine what the Chief of Police had screamed in Tyler's ear. The police may overlook my indiscretions, but I wasn't immune.

What the fuck was going on with her? An inferno of rage blazed inside me and yeah, it was directed at her. I was so pissed off I was afraid to speak.

Unable to sleep, I'd come back to the hospital to sit with her. That was until they tried to stop me from seeing her and then the straps holding her down like some fuckin' animal.

I felt her eyes on me as I strode into the elevator and pressed the PH button.

Shit, I felt as if a gun was aimed at me from miles away. I followed my instinct, and I'd never had it let me down—until now. Now, it fucked with me because I'd left her in the hospital when I shouldn't have. I hated the feeling of uncertainty of what the hell was going to happen here with Georgie. I lived by doing and never second-guessing. You're dead if you second-guess.

Now, we deal.

A motto we lived by when bad shit went down. There was no point wondering what the fuck you should've done or could've. Bad shit happened. Fucked-up happened. Deal with it and move on.

But suddenly, dealing with whatever was happening with Georgie was not so cut and dry.

CHAPTER EIGHT

Georgie

I WOKE UP in his bed having slept all day from the sedative. The last I remembered was being held in his arms in the elevator. When I sat up, I saw Deck sitting in the black-leather chair in the corner of the room, a book in hand and one leg casually crossed over the other. He looked completely relaxed and so not like Deck.

He quietly closed the book and set it on the dresser beside him before a creak of leather sounded as he stood. I couldn't take my eyes off him as he strode toward me, stopping when his knees touched the side of the bed. He reached forward and my heart slammed into my chest as he put his hand on my head and smoothed my hair back.

It was the most calming, sweet caress I'd ever experienced, and the heat in my body rose as I took him in. It also scared me as to why he was so calm.

"I'll make you something to eat while you shower."

I expected him to pound me with questions. This … this threw me completely off-balance.

There was literally nothing in this world that smelled better than him. It was as if inhaling his scent wrapped my lungs in the comfort of home. I hated that I felt that way, yet after all these years I concluded nothing was changing it.

I loved Deck. Had since I was sixteen and no matter what fucked-up shit was in my head—I always would. But our chance had been destroyed by the fucked-up world we lived in. And yes, by the choices I'd made.

Before he could move away, I grabbed his hand. The coarse feel of his skin sent a wave of desire through me. I needed this connection with him. To feel him. To know he was real, that *this* was real. Because my life was anything but and suddenly, I needed it to be. "Why do you keep saving me when all I do is disappoint you?"

Deck's brows lowered and he tried to slip his hand from mine, but I tightened my grip. His scowl intensified. "Georgie. Don't." I let his hand go. "Take a shower. Tyler brought over some things for you while you slept. They're in the bathroom."

I felt every single word hit me in the heart. It was Deck stomping on my chest with his combat boot and watching as it squished my heart into a pancake. He didn't even want to touch my hand. Yeah, well, what did I expect?

He walked to the door.

Maybe that was why it was so much easier to be someone I wasn't. He rejected *her*, not the real me. I could push it away and drown it out. But now, it was like my two worlds were colliding and I had no escape.

He stopped in the doorway and then without turning said, "No more lies."

I inhaled sharply and he must have heard me because his shoulders tensed. But he didn't look at me; instead, he walked away.

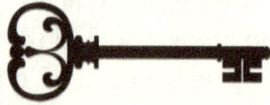

THE WARM WATER ran over my skin like a heated silk sheet then pooled at my feet. I leaned up against the tiled wall and closed my eyes, his words repeating over and over in my head.

Telling the truth wasn't so simple. Never would be and yet …

The bathroom door opened.

I forced myself to remain still as Deck walked in.

I swallowed then licked my lips as my heart began to pound. He leaned against the counter, crossing his arms with his head tilted slightly down as if he were looking at his feet. Unusual for Deck; he met everything head-on without hesitation.

The water hit my breasts and my nipples hardened. Between my legs fluttered with tingles and I knew if I touched myself, I'd feel the slick moisture of what Deck did to me without a single touch.

I did the only thing I was comfortable doing when in a situation which made me uneasy—I used my sass. "You going to stand there or join me?" I was a little surprised that even through the fogged door, I saw his jaw clench.

"You've been lying to me."

I froze for a second, swallowed then picked up the shampoo bottle and pretended to be unconcerned as I squirted the coconut-smelling liquid into my hand. "Jesus, Deck, are you really going to bring this up while I'm in the shower naked with you standing two feet away?"

I closed my eyes and began massaging my head.

The shower door opened and suddenly he was standing a foot away. "What the fuck is going on?"

Now, *this* was the Deck I expected, yet I was still unprepared, especially naked in the shower with soap all over me. Maybe the sass hadn't been a good idea.

I was uncertain what he knew, didn't know what lies he was referring to. There were so many I didn't even know myself what part of me was the truth and what wasn't. But revealing any of the truths had consequences—*he* warned me, and I'd known the rules when it all began. At the time, I never thought Deck was coming back.

His gaze trailed down my naked, glistening body and I felt as if it were his fingertips. Goosebumps bristled and my knees weakened. Our eyes met, and I recognized the desire in the depths of his.

I wanted him so badly it was pathetic, and I hated myself for it. We stared at one another for several seconds; the only sound was the water peppering my flushed skin.

He stepped under the spray and blocked it from hitting me as he came in close, stopping only when his jean-clad thighs brushed against mine. I glanced down at his bare feet and then slowly back up again. He was watching me. And it was taking every part of my strength to deny him.

"Deck ..."

"No." His hands came down on my shoulders and his fingers tightened. I winced under the pressure. "When you open your mouth, I want the words explaining why the fuck you're not currently shaking and trembling and going through withdrawal."

Shit. I'd been so freaked out over the purge, then the hospital and the dream that I hadn't even considered the reality that Deck would realize my drinking had been a lie. I'd thought he'd been referring to the cuts on my body. But after no drinking for over thirty hours ... an alcoholic would have withdrawal symptoms, the shakes being one of them.

I opened my mouth to deny, to make up some shit story I knew he'd see right through, but I had nothing. I couldn't even begin to figure out a story that would remotely explain except for the truth, and I couldn't give him what he wanted. What *I* wanted.

He slammed his fist into the tiled wall above my head. The look on his face was one I'd never seen before—ravaged. "Damn it. Talk to me."

Oh, God. I wanted so desperately to tell him everything. I was cracking and yet I had nothing to give him. I couldn't. It could kill him, and I'd never take that chance. It was all I had to give him.

Water dripped down his face, clothes soaking-wet, lips tight and yet in his eyes, I saw hurt. He was wounded and that was worse than the disappointment and the anger.

I didn't care what happened to me; I was past that. What I cared about was the threat to Deck, because it was real. It had been pounded into my head since I was sixteen what would happen if I ever told anyone. Then when Deck came back, it was reiterated specifically for Deck. And *he* was the one person in this world I knew was capable of killing Deck. "Don't ask me. Please."

"Christ." He pushed off from the wall and turned to leave. I reached for him; I didn't know why. I should've let him go, but I needed him. I always did and now more than ever because I was crumbling. It wasn't fair what I was doing to him, but I'd found out real young that life wasn't fair and you had to suck it up and do what needed to be done to keep those you love safe.

The second my hand curled around his arm, he violently spun

around. I thought he was going to push me away from him but instead, he pushed me against the wall then pressed his body hard against mine. His hands locked my wrists on either side of my head on the tiles.

He groaned just before his mouth crushed mine.

It was an assault. It was him wanting to hurt me. It was Deck taking and me submitting. Pain and need. It was being fed after starving for years. My thirst for him was so strong and unable to be quenched. I felt the tears streaming from my eyes as he continued to kiss me, tongue driving into my mouth. No forgiveness. No mercy.

Nothing prepared me for this kiss as he made me his, taking from me every ounce of myself and giving it to him. I sagged into him, my mouth sore and painful at his aggression.

It was what I wanted. What I expected from Deck. And yes, I deserved it to be painful. I wanted it to be painful, so it would make it *real*.

He abruptly broke away, but his chest remained against mine as we both breathed hard. His grip on my wrists tightened. I panted and stared at him, my vision blurred from the tears and the water that continued to pound into us. I closed my eyes, unable to face him knowing I'd lose the one man I wouldn't survive without if I told him. But if I didn't … I'd lose him anyway.

"Look. At. Me."

I took my time opening my eyes and when I did, more tears escaped, sliding down my cheeks. It was then I saw his shoulders slump and it was like something cracked in him. I didn't know how I knew, but Deck … I knew Deck, and I saw it with the way the tension around his mouth eased. How his hands uncurled. How his eyes softened as if the dark brown melted to warm milk chocolate.

"Baby, I can't help you without knowing what's happening."

And that did it. A sob escaped and I lowered my head. I never expected his touch as he moved in and took hold of me. The comfort it gave me released the cries. His arms were warm and yet hard as he wrapped me in his cocoon of protectiveness. It became a release of everything.

It was like when I went to the shed and let go of all the emotions, except … there was no cutting. No memories. Just Deck. I felt safe with him, always had. No matter what haunted me, what lies I lived, Deck was my real.

The weight in my chest lifted as he held me and I cried. It wasn't for me. It was for him and what I was doing to him. I had to protect him. This man who stole my heart at such a young age. But I didn't know how anymore. I was afraid I couldn't and that … that terrified me.

There were no words as he cradled me against his chest for a long time, his hand caressing my hair, water beating into his back and making a smacking sound as it soaked his shirt. "I can't lose you," I mumbled against him.

His arms tightened and he kept his hand on the back of my head to keep me from looking up at him. He didn't say anything, and that scared me because Deck would never lie. He was his word. He was the type who would tell a girl she looked like shit if he thought she did.

And I was a complete lie.

Fresh tears spilled, indistinguishable from the water. He pulled back and I caught a glimpse of his face before he turned away. Haunted. Broken. God, was there fear in his eyes? Then that steel shield dropped, he became the Deck I was so familiar with. He was shutting down.

We were a lot alike. I hid behind a false persona, and he blocked his out.

I stood in the shower for a few minutes after he left, the water now cold, but I felt nothing. Nothing except Deck's mouth still tingling on mine.

DECK

I PEELED OFF my wet clothes, tossed them on the bed, and then walked over to my dresser, taking out a fresh t-shirt and pair of jeans. I heard the water shut off and the sink tap turn on.

I sat on the edge of the bed and leaned over, putting my head in my hands. Fuck. I kissed her. I'd held off for ten goddamn years. Ten years. Yet when everything was a complete fuck-fest … I kissed her.

Jesus, everything was in chaos and I hated chaos. I grunted—chaos. Bad choice of words. Fuckin' Connor. It was killing me not to go after him. He was alive somewhere and yet he didn't want to be found. Well, he was getting his wish. I had to deal with Georgie; then maybe if I could find a way to keep her safe from Connor's threat, I'd go after him. Maybe I'd even ask Kai to help. He knew the worst scum in the world and might be an asset.

I'd watched Georgie sleep all day. No shaking. Trembling. Hands steady when she woke. Not one withdrawal symptom. I'd fuckin' waited for it. I'd called the doctor I used for my men just to be sure because I couldn't believe what I was seeing. She lay peacefully all fuckin' day.

Georgie should have been a washing machine on spin cycle having not had a drink. There was no opportunity for her to have any, so that meant …

The relief she wasn't an alcoholic was overwhelming. But then … then the crushing reality of what that meant sank in. The confusion as to why she'd pretend to be an alcoholic. The hurt. Yeah, it fuckin' hurt like hell she'd been playing it up like she was. The bottles in her purse. The constant partying and the slurred words and stumbling.

What the fuck was going on? I hadn't intended on talking to her naked in the shower. I hadn't intended on opening the shower door. Shit, I hadn't intended a lot of shit with her.

I wanted to strangle her, and yell and force her to tell me. I had gone into the bathroom to do just that, but then I opened the shower door and saw her. She looked so … vulnerable and fragile. I hated her for whatever bullshit she'd been feeding me, us—everyone. But the protective instinct to hold her and take away the pain I saw swirling within the depths of her eyes …

I crashed. I fuckin' crashed.

I kissed her and broke down that last wall which had been teetering for years.

My cock had never been so fuckin' hard, and yet I wasn't even thinking about sex. I was thinking about her, the girl, the woman, the sassy smartass chick. I wanted to take the pain I felt in her away with my kisses. Carry her to my bed and hold her until she fell asleep in my arms. Wake up to her messy, blue-streaked hair and her smart-ass remarks. Then I wanted the girl I'd lost so long ago. I knew she was still part of Georgie. The sweet, innocent girl who tried to please everyone, who wasn't broken and filled with so much anger and pain and trying to numb it with all the bullshit.

Jesus. Had I driven her to this? Why would she pretend to be something she wasn't? I'd wanted her for so long, the lines were now blurred. She was almost an obsession. I knew it, and my men fuckin' knew it.

The reason I could never have her was so faded into what I wanted and needed that I was uncertain if it was even the real reason anymore. At first, I tried to do what was right and keep my word to Connor, but now … now, right was being washed away. There was no right anymore. Except, what right did I have bringing her into my fucked-up world?

The door creaked and I raised my head. Georgie stood, wearing baggie, grey track pants and a loose pale-pink, V-neck shirt. I saw the transformation. She'd pulled herself together and was all sass now, but I was going to tear her back down again. I needed the truth, and if I didn't get it then I knew my only other choice—walk away.

"Really, Deck?" She gestured to her clothes.

I felt a pull on the corners of my lips. All this bullshit happening and she could still manage to get me to smile. "That's all you get." There was always a purpose to what I did and getting Tyler to bring a bag of sweats and baggy t-shirts was a damn good one. Didn't really work, though; she still looked fuckin' hot as hell.

I watched her think it over and it was cute. Yeah, she was ignoring the big picture here. She was debating whether to push the issue or let it ride. Georgie was good at pushing, but she was smart as hell and knew when to shut her mouth, too.

"I feel like ice cream."

And she was letting it go, probably scared I was going to start in on her.

And I was. I just wasn't doing it right now.

She cocked her hip and put her hand on it. Fuckin' track pants were supposed to do nothing for her body and yet … "Strawberry. You have any? I was thinking about putting it all over my body and having you lick it off." And there was the flirty sass she was hiding behind.

I stared at her for several seconds as my cock swelled just thinking about that image. Her lying on her back, hands above her head, squirming beneath me as I covered her body in ice cream, then inch by inch licked it off until only one place remained—between her thighs. She'd arch up toward me, begging to give her what she wanted yet I'd deny her until she submitted to me completely.

Georgie's complete and utter submission.

Yeah, I'd get it from her.

I lived by instinct. It drove me, protected me and it was going to be my breaking point. Because Georgie standing there, sober, beautiful and … Jesus, she looked innocent and sweet and sassy and stubborn.

"Or we can do your cock instead. My mouth—"

"Stop." I needed her to stop before I tossed her on the bed and fucked her.

Trying to cover up her vulnerability wasn't going to work anymore. I was an expert at getting the truth from people. I knew the tactics, and I was going to use them against her. I'd let her stir. Feel uneasy. Uncertain as to when I'd pounce. And I *would* pounce and it would be hard. "It's in the freezer."

CHAPTER NINE

Georgie

H E HAD MY strawberry ice cream? Deck didn't eat ice cream, but he had my favorite in his freezer. Two possibilities came to mind: either Deck bought it knowing I loved strawberry ice cream or he was a closet strawberry ice cream eater.

I opened the freezer and there it was. It was like opening a present on Christmas morning for two reasons. One, it was my favorite and two, because Deck had my favorite in his freezer. I found an ice cream scoop in the second drawer down, and I placed it and the container on the counter just as Deck walked into the kitchen. He was wearing his jeans low on his hips and a plain, black t-shirt that showed off every contour and accentuated his tatts. He came in close … real close, then reached past me into the cupboard and pulled out a bowl. Then I heard the scattering of utensils and the drawer banged shut.

The spoon clanged in the bottom of the bowl as he set it down in front of me.

"You have my favorite ice cream." It was a statement more to me than him. It was a revelation that this one small truth about me—Deck knew about.

He picked up the container, took off the lid, ripped the plastic from the top then grabbed the scoop and started dishing ice cream into the bowl. Swirls of vanilla and strawberry lay in the bottom in three large balls. He pushed the bowl toward me.

"I'm making pasta. Eat your ice cream."

I stared at him then the ice cream for several seconds then slid it to the other side of the counter and sat down on a bar stool.

I kept my head down while I ate, not sure why this was hitting me so hard. So what? Deck had known me for years, so he must have known. It wasn't a big deal. The thing was—it *was* a big deal to me. Because not only did he know, but he made sure it was here for me after the shit went down. He knew it was my comfort food, and I needed comfort because what Deck was doing … keeping me on edge … not confronting me … trying to throw me off balance … It was working.

Deck's bare feet padded across the ceramic tiles as he moved through the kitchen, completely at ease while I was silently freaking out. *He* told me I could never be Chaos when I was with Deck. I was the girl who fell in love with him. I was the woman who still loved him and one day it would be my destruction. Of course, *he'd* say that. The guy was guarded, mistrustful and his morals were questionable, but not once had he harmed me. Even the cutting he did once a year had been something he had refused to do at first. That was until he found out Tanner had done it to me that first time and the cuts had been pretty bad. After that, every year *he* met me on that day.

Deck's voice cut into my thoughts. "You came home from school one day, dress stained with what looked like ketchup, and you had a French fry in your hair." My spoon clinked into the bowl and I stared up at him, but he wasn't looking at me; he was cutting up mushrooms and peppers on a cutting board with his back to me. "The pins from your hair had fallen out and it was all windblown and knotted."

I used to be teased for being perfect all the time. Clothes always tidy and neat, hair tied back. I was the teacher's pet, the girl who was quiet in class and always got an A. But, often, I'd come home crying because the bullies had done something to me.

I remembered the day Deck was talking about. A group of boys in my class waited for me to come out of the side door of the school.

I always used the side door to avoid them, but they figured it out. As soon as the door opened and I saw them all standing watching me with big grins on their faces—I knew. It was too late, though. The bucket of slop came down on me from a window above. It was the cafeteria garbage, and I was covered in the remnants of the entire school's leftover lunch. I took off crying, their laughter ringing in my ears as they chanted 'Trashy Georgie'. It became my new nickname for the rest of the year. Even worse was that some people thought I was called that for another reason and so I was considered a slut, too.

When I did get home, I'd stood outside the house for several minutes, drying my eyes and cleaning myself off as much as possible. I was thankful at least we hadn't had any gravy at lunch that day. I walked in the house and saw Deck sitting on the couch playing a shooting video game with Connor, and I nearly ran back out. I didn't want him to see my blotchy face and red-rimmed eyes.

"I knew you'd been crying the second you walked in the door. I also knew you were trying to hide it." Deck threw the vegetables in the frying pan and they sizzled and hissed under the heat.

I didn't want to talk about this.

"Connor saw it, too." Yeah, but it had been Deck who'd nudged him in the shoulder and drew his attention away from the video game so he'd look at me. It took two seconds for Connor to reach me. He gave me a hug and quietly asked me what was wrong. I told him I tripped and fell with my lunch tray.

I knew he didn't believe me, but he saw my pleading eyes and let it go. My brother was good at reading me and he knew if he pushed, I'd be a crying mess and I hated that.

Deck didn't. No, he got up off the couch and stalked toward me as if he was the lion assessing his prey. When he stopped in front of me, he looked down at my dress, picked the French fry from my hair and met my eyes.

I think I fell in love with him right then. Actually, I knew I did. It was the way the warmth of his eyes penetrated me; it was as if he were wrapping me in his protective shield and nothing could get to me.

"You got me a bowl of strawberry ice cream."

He nodded. "And you sat cross-legged on the chair at the kitchen table, trying to hide behind a curtain of hair. You had a smudge of something on your face just above your cheekbone." I'd been mortified later when I'd gone in the washroom and seen what a mess I was … well, a mess to my standards, but the actual garbage hadn't done much damage except to my emotional wellbeing. The worst part was Deck seeing me like that. "You shovelled in that ice cream so goddamn fast I swear you must have had brain freeze a million times over."

I did. But I wanted to eat the ice cream as fast as I could and escape Deck's scrutiny. Even from the other room, I saw him talking quietly to Connor, but his eyes never left me.

"What were you telling him?" I'd always wanted to know.

"That no fuckin' way had you tripped, and if he didn't kick the ass of whoever was bullying you, I would."

But I never told Connor who was responsible despite him badgering me. A week later, they were deployed overseas.

I never saw Connor again.

"You were sixteen," Deck said. "And I shouldn't have wanted you, but fuck …" I jerked my gaze to him. *He wanted me? The quiet, spindly girl who was afraid of her own shadow?* "Connor saw it, too. There was just something about you … so stubborn … determined to be strong. Yet, vulnerable and fuck, babe … so goddamn beautiful."

He thought I was beautiful. "I wasn't stubborn or determined."

"Yeah, baby. You were."

I stiffened. "I wasn't." I was a wimp. I was tortured for months and never did anything about it.

"You were."

"I wasn't, damn it."

"You done arguing?" He glanced at me over his shoulder, his tatted arm flexed and tense as he held the frying pan.

"Yeah." I was feeling shaky and uncertain … no, it was way more than that. I was totally fucked up because Deck had wanted me back then. "You never saw me like a kid sister?"

Deck snorted. "Fuck no. Jesus, babe. I just fuckin' kissed you."

"I know, but back then—"

"No. Never. Now, go set the table."

I stared at his back, his shoulder muscles flexing as he stirred the vegetables, the ink on his arm catching the sun's sinking rays through the large bay windows above the sink. I knew each one of the tatts. Over the years, he'd extended the tribal design from his elbow up to the side of his neck. I felt heat rise on my cheeks as I thought about my fingertips sliding over the contours of his arms, tracing each then kissing the side of his neck where—

"Georgie."

I jerked my gaze from his neck up to his eyes. Shit, his eyes were narrowed and lips tight and Jesus, it was as if he had the reflection of fireworks blazing in his pupils. My heart sped up and my chest rose with every ragged breath.

He was looking at me as if he'd devour me, and it turned me on so goddamn much the moisture between my legs became wet and shivers became trembles.

"Table." It was one abrupt word, and yet it vibrated through me as if he'd just made me come with the flick of his finger.

I swallowed. Then I stood on my quivering legs and got my shit together because being undone by Deck was dangerous. "Yes, sir." I saluted and winked at him, trying my best to hide everything I was feeling with my usual sass. He scowled and turned back to the stove.

I set the table while Deck finished cooking. When I was done, I watched him from the other room and it didn't help me any when the image of him naked wearing a white apron came to mind. Then he turned, caught me staring, and I felt the heat in my cheeks. Shit, he was throwing me off-balance with everything he was doing.

He came toward me with a plate of steaming pasta, eyes locked on me.

I licked my dry lips and his gaze followed the action of my tongue as he set the plate down on the table between us. I knew I couldn't be wrong in that Deck wanted me right now.

"Mmm, looks delicious." I leaned over the table to peer at the pasta. "I didn't know you could cook, sweetpea."

Deck's eyes went from my breasts that, despite the too-big t-shirt, were accentuated with the way I was leaning and because I was turned on. I knew my nipples were showing because I didn't put on a bra.

He scooped a large amount of pasta onto my plate, way more than I could ever eat. "Because you don't. Just like I obviously don't know you."

Fuck. I had to steer this away from me. I sat back in my chair, crossing my arms. "And that's whose fault? You've never told me anything about yourself." I had stopped asking about his family a long time ago.

"Nothing to tell."

"And I *do* know what type of person you are. That's all that really matters anyway."

Deck snorted and shook his head while he filled his plate.

I said quietly, "I do know you, Deck. I know you like control. That you can't stand to be in a situation where you don't have it. I know you organize your shirts in your closet by color. That everything has to be in order. That you have a maid come clean your place once a week and she's here illegally and you overpay her so she can feed her family." That little tidbit I'd had to dig for because Deck kept that real quiet. She didn't even have a routine as to when she came—completely unpredictable.

Deck picked up his fork and spoon and began twirling his pasta as if he wasn't hearing a word I was saying. "How I keep my clothes and pay my maid is not knowing me."

"You protect me because you won't break your word to my brother. You always tell the truth and your men are like your family and you'd give your life for them."

The clang of his fork hit his plate as he dropped it. "If you want to go there, we can. I was giving you time to get your shit together, but we can do this right now."

I put my head down and started eating my pasta. He hadn't been giving me time. He had a method to getting answers. Shit, he tortured men for answers or he watched as Vic did it and from what I heard, he never failed.

"That's what I thought."

I glanced up from the corner of my eye and saw him pick his fork back up, twirl a forkful of pasta then drop it again and shove his plate away. He got up so abruptly his chair fell over, and then he strode to the sliding glass door, yanked it open and walked out onto the large terrace.

My body wanted to go after him, to soothe the anger pulsating from every pore in his body, but I *did* know Deck. I knew him well enough to know if I pushed him when he was like this, I'd push him in the wrong direction.

I sat and waited for him to come back, but he'd disappeared around the side of the patio where I couldn't see him through the windows. I shovelled the pasta around on my plate, starving but unable to eat any more.

I finally cleared the table when I realized Deck had no intention of coming back to eat with me. I took my time cleaning the kitchen, enjoying the tedious task since I was silently freaking out. God, I wanted to explain everything so badly it made me sick to my stomach. I was trapped and somehow I knew this day would come, I just thought ... shit, I didn't think. I hid. Deck had left for two years. I never thought he'd come back and by then it was too late.

I was leaning over the sink scrubbing the frying pan when I felt him behind me. Then his hands rested on my hips and I closed my eyes as the feel of him sunk into me. My heart pounded and shivers tickled my skin like the tip of a feather.

His breath swept over the right side of my neck as he spoke, "He asked me to protect you and ..."

I knew exactly who he was talking about—my brother.

"I finished up my two years with JTF2 after he died. The missions ... they helped me grieve. They eased the rage threatening to drive me over the edge. I got out as soon as they let me."

He leaned in closer so his thighs were up against me. "Connor also made me promise to never touch you. His exact words, 'Hands off my little sister. Don't date her, kiss her, and sure as fuck don't fuck her'."

My breath hitched and I dropped the frying pan into the sink, the water still running.

"He knew I felt something for you." Oh, God, tears filled my eyes. "Connor wanted a guy for you who didn't have a high probability of dying. I kill for a living. I don't have a family. And I most likely *will* die on one of these missions."

A tear slipped from its confines. "Deck." My voice quaked, "I'd rather have you for a day than never have you at all."

He spun me around. "He's right, Georgie. I'm not what you need."

"You don't know what I need, damn it." I hadn't meant to shout, but I was falling over the edge with no way back up. I was the one who had it bad for Deck and I was going to hurt him if he knew the truth. My entire life was a lie. Except my love for Deck. That was never a lie.

He grabbed my forearms before I could place my hands on his

chest. He scowled as he looked down at me. "Connor wanted better for you. I want better for you."

I met his dark tormented eyes and said softly, "You're my better, Deck." Before he could respond, I ducked under his arm and I walked away.

He let me.

CHAPTER
TEN

I FELL ASLEEP in the lounge chair on the terrace overlooking the plunge pool, but when I woke in the morning, it was in Deck's bed with my back against his chest, his hand beneath my shirt, fingers softly stroking my abdomen. I also noticed I had no jogging pants on, just panties, meaning he must have taken them off at some point. I felt the weight of his warm, hard thigh over the top of mine and his lips nuzzled into the crook of my neck.

I'd never felt so complete as I did at that moment. This was how it was supposed to be. Ten years of never getting this because … because each of us lived by our word. Him to my brother. Me to … *Him*. But keeping my word was different than Deck, I was forced to.

And now … I had to tell him something. Deck wouldn't have it any other way, and God, I wanted to tell him every single thing, but … I couldn't lose him. But how couldn't I? He'd figure it out anyway and then … I didn't want to think about Deck ever being killed especially because of me.

He already knew I wasn't an alcoholic but the rest … Deck was unpredictable and I had no idea how he was going to react. It terrified me to think I'd never have this again. That this moment was going to be lost to the lies. That he'd leave, but most of all, that he'd be hurt. And *I* did that to him. It would be my fault.

His arm tightened around my waist. "Your heart beats any faster, I'm taking you to the hospital."

Of course it was. I could pretend with anyone—except Deck. Hence the drinking cover-story idea. If I was drunk or pretended to be drunk, then it relieved some of the pressure of Deck finding out what I did for *him.*

Everything had changed. I had nothing to latch onto, to pull me from the inevitable despair that was coming.

"Need answers, babe," he whispered, his graveled morning voice vibrating against my neck.

I was sure this was some kind of tactic. Have me in bed in his arms all groggy and snuggled into him. Shit, it was a damn good tactic.

"Yeah. I … I don't want you to get hurt." In more ways than one. Emotionally because of the lies and physically because *he* made the rules damn clear.

"I'm pretty fuckin' tough."

I did a half-laugh and he tightened his hold on me. Who would've thought Deck could be sweet, but he kissed the top of my head then gently caressed my abdomen while his other hand slowly stroked my hair. Calm. Serenity. It was not what I had in my life.

"Not tough enough for this." At least I didn't think so.

"Georgie, this is how it has to play out. You know that. We can't dance around this shit any longer. I know it's big, and I know I'm not going to like it, but we deal and move on."

"I can't have anything ever happen to you." If he died because of me, I'd never survive that.

"If you don't tell me, I *will* find out. And then it will be worse."

He was right. I knew it and yet, I didn't even know where to start. Maybe if I told him some of it? It would satisfy him and still keep the truth hidden, which would protect Deck against *him.*

"What happened after Connor died? After I left?"

I stiffened and turned slightly so I could look at him. "How did you know?"

He sighed and kissed my forehead. "I don't. But I have a feeling that whatever *this* is—that is when it started. When I came back you were different. Colder. Innocence gone. Harder and sassy as hell. Too much sass. I figured, it was you trying to break free from the perfection you used to live under, but you went one hundred eighty degrees in the opposite direction."

I nodded. *Yeah, that was because I'd been broken and had to live with pieces of myself.*

His hand stroked my abdomen slow and steady and his breath whispered across my ear. "Let me in, babe."

I linked my fingers with his. If I told him about Robbie, maybe he'd leave the other alone and I could still keep him safe. "I was a mess after Connor died. Think you know that. I just didn't care about anything anymore. My parents wanted life back to routine as soon as possible, but the reality was nothing was routine anymore. My mother cried all the time. I rarely talked and when I did it was … well, sarcastic and mean." I swallowed and took a deep breath. Deck continued to stroke my abdomen, soft and rhythmic. "He was a senior at my school." His hand stopped moving and I could feel his heart skip a beat and then pound harder. "I don't know why he picked me … but he did. Maybe I looked vulnerable. Easy prey." I stopped for a few seconds, hating that I had to give Deck this part of me that was weak and pathetic.

"What did he do to you, Georgie?" His words were coarse as if he had trouble getting them out.

I told him about Robbie, the words coming out as if I was reading them from a book. It was the only way I could speak. I felt the tension in him, the stillness. He continued to soothe me, but it wasn't me who needed soothing anymore. I knew without looking at him every word I spoke made him angrier than I'd ever known him to be.

"When did it stop?" His voice was barely controlled, a chord of tones strung so tightly it could snap any second.

"He was arrested for selling drugs at school. I never saw him again." When the police pulled up to the school with their lights flashing outside the window, I knew. I knew Robbie was leaving and ten minutes later, I saw him handcuffed and being led out to the car. I knew who had called the police on him and I knew Robbie would have hard drugs in his locker as proof because I put them there. It was enough to be considered a dealer.

The police car drove away and it was as if the door to a trap had opened and I was set free. I put my head on my desk and sobbed so hard the teacher ended up taking me to the infirmary and called my parents. My mom came and picked me up, but I told her I was crying because of my period pains. She believed me, and why wouldn't she? I was always their little princess.

After that day, I could breathe again. For months, I'd been afraid. Terrified to speak to anyone, to run, to not run. To do anything except suffer. I'd never take the risk of anyone I loved dying—never.

"Do your parents know?"

I shook my head. "No. I never told them."

He had been the one to call the police. *He* was also the one who gave me the drugs to plant in Robbie's locker. He told me going after Robbie for what he did to me and to other girls would mean going to court. It would be a long, drawn-out battle and I'd have to tell everyone what happened to me. Plus, there was always the possibility they wouldn't have enough proof and he'd walk. So, Robbie went to jail for drugs and I was finally free of him. That was all I cared about at the time.

"Why? Why didn't you tell them? Jesus, you could've called my unit. Someone would've got hold of me." He turned over onto his back but took me with him, flipping me over so I was half on top of him. His arm was still around me preventing any escape, and his other was over his eyes.

"He threatened my mom, said he'd cut out her throat if I ever said anything. I was sixteen, Deck … I believed him. It started only a week after Connor died and I was vulnerable, depressed and I felt … alone." My cheek rested on the tribal ink drawn into his chest. "And scared." Deck squeezed me.

"I would've killed him." And that was the issue. I knew that. Even at sixteen, I knew Deck and Connor—if he'd been alive—would've killed Robbie and ended up in jail themselves. It wasn't something I was willing to risk even if I *had* considered trying to get hold of Deck.

I nodded and my cheek rubbed on his chest.

"Where is he now?"

"I don't know." I didn't. *He'd* been looking for Robbie ever since he left prison.

I felt his body stiffen. "I'll find him."

I sat upright, putting my hands on his chest. "Deck, no. You don't

107

understand—"

His brows lowered over his darkened eyes. "Oh, I fuckin' under-stand. Some guy tortured you for months when you were sixteen. A fuckin' disgusting lowlife who doesn't deserve to breathe air." He threw his legs over the side of the bed and reached for his cell.

"Damn it, no." I leapt on him and knocked the phone from his hands, causing it to slide across the floor. "You can't."

"What the fuck, Georgie? You expect me to hear about some fucker who tortures you for months then sit back and do nothing? No fuckin' way in hell."

He went to get up and I grabbed his arm with both hands. He ig-nored me and kept walking, and I scrambled after him. Years of lying, deception, doing things I didn't want to do, all of it was slipping away. All I could think about was Deck being killed because of this. If he started digging …

"Deck. I need to do this."

He was halfway leaned over to pick up his phone when he froze and straightened while looking at me still holding his arm. "Do what?"

My hands slowly slipped from him and it felt as if I was being suf-focated by my own breath. Would he understand? Would he walk away and never see me again? I couldn't bear to think of it.

I thought of the only thing which came to mind and it *was* the truth, just an omission of a few things. "I have someone looking for him. Please, Deck. I don't want you involved."

His eyes widened with surprise and shock. Why wouldn't he be? Deck had no idea we'd been searching for Robbie for years. That I was Chaos and did … assignments for *him*.

"Stay right there." Deck snatched up his phone and started walking from the room, the phone to his ear. "Tyler," he snarled.

I was unravelling. Every part of me was being splayed out in front of the one man I'd loved all my life and I felt—gutted. I felt weak and vulnerable and he was taking my power away.

"Damn it, I waited for you to come back," I shouted. "To see your car pull up to the curb, to be waiting there in the morning when I looked out the window. But you weren't. You never came." I took a deep breath and tried to steady my voice for the blow. And it would be a huge blow to Deck, but he was going after Robbie and would soon find out everything. I couldn't let him go in blind. He'd be killed. I had to tell him. "But Kai did."

He stopped. The phone lowered and I heard Tyler yelling on the other end. He kicked the bedroom door closed, then slowly turned. For a second, I saw the shock, eyes wide and mouth dropped open, and then it changed completely. His eyes darkened and narrowed—unyielding, and mixed in was a sneer of disgust. There was no sexy anywhere in him because his intimidating stare overrode the sexy.

"Kai?"

I swallowed then nodded, but I really felt like denying it and then running for the door.

"You fucking him, Georgie?" With the way his hands were clenching and unclenching, his jaw tight and his eyes hard … Deck was holding on by a thread.

I shook my head. "No. It's not like that."

"So, it's like *something*? With Kai? The unstable fucker who was at an auction buying sex slaves? Who doesn't have a fuckin' history? Who no one trusts? Who handles a knife like it's part of his hand. Whose morals border on—" He stopped abruptly, his eyes glaring into me so fiercely I looked away. A deep, resonating growl emerged from his throat. He tossed his phone on the dresser and I jumped when it made a loud clang. "Tell me he didn't put those cuts on you."

Shit.

"Tell me," he shouted. This was Deck out of control. The Deck I never wanted to know. The Deck I didn't think anyone wanted to encounter—every muscle tense, hands clenched into fists, jaw hard and determined with the heat of fury pulsating off him.

"I can't," I whispered.

Deck nodded and it wasn't the reaction I expected. I actually no longer knew what to expect. This was unpredictable Deck. He walked over to his dresser, opened the drawer and pulled out a knife and then a gun. I heard the clicking and snapping as he checked the gun then slid it in the back of his pants.

"Deck?" He ignored me, grabbed his cell and put it in his pocket then headed for the door. "Deck. What are you doing?"

"What the fuck do you think I'm doing, Georgie? Stay here. You leave my place, you won't like what happens." He yanked open the door and strode out.

I ran after him. "Deck, I asked him to. I asked Kai to do it. Please, I know it sounds screwed up and it is, but please, don't go after him. Please."

He stopped and turned to face me. "You fuckin' asked him to? Jesus. Why the fuckin' hell would you do that? Why, damn it?"

I looked at my feet as I said, "It made the pain go away."

"No, it fuckin' didn't. It kept it alive. He kept it alive and made you relive it." He strode toward me, grabbing my arms. "Look at me."

I did because I just wanted Deck to give me something to hold onto because he was right. I was holding onto what happened to me so I'd never forget it. To release all the emotions I had built up in me for that one day.

"I lost you a long fuckin' time ago." His fingers tightened and he stared at me for several seconds before saying quietly, "Come back to me, Georgie."

My breath hitched.

His eyes softened. "Baby, come back to me. Stop pretending. Stop hiding. Trust me."

I wished I could, but nothing in my life was simple since Connor died. If he went after Kai … "Please, don't go after Kai."

He snorted and abruptly shoved me away from him. "Why? Because you love him? You can't bear to see him hurt? Well, don't worry; I'm not going to hurt him, Georgie. I'm going to fuckin' kill him."

"No!" I yelled as he opened the door to his penthouse. I ran after him and slammed into his chest as he hit the elevator button. "No. He'll kill you, Deck."

The elevator dinged and the doors opened.

He shoved me aside and walked into the elevator.

CHAPTER
ELEVEN

AS SOON As the elevator doors closed, I ran back into loft and searched through the bag Tyler dropped off for me. I felt the familiar, hard plastic at the bottom and yanked out my phone. Three missed calls. One Emily, one Kat and one unknown.

Shit. Unknown—Kai. I pressed in the code to get through to his number and dialed.

Please answer. Please.

"A tad dramatic, wasn't it? Might want to curb the drinking for real, Chaos. I would prefer if you lived."

I didn't have time to word-play with him. "He knows."

Silence.

It sounded like he was opening a door and then the whoosh of traffic. "Knows what, Chaos?"

"About Robbie and then …" Shit, Kai always said he'd end me then kill Deck if I ever told Deck what I was doing. Not sure what 'end' meant, but with Kai it could mean kill, torture, emotionally destroy or put me in a space ship and send me up into the universe. I didn't care. He could do whatever he wanted to me as long as he left Deck alive.

"Then?"

He was calm, but the charm I often heard in his voice disappeared. "He saw me at the hospital, Kai. He saw the chart. The cuts."

"And you gave him a plausible explanation."

"God, Kai … Deck isn't fuckin' stupid. The only reason I've gotten away with this is because he's been thinking I'm an irresponsible drunk. Now he knows I'm not."

"And how did he discover that little tidbit, Chaos?"

"You figure it out, asshole. I'm staying with him. I don't have a single withdrawal symptom." I held the phone between my ear and my shoulder and pulled on my sweatshirt. "Kai, he's coming after you."

"You really fucked things up, didn't you, Chaos?" I heard Kai shuffling something around and then a car door slammed and the wind whistled through the phone. "I told you what happens if he finds out."

I stood frozen in place, tears pooling in my eyes. "Please, Kai. Don't. I'll do anything. Please don't kill him. It isn't his fault; it's mine. Do what you need to me, but not him. Please, not Deck." I took a deep breath, attempting to get my shit together, my insides balled up like tangled wire.

Kai chuckled and I always hated when he did that. It was as if nothing ever concerned him even when I was begging for a life. Even after I tell him Deck, an ex-JTF2, the most elite task force in the world, was coming after him—he laughs? "I'm hurt, Chaos. Where is your concern for me?"

I threw on my jogging pants, grabbed my wallet and ran for the door. "Don't be a dick. Does he know where you are? You must keep tabs on him, a GPS maybe?"

"You think very highly of me. But no, I don't have tabs on him. I have tabs on you and whenever Deck is in town, he is with you. So, it's pretty easy to know where he is." Not really true. Well, sort of true. I stayed here usually whenever he had dragged me out of some bar or party, and we had the same friends, so he was often with me if he was around.

When he was in town, he always came to my Sunday brunch, but none of his men ever did. I knew Kai had a tracking device in my phone, car and I suspected other places. Ended up being really useful the day the scumbag sex-trader Alfonzo had kidnapped me, Emily, and the girl London. If Kai hadn't been able to convince Alfonzo to meet the guy responsible for transporting girls, Kai still would've known where we were.

I stopped bitching about it after that day. So, I'd lived with two dangerous men who kept tabs on me … you'd think I'd feel safe. Yeah, well, nothing about Kai was safe.

I slammed the door of the loft and pressed the elevator.

"Chaos, calm down." I was breathing hard in the phone. "Think about what you're doing." The elevator dinged and the doors opened. "Chaos, sit the fuck down. Now. Do not get in that elevator."

I watched the doors close again and then I slowly slid down the wall of the hallway until my butt hit the floor. I bent my legs and dropped my head between them while I took long, deep breaths trying to get control of the panic.

I was never so freaked out as I was at this moment. But when it came to Deck, the thought of losing him, it was like a light switch went on and all my emotions went haywire. Kai's voice cut into me. "Remember everything I taught you, Chaos. You need to find that now." He kept his voice low and soothing, rhythmic. "Nothing gets done if you panic. You know this."

I didn't know what I was doing. I had no idea where Deck went, and I was chasing him. It didn't make sense. I wasn't making sense. What the hell was I doing? "Don't hurt him," I said quietly. "Don't hurt him."

"Go back inside and wait for him."

My breath caught in my throat. "You said you'd kill him if he ever knew."

"Yes. And that was the truth, but things have changed slightly. I'll come by tomorrow and we can have a chat."

My grip on the phone tightened. "What? Are you crazy?" Yeah, Kai was a little crazy.

Kai sighed. "I'd rather be the hunter than the trapped prey, my dear."

"He's going to kill you. Jesus, you're going to kill him."

He laughed. "Chaos, you have quite the imagination. Firstly, Deck won't kill me and secondly, I won't kill him—yet. Besides, I like you, Chaos. I'm thinking if I killed him, you'd probably try and kill me. And I really don't want to have to kill you."

Then the phone went dead.

I sat outside the elevator for a long time. Every time I heard it ding on other floors, I'd look up, my heart racing. Hoping he was back, praying he didn't do anything reckless. But Deck was never reckless—until I saw him tonight. His face, it was like I'd stabbed him in the stomach with a dull blade and then slowly turned it. His shock. His disbelief.

In one sentence, I blew up everything he thought about me. I told him another man cut me and I'd asked him to do it. God, the look on his face. Surprise and rage burned like an erupted volcano in his eyes. I deserved his hate. His disgust. Fuck, I was disgusted with myself.

It was just after midnight when the elevator doors opened and Deck stepped out. I was half-asleep, my neck sore from tilting back against the wall. I jerked upright and then scrambled to my feet.

"Deck." He looked perfectly contained: clothes neat and tidy, face tight but that was usual. He had a Band-Aid on his arm but the rest of him … no blood. He had all his limbs and he was standing.

I felt the familiar butterflies fluttering in my stomach at the sight of him. No matter what shit had gone down between us, whenever I set my eyes on him … it was the same feeling.

The only real man worth having and yet … it was his eyes which stabbed each butterfly and had them falling dead in the pit of my stomach. Then his gaze flicked over me dismissively like I was an ornament he didn't like in his foyer.

He strode past and opened his door, leaving it ajar. That was a good sign; at least he wasn't locking me out. I followed him in then clicked the door shut behind me and leaned against it.

He ignored me for several minutes as he helped himself to a bottle of water from the fridge, chugged it back then left the empty container on the counter. That was unlike Deck; he always kept order. His home was spotless and he put everything in its place.

He walked over to the window and stood quiet and still, staring out at the darkened sky. I waited, knowing he might kick me out any second, never wanting to see me again. I felt sick to my stomach thinking about it, wondering how I could make this all go away. But whatever he decided, I deserved it. I deserved his hate. I just had to make sure he stayed safe.

His voice was rough and hard as he said, "Take off your shirt, Georgie."

"What?" *What the hell?* A million thoughts raced through my brain as I tried to think of where he was going with this. Did he want to see the cuts? See what Kai had done?

He slowly turned and looked at me. "Take. Off. Your. Shirt."

My eyes felt like they'd been zapped as they widened with surprise. There was that distinct wave of heated bliss charging through me like soldiers attacking their enemy with torches.

He walked toward me. I considered running, but I'd do anything Deck wanted right now. I was turned on and terrified at the same time. My hand on the doorknob twisted.

He kept coming until he was inches away and when he took a breath, I could feel his shirt touch mine. He leaned into me, hands resting on the door above my head, trapping me. "Do you ever listen to instructions?"

I trembled because I was thinking about him kissing me when I should have been thinking about what he was doing.

"I'm going to fuck you, Georgie." My breath hitched and an intense ache grabbed me and held so tight I shifted uneasily. The drumming of my heart was so violent I thought it might spike out the top of my head.

"I … I don't understand." Why was he doing this? Ten years I'd wanted to sleep with him. Ten years and suddenly after I told him bad shit … horrible shit … shit I wasn't even finished telling him … he wanted to break his word to my brother and sleep with me?

He smiled, but it wasn't a pleasant smile. It was kind of cruel and all-knowing with lips pursed together and slightly pulled up in the corners. So not Deck. "You don't understand how to fuck? Or you don't understand what I said?"

"I don't understand why you want to."

"Oh, you will. You'll understand so fuckin' clearly it will make your head spin."

Oh, shit, his voice was low and husky and reminded me of the muffled roar of a souped-up shiny black Mustang. The rough denim of his jeans rubbed across my pelvis and I wanted to rip them off and feel the heated bliss of his skin against mine.

"Never known you to be speechless." He hadn't touched me yet—well, if I didn't count his eyes driving into me. "You want this, Georgie? Because I had the impression you did. This is me." He leaned in closer, so his lips were next to my ear. "Do what I say and take off your fuckin' shirt or walk out that door and never come back."

Jesus. I was so stunned I stood there even when he pushed off the door and stepped away. I knew Deck. He didn't make idle threats, and I suspected he'd even open the door for me if I refused him.

There wasn't a chance I'd ever do that.

I grabbed the edges of my shirt, pulled it over my head and let it slip from my fingers to the floor. I heard his intake of breath as he looked at me. His expression remained the same, unwavering and hard, and it made my legs quiver like rubber bands. I leaned back onto the door for support and it pushed my chest out which sparked a smoldering flame in his eyes.

"Bra."

Why hadn't he kissed me? Touched me? Why was he making me undress as he stood fully clothed, even wearing his boots? What was this?

"Deck, why—"

His brows rose and I swallowed then reached behind me and grabbed the clasp of my bra. The hooks came undone and the straps slid down my arms as my bra fell forward. His eyes were on mine until I let the bra fall. Goose bumps spread across my skin as his eyes drifted down to my chest and I suddenly felt vulnerable. I didn't like that, and I went to cross my arms when he grabbed my wrists.

"No." Deck let me go then nodded to my jogging pants.

I swallowed, bent over and took them off, leaving them on the floor beside me.

He waited.

I stood half-naked against his door while he watched me. It was thrilling as much as it was unsettling. And I was completely turned on and confused that I was turned on by it.

He didn't need to say anything; he merely looked at my panties.

I didn't want it like this. I wanted passion, him grabbing me and ripping off all my clothes, not him standing there while I undressed. This wasn't even remotely like my fantasies. Well, except for the fact I was burning up and aching with so much anticipation for his touch that I was afraid I'd collapse.

"Kiss me, Deck." I wanted him in my arms, to hold me, hear him groan, feel his hands on me.

"You can't do what I ask then get out." Deck turned on his heel and strode down the hall.

Fuck. God, what was I doing? But I found myself running after him and saying, "Okay. Okay, I'll do it."

He was already at his bedroom door and I sighed as my words stopped him and he turned. My skin was on fire and it wasn't from embarrassment as his eyes roamed over my body as if he was contemplating whether I was worthy of him.

When he leaned back against the doorframe and crossed his arms, I knew exactly what he was waiting for. I slipped my fingers into the bikini straps of my white panties and slowly dragged them down then stepped out of them. I lifted my head and stood up straight, cocking my hip as I put one hand on it.

I waited. There wasn't anything else I could do because I wanted Deck. It needed to be him. I'd waited ten years for it to be him, so I'd stand and wait for the next ten years if Deck had his eyes on me like he did at this moment.

His arms uncrossed. "Perfect."

My insides went haywire as he strode toward me. Could a body be set into flames from a mere look? Yes. Hell yes, we were talking about Deck here.

He stopped a foot away and I was screaming for him to come closer. I wanted to beg. *Jesus, did I just say that?* All my internal thoughts were screwed up and I had no idea what I was thinking except the beacon of 'kiss me' flashing relentlessly.

"Look at me."

I thought I was, but I was staring at his tatted chest, willing it to come closer. The smartass in me wanted to defy him after all the orders he gave me. However, the desire was too overpowering, and I knew if I gave him any smartass he'd turn and leave without a single backward glance. I wouldn't risk it.

I met his eyes and the dark steadiness I always saw was lit with a smoldering flame. Okay, I could get some power back here. I opened my mouth. His brows lowered and I quickly slammed it shut. Maybe not.

"If this happens, there's no going back." The creak in the floorboards sounded and a shiver raced through me.

What did he mean 'no going back'? "What exactly does that entail?"

His lips pulled down in the corners, and I knew he was a little pissed off. Add the sudden tension in his shoulders with it and he was angry. *Okay, what the hell?*

"It entails everything." He stepped closer and when his hands curled around my upper arms, the ache between my legs became unbearable. "You ready for that?"

I decided I wanted to be brave because I was feeling insecure and needed some of it back. "Kiss me and I'll let you know."

There was a twitch at the corner of his mouth and his fingers slid down my arms in a slow glide, the roughness against my smooth skin like silk and sandpaper. They moved up again and tightened. I couldn't read him, damn it. Deck was a complexity I hadn't figured out and probably never would.

His one hand caressed up to my shoulder and then to the curve of my neck until his fingers cupped the back of my neck. I lost my balance as I swayed into him, each molecule drawn toward him.

With one swift pull, he dragged me into him and then his head tilted and my lips met his. It was hard and soft and holy shit, it was alarmingly better than the kiss in the shower. His tongue slid across my teeth and then pushed past, entering the warmth. His arm went behind me, preventing any escape, although I didn't even consider escaping.

My hands found their way around him and I caressed up his back until my fingers gripped his neck. It was cathartic as I felt the vibration of his groan and the sensation zapped my skin, sinking between my legs. His kiss deepened, if that was possible. He pulled my hair and I had no choice but to tilt my head back.

His kiss was an invasion. I got what he meant by 'no going back'. He asked me if I was sure because Deck was taking and I had to give or be taken. The thought turned me on more and I kissed him hungrily as if starved for him.

I had been starved for him.

Ten years. Ten friggin' years this man had been in my head trampling me and now I was tasting him, feeling him. I knew Deck didn't do half-ass; it was all or nothing.

He groaned then pulled away. I tried to tug him back, but he wouldn't let me and instead, I ran my hands down his solid back to his jeans and then down further to cup his ass.

Deck was eight years older than me, and I may have been inexperienced when it came to the actual sex part, but I'd done other things with guys and I knew what they liked.

His eyes drove into me as he tightened his grip in my hair. "Everything."

I had no response because I didn't know what he meant, but I'd do or say anything he asked. I wanted him to be lying on top of me and sinking inside me before I melted. "Baby, I need you."

"I like it when you call me that."

I bit my lip. "I know."

He gave a curt nod and walked me backward until I felt the bed behind me and I fell, bouncing onto the mattress. I winced when my back hit the bed.

He saw it. "The cuts?"

I nodded. "But they're fine."

He watched me for a second as if assessing my words. "I won't be gentle."

I didn't think he would be. "I know."

Then he said, "Your sass stays out of the bedroom tonight."

I got up on my elbows, which made my breasts stick out, and I noticed his eyes widen. The reaction was quickly covered up again with his steady resolve. I knew Deck had some real emotional scars, and I wondered even in the heat of passion if he'd let them go. If maybe I'd see a hint of the unshielded Deck.

Holy shit, this was happening. I licked my upper lip as he took off his shirt and my eyes took in the deep valleys and hills of his naked chest and abdomen. There was a hint of a trail of hair that led down to … his fingers popped open his jeans button. The zipper slid down and with the sound came a wave of sparks hitting my lower belly.

I was going to see Deck naked. Damn, fantasy comes true. I needed oxygen fast. I watched him pull down the denim and then step out of them.

Muscular thighs, a scattering of dark hair, the taut calves, which had that distinct, flexed whatever it was called in the back of his legs. Legs I needed around me—tight. But more than that, I quivered as my eyes hit the hard swelling pushing against the black material of his boxer briefs. There was no hesitation as he pulled those off, too, and his cock sprang free. For a second, I thought of scrambling off the bed. *How the hell did something like that fit inside a girl?*

"Open your legs, Georgie."

His voice cut through my thoughts of his cock pushing into me and I stared up at him, gaping. "Huh?"

There was no uncertainty in him as he stood tall, confident and completely naked in front of me. I shouldn't have thought any differently. I mean, Deck was the team leader of an elite force of men who were just as dangerous as he was. Shit, he took out bad men—real bad men who had real bad friends, and yet Deck never looked emotionally exposed for a second.

His stance widened and he watched me, waiting for a response. A response … Right, legs. Open legs. He knelt on one knee between my legs on the bed. His body followed and I closed my eyes with complete and utter relief as his weight finally came on top of me. It was liberating. It was truth. It was real and for a moment, I forgot who I'd become over the years and became the innocent girl who fell in love with a man she thought she could never have.

His hands immediately took mine, placed them above my head and locked them. It was a power position, and I think I always knew this was how it would be with Deck. He'd never yield to another and that included during sex.

Then he kissed me and my legs wrapped around his hips. His one hand kept my arms locked above my head while his other stroked down my side until he was grabbing my thigh, hitching it higher on his waist. The strain on my muscles made them quiver and shake.

Deck didn't let up as his mouth took mine, tongue invading, and I opened to him. It was complete surrender and it was … rescuing. I let go and gave him all I refused to give to anyone else.

"Jesus." The drum of his voice broke through my haze of desire and I sighed under his mouth. "That's it. Give in to me." He trailed kisses down my neck to between my breasts and squeezed my thigh. "Leave it there." He moved his hand and cupped my breast, his thumb rolling over my nipple.

"Oh, God," I moaned, every part of me shaking and aching and coursing with the tantalizing heat of Deck. He pinched my nipple—hard. I arched, eyes closing. It hurt like hell but then … then the heat of his mouth soothed the pain and I moaned. His teeth tugged then bit and I gasped.

"Let go." He drew the sensitive nub into his mouth and suckled.

"Deck." I didn't know why I was saying his name out loud. Maybe because I needed to hear my own voice to know this was real. "Please. Fuck me." The throbbing between my legs had me pushing upward into him, wanting more.

"Never thought I'd hear those words from your lips, Georgie." Deck moved to my other breast and gave it the same treatment and I swear I was panting like a friggin' dog by the time he was done.

"I've always loved you." His head snapped up at my words and there was a tightening of his lips as his brow furrowed.

"Georgie." His voice was hard and unrelenting, and I was uncertain what he meant by saying my name like that. But I soon didn't care because his hand cupped between my legs and his finger slid into the wetness. "Fuck," he groaned then slipped two fingers inside me, firm and deep.

The sudden intrusion was uncomfortable. I had a vibrator but I never put it inside me. This was two fingers, and I was uncertain how anything bigger, like his cock, was going to fit without tearing me apart.

He froze. It was every muscle tensing, sniper mode. Even his fingers inside me remained still. He let go of my wrists and grabbed my chin. "You a virgin, Georgie?"

"Well, if you mean have I ever had a cock inside me—no."

His eyes narrowed, jaw pulsed and he looked intense. He tightened his grip on my chin. "Why?"

Because I had been a girl with a crush that got out of hand. I'd tried to have sex, but I always stopped before it got too far. It never felt right.

He pushed his finger in me a little further. "This," he said. "You were going to give it to Lionel?"

I shrugged. That had been the idea that night, along with my assignment. I had some explaining to do about Lionel, but with his fingers inside me, I wasn't saying shit.

"Georgie," he warned.

I was losing the ache and it was being replaced with pissy. "Seriously, Deck. You're bringing this up now with your fingers inside me and your cock hard against my thigh."

"Were you?" He kept his voice calm although it was laced with anger. I knew Deck well enough to know this was really pissing him off. "I'm putting my cock in you no matter what, but I want to hear it from you."

"God, do you have to take every ounce of pride away from me?"

"It's not pride I'm taking, Georgie. It's every fuckin' thing. Told you that. We don't go back from here. The bullshit you've been throwing around ends. The lies," he paused and I flinched under him, "now I get to stop it."

"Stop what?"

He ignored me. "Were you?"

His fingers curled slightly inside me and I clenched around him. His brows lowered and he scowled. "Fine. Yes. I thought about it, but I couldn't go through with it. I wanted it to be you. It had to be you. I knew since the day I came home from school and you gave me that bowl of ice cream. You scared the crap out of me, but that moment ... I saw something in you. It was so clear to me, the sweetness lingering in your eyes, the concern and yeah, the anger was there, but it was all for me."

Deck let go of my chin, his mouth slamming down on mine and our lips came together in a welding of heat. His thumb circled my clit and I moaned as the ache turned to an intense throb and I tightened around him.

His weight grew heavier still and his hand roamed across my skin, touching every part of me as he kissed me. I bit his lip and he growled, the pressure of his thumb stopping. I arched into him, shifting to the side, trying to get him to rub me again.

He pulled back and I was suddenly cold as his body left me and slipped off the bed. He picked up his jeans, reached into a pocket and pulled out a square package. He ripped it open and I watched as he slid the condom on.

Our eyes met. "You trust me?" he asked.

He was the only person I did trust.

"I need to hear you say it."

Goddamn, Deck. "Yeah. I trust you."

He gave a curt nod and then he lifted me up, placing me further up on the bed. His heat covered me again and I instinctively wrapped my legs around him while he teased me with the tip of his cock before he rubbed it against my opening. Then he flexed his hips forward and he slipped inside.

His eyes never left me as he edged in further. I closed my eyes at the unfamiliar intrusion.

"Relax." It was an order and I wanted to smack him, but instead, I did exactly like he wanted and my thigh muscles loosened.

He pushed further in and I moaned at the discomfort and the pleasure. His fingers began playing with me again and the tension in my belly started to build. Soon, it was me arching and pushing him in further.

I'd gotten myself off numerous, okay, thousands of times, but having Deck inside me and the pressure, the pulsating—it was completely different. Overpowering. Jesus, Deck was overpowering.

He lowered his mouth over mine and I sighed, loving the harsh assault. Then his hips shot forward and my cry vibrated into his mouth.

Holy hell, it was like a knife just ripped through me. I tried to get away. I wanted him out of me; it was uncomfortable and hurt and I didn't like it.

But Deck remained still on top of me and kissed me. Then when I stopped fighting, he trailed kisses over my face. "That's it. Breathe." He caressed my hair and it was the sweetest gesture I ever had from Deck. I leaned into him and closed my eyes, letting my body adjust to the thickness of his cock deep inside.

"You good?"

I still throbbed but it wasn't as bad now and when his finger started playing with me again, the pain and discomfort was replaced with pulsating and building. I tilted my pelvis and he got the hint, moving slowly and steadily inside me.

"Baby," I moaned as he slipped in and out, wetness clinging to him.

He lifted up on his hands on either side of me and then pulled out further and pushed hard in again. I groaned as a wave of need catapulted into me; it was like a mini-orgasm.

He did it again and the sensation of his rough thrust into my velvet softness had me meeting his movements so our bodies slapped into one another.

"Fuck." Deck pumped faster when I met his need with my own.

I held onto his arms. "Harder."

He did. Again and again. I screamed as the wave of sensations took

123

my body and threw it off the ledge. I was falling and Deck just kept going, pushing, shoving then suddenly he groaned as he thrust deep one last time.

I lay beneath him for several seconds, taking in what just happened. "Epic," I breathed in a rough whisper.

His body quivered and the strain in his face was gone as he stared at me as if I was a stranger.

I raised my hand and stroked the side of his face. "Baby?"

He turned his head and kissed my palm then rolled off me and got up. He walked into the bathroom then came back, unabashed by his state of nakedness.

He stopped by the bed and looked down at me. I felt the tension; it was as if a cold veil had descended over him. He picked up his jeans and slid them on. "Your back okay?"

"It's fine, Deck. They were minor cuts, not a big deal." Kai was insistent on making sure they were minor, unlike Tanner's that first year.

His brows drew lower over his eyes. I didn't think he liked that answer. He didn't say anything for a few seconds and then he said, "You're telling me fuckin' everything."

I sat up.

A sliver of fear made its way through my satisfied body and I grabbed the sheet to cover myself, not from discomfort but because I was chilly. All the heat had left me and the blood in my veins was running cold.

He ran his hand over the top of his head. Shit. He looked—edgy. Then his eyes met mine again. A shiver coursed down my spine at his rigid, determined eyes. "You just give yourself to me?"

I didn't know where he was going with this, but I nodded. "Yeah."

He paused as if thinking on his next words. It wasn't often Deck hesitated; he was direct and honest, no need to be careful with his words. "You understand what that means?"

"Not really." Because I had no clue what was going on in his head right now. We had sex. Deck broke his word to my brother, and I had some serious lies he was still digesting.

"You should've before you spread your legs for me."

"Jesus, Deck." I wanted to flip him the finger then beg him to kiss me. Both were not a good idea at that moment.

"It means you're mine—completely. There's no running. No going back. And sure as fuck no lies. You have an issue, we talk. You have a problem, I'll deal with it. If I need you to do something, I expect you to do it."

"Whoa, back way up."

His brows rose. "I asked if you were sure. You said yes. There's no backing up. I didn't hang around torturing myself for eight goddamn years just to take you and have you tell me to back up. There's only forward with me. You knew what you were doing. I'm not letting you go, and that involves telling me everything." He strode toward the door. "And I want it all."

I didn't know why I was shaking. Turned on? Scared? I'd go with a combo.

"What's his full name?" he asked.

Shit. This was the last thing I wanted, but I'd opened this can of worms and they were slithering all over me. Deck was taking over.

"Robbie Krovakov."

His body stiffened and he reached in his back pocket and pulled out his phone.

"What are you going to do?"

He had the phone to his ear as he turned to look at me. "Stay here. When I come back, I expect you to be naked in bed waiting for me."

My eyes widened.

"You have something to say?"

I shook my head.

Then he left.

CHAPTER TWELVE

DECK

I STRODE OUT of the room. "Robbie Krovakov. Went to Georgie's public school, German Mills. Find his location. I'd check the local penitentiary first. And Vic, this guy is mine." I hung up and shoved the phone back in my pocket.

I walked into my office and started up my laptop, checking through any correspondence I'd had with Kai.

The truth was I was in my office to get away from her before I crashed and lost everything of myself in her. I got what I wanted. I made her mine. There was no backing down now, but what I wondered was if either of us was going to be able to handle it. I was feeling so fucked up after that. … Jesus, being inside her, feeling her, kissing her, it was like a brilliance of colors had burned through my darkness.

I tried to concentrate, but all I could think about was thrusting inside Georgie. Feeling her tightness around my cock, how she stood in front of me and stripped. How she dug her nails into my back as I slammed into her over and over again.

She was a fuckin' virgin. A virgin. Unexpected and … it was a gift.

Despite all the lies that surrounded her … she saved that for me. Jesus. I may have never … fuck Connor. Fuck everything. She was mine now, and I was never letting her go.

My cock hardened as I thought of her lying in my bed right now, uncertain and a little scared, as she should be. I was still reeling with anger at her, at Kai and at myself for not seeing this. The drinking had been a lie? Fuck. Had I been so determined to keep her at a distance I missed what was staring right at me? I knew Georgie, at least I thought I had. It never sat right with me about the drinking. Georgie was stronger than that.

"Damn it." I slammed my laptop shut and leaned back in my chair, the creak of leather and my groan melding together.

I hadn't shut the door and I looked up to see Georgie standing in the baggy sweat clothes I had gotten her. She leaned back against the doorframe so I could see her side profile, her leg bent so her foot was resting on the wall. And she looked sexy as hell.

She also didn't do as I said. Complete opposite, in fact. I hid my smile because I sure as hell didn't want her to see it.

Even with blue streaks or whatever fuckin' color she dyed her hair, I thought she was beautiful. Hadn't changed since the day I met her. Her, too young to do anything about it, and me who'd become a killer who had seen far too much bad shit to ever let a girl so innocent into my life.

My men from Unyielding Riot were the same; seen and done more than most humans could even bear hearing about, let alone experience firsthand. The path we were on was a rocky one, and I expected Connor was on one that there was no way back from.

Fuck. Georgie could never know about her brother being alive. I sure as hell didn't like starting what we had with a secret as big as this, but Connor wasn't her brother anymore. There was only harm in telling her about him right now.

She was fiddling with her hands. Not her usual cocky, sassy self. And it reminded me of the girl I'd watched eating the ice cream.

"Told you to stay put." And I also knew Georgie rarely followed instructions.

Silence.

"Also told you to be naked."

I saw her teeth snag her lower lip then slowly let it go. "Why do you want me now? I lied to you. I pretended to be someone I wasn't—"

"Stop."

She clamped her mouth shut at hearing the hard edge to my one word. I wanted her again so badly it was clouding my judgement on what I had to do here and yet ... the years of waiting, of never thinking I'd have her, overtook needing answers.

My cock swelled so hard it was painful. Jesus, yes. I'd fuck her for the next week straight if I could. She lifted her head and her veil of hair parted as she turned to look at me. Damn it, she knew exactly what she was doing looking like that.

"Come here."

She walked over to me and I appreciated the sway of her hips and the slightly parted lips. Thing was, Georgie was sexy as hell and she didn't even know it. Yeah, she played the part with her sass, but beneath that laid a vulnerable girl who hid behind a web of lies.

But what Georgie needed right now was to know who was in control because this bullshit with her had ended.

"Sit on my desk." I pushed my laptop aside then my chair back as she came to stand in front of me. She placed her palms on the edge of the desk then slid her ass up onto the mahogany surface. I rolled my chair forward until I could touch her hips and then I jerked her to the very edge. "You sore?"

She shook her head. I raised my brows and she amended her answer. "A little."

"Then I'm not fucking you." Her look of disappointment made me smile, and for a second, I felt the sweet elation swim through my veins. It was unfamiliar and warming. Fuck, I liked it—a lot. "Up." I spanked the right side of her butt and she raised it so I could tug her sweat pants off her ass then repeat on the other side. I dragged them slowly off her legs, letting my fingertips skim her soft skin.

I noticed the goose bumps and her eyes closed briefly as she tilted her head back. I dropped the pants to the floor then ran my hand up her leg to her inner thigh. "Lie back. Eyes closed."

She was breathing hard now, anticipating my next movements. I didn't like anyone knowing what I was going to do; it made me predictable and that was dangerous.

I got up and heard her breath hitch. Fuck, I'd like nothing more than to pound my cock into her right now, or have her mouth on me while I pushed down her throat.

But she needed a lesson and I intended to give it to her.

I walked away.

I heard the movement, didn't even have to turn around to see she was starting to get up and say something.

"Eyes closed. Do not move until I tell you. And if my instructions aren't followed this time … you know where the door is."

Then I closed the office door to make it seem like I left her and quietly sat in the corner of the room and waited.

Georgie

I TREMBLED AND shivered as I lay back on the desk, my legs naked and hanging over the edge. I kept my eyes closed because if I opened them, I'd get up and run after him and Deck was doing this for a reason. I knew he'd never hurt me. I knew he'd look after me and in a way, the anticipation of leaving me here made me want him even more.

I felt the aching between my legs build as I lay there. Throbbing. Pulsating. I knew I was getting wetter and suddenly wished I'd been wearing panties. My mind was reeling with thoughts of Deck, of his cock inside me, his hands on my skin, lips on my mouth and then trailing down my skin, tasting me.

My body jerked and I parted my legs a little more, wishing a window was open and a breeze would hit me between my thighs. I was dying to be touched so badly I put my hand on my chest and was about to circle my nipple when his abrupt tone from behind stopped me.

"No touching."

Shit, I'd thought he'd left the room. My eyes flew open, but I couldn't see him. I opened my mouth to beg him, but he must have suspected.

"Shhh." His rumbling sound sent a wave of desire through me and I moaned, my hands flat against the hard surface of the desk, wanting to grab hold of something, anything.

"Keep your eyes closed." Then I heard the rustling of clothing. Was he undressing? I bit my lip so hard I tasted blood. Something hit the floor. Shoes? Had he been wearing shoes? Or a belt? A cold shiver raced over me and I almost bolted upright to look. I didn't like the idea of a belt anywhere near me and I had to consciously stop myself from running. I trusted Deck, more than anyone in my life. I may have kept things from him, but it was to protect him.

Then his footsteps walked across the room, the easy, confident stride I knew so well and could recognize even blind.

A latch clicked open. The slide of wood against wood sounded and the smell of chlorine from the plunge pool wafted into the room on the wings of the summer breeze. It tickled my face and I moaned again as my legs quivered.

"How wet are you, Georgie?"

I knew I was soaking. I could even feel a drip on my inner thigh and he hadn't even touched me yet.

"I need you to answer me."

"Wet. I'm really wet."

I nearly bolted upright when he was suddenly there, his finger slipping through my wetness as if checking to make sure I was telling the truth. He must have anticipated my reaction because he put one hand on my chest to keep me steady as I tried to arch my back off the desk.

"Nice to see you're not lying to me."

Then his touch disappeared until I felt his finger tracing my upper lip. "Open." I did and I tasted myself as I suckled his finger. He suddenly withdrew and his mouth replaced it. For a moment, it was soft as his tongue swirled and tasted the remnants of me, but then like a trigger going off, his weight was on top of me and he slammed his mouth on mine.

Taking.

Claiming.

Fierce and almost angry.

His chest was naked against mine, but the rough denim of his jeans rubbed against me. His fingers curled into my hair and pulled as he tilted my head slightly, a harsh assault as if he couldn't kiss me hard enough.

He was aggressive as he ground into me, the edge of the desk cutting into my upper thighs, but I didn't care because I wanted Deck like this. It was him being out of control and Deck was never out of control. I made him this way, and it couldn't have turned me on more.

He growled low then pulled back. "Keep your eyes closed." He sounded like he had some control back as his weight lifted off me, but I could still hear his heavy breathing and knew he hadn't left me again. What I didn't know was what he was going to do next.

Then I heard the creak of the leather as he sat in his chair again, the wheels rolled over the hardwood. Was it closer to me or further away? What was he doing?

"Open your legs wider so I can see your pussy glisten."

I swallowed and did what he wanted, my stomach on a never-ending roller coaster ride.

"Wider."

I did and felt the strain in my thighs at the position. It wasn't painful, just uncomfortable when all I wanted to do was lock my legs around his waist and feel his cock inside me again.

"Good girl." I felt his lips kiss my inner thigh and I nearly leapt off the desk and jumped him. Instead, I sucked in air and moaned, about to say his name when he moved away again. "Do you like this, Georgie?"

I nodded. I'd never been so turned on in my life, and I had a lot of books and a vibrator I had used for my fantasies of Deck. But never had I had a fantasy like this.

"Do you want me?"

"Yes." It was a breathless begging.

"You'll never lie to me again, will you?"

I shook my head. He knew damn well I'd say anything right now.

"One lie and this ends. I walk. And Georgie, I'm not coming back."

I stiffened. Now that I had Deck, I couldn't ever imagine not having him, but it was going to be hard as hell explaining the purging. He'd never understand why I had to do it. Shit, I didn't understand it. Kai seemed to. The charming bastard had one hell of a fucked-up mind. I didn't even want to know what had happened to him to find out why he was the way he was.

"You want to come?" Deck asked.

"Baby, my clit is a grenade with the pin pulled."

He chuckled and I almost opened my eyes at the unfamiliar sound. Deck rarely chuckled and the warmth filling my chest was as if I'd been handed heaven in the palm of my hand.

Then his tongue flicked across me and I sighed with relief. His hands gripped my thighs and he was licking between my folds, tasting, as the rumble of his groan vibrating against me made me arch into him. His hands tightened on my thighs and opened my legs even further.

Circling, suckling then roaming slow and hard over my moisture. His hand left my leg and then his finger shoved inside me and I cried out. The pressure built into a cavalcade of emotions as he pressed in and out while his tongue flicked and suckled repeatedly until I screamed out. Arching into him and grabbing his head, my hands curled into his hair.

He kept going, pressing my orgasm out longer until I was so sensitive I was pushing his head away. He growled at me and grabbed my wrists, forcing them down hard on the desk and locking them in place. Not even for a second did his tongue stop.

My legs quivered and were closing in on his shoulders as I wiggled to get away from his mouth. "Deck." It was hurting. Uncomfortable. Almost painful until suddenly it stopped and I felt the familiar pressure building inside me again.

"Oh, God. Oh, God!" It hit me like a bolt of lightning and I banged my head against the desk as I came again, fighting against his hands as my body arched and tried to curl into him.

Finally, he gave one long, slow lick up me then let me go.

CHAPTER
THIRTEEN

DECK

I WANTED TO shove my cock into her so badly it was like trying to stop myself from drinking a glass of water in the middle of the desert. I had no doubt she wouldn't complain, but I knew she had to be sore after I fucked her like a crazed animal and she'd been a virgin.

Jesus. A virgin. I may have kept men watching her, but I never suspected she hadn't had sex before. She talked like she did. I'd hated it when her mouth would run off about fucking, licking or anything sexual. She even flaunted Crisis, the sex-crazed guitarist in the band Tear Asunder. Nearly sent me over the edge when I saw her arm around him.

Crisis may be a flirt and a slut, but he wasn't stupid and he'd backed off Georgie despite her protests. I had wondered if she'd ever slept with him, though. Now, I knew, and I realized the tightness in my chest was gone. She was mine. Completely.

I sat back in the chair and watched as she slid off my desk then reached over and slipped on her track pants. Looking at her now, it wasn't painful like it had been for years. Now, it was … freedom. For today—tomorrow. For-fuckin-ever.

She climbed onto my lap, her knees on either side of me, arms linked around my neck. I put my hands under her ass and held her. I could already tell she was going to be sassy. Georgie had this sparkle in her eyes that was like the brightest fuckin' star in the sky. Then she'd get this little pull at the corners of her lips; it was subtle now and I liked it better. Sometimes, I'd watch her and it was exaggerated, and I thought it had looked forced. Now … now, she looked at ease, even after putting her through the patience game of sexual denial. Nearly destroyed me and I'd be having blue balls for the rest of the afternoon.

I'd take it. Anything to see her like that, wet with her legs parted and quivering. Chest rising and falling as she waited for me to give her what her body was begging for.

Her fingers curled into my hair at the back of my neck. "Cupcake status has changed. You're the fucking cake and the icing with those little red things on top."

I chuckled. "Cherries." I didn't know where she got comparing men to desserts from, but it was Georgie and I thought it was adorable. *Fuck, I said adorable. Shit.*

"And the red ants … I take that back."

My brows rose. "Red ants?"

She shrugged. "Yeah, I thought you were really uptight and could use some red ants up your ass. Well, you *are* uptight, just a different uptight."

I laughed throwing my head back and my chest rumbling with a deep, rough sound. Georgie was staring at me with wide eyes and open mouth. "You say anything else about me?"

"Sure, but the judgement it still out."

I tightened my hands on her ass and squeezed. She yelped and I grinned.

"Fine. I may have said I thought you were a boring missionary-position kind of guy."

I'd never laughed so hard in my life because that was the furthest from the truth and had been one of the many reasons I'd kept clear of Georgie. I was demanding, controlling and most of the time I liked it hard and rough. I wondered if that was part of the reason Connor never wanted me with Georgie.

A wave of pain hit me as I thought of my friend who was no longer the carefree, smiling guy I'd once known. Then I pulled her close and kissed her forehead. Jesus, I'd wanted to do that for so long. I didn't realize how badly until right at this moment. She'd always been mine, but now I owned her and no other was getting a piece of her. Kai, I'd have to deal with—fast.

"I need to see Robbie again, Deck."

I stiffened. "No."

"You can't take that away from me." She pulled back a little and her hand stroked down my arm over my ink, her finger tracing the images.

"Georgie." I got up, taking her with me and setting her on her feet before walking away. "No."

"Deck—"

I stormed back toward her and grabbed her by the shoulders. I knew my fingers were bruising, but I was so pissed off even thinking about Georgie getting close to that bastard. Getting close to anything as tainted as what I was going to do to that sick bastard.

"Out of the question. Not up for discussion. I know you think you need to, but the answer is no. I don't want you anywhere near that piece of shit."

Her voice was soft as she stood in front of me, meeting my eyes and not once wavering under my intensity. "I need this."

I abruptly let her go and walked away then kicked out at the small glass coffee table. The vase in the center teetered for a second and then toppled over. "You're already on shaky fuckin' ground, Georgie. Might want to curb the wants and needs."

She placed her hands on her hips and glared. "My ground has been shaking for years; I'm used to it. You can't tell me what I can and can't do."

"Damn right, I can."

"Why are so you angry over this?"

I strode to the door. I didn't know why. Her mentioning going near Robbie had made it so real. The fear she'd lived in. The pain. Then her need to purge. Jesus, I hadn't protected her at all. And I knew that was the reason I was so angry. "Whatever shit you have with Kai has ended. Ideas about going near the bastard who hurt you—ended. And this is the end of the discussion."

She got red in the face and if I wasn't so mad, I'd think it was adorable. Shit, it still *was* adorable. *There I go again with adorable.* What the fuck was happening to me? "I'm not the girl you think I am, Deck."

And that right there pissed me the fuck off. Because no matter what lies she spun, she is the girl I knew. The weak, drinking, insensitive girl was never Georgie. It was why I'd always been able to resist her. I didn't like that girl.

"Yeah, you are. You're everything I knew you were but were fuckin' hiding from me." I kept my voice real quiet and controlled.

She stormed toward me and for a second, I thought she was going to slap me—or at least try to. But I saw the fire in her eyes and it wasn't just anger, it was heat.

Georgie leapt on me and wrapped her legs around my waist and then her lips were up against mine. It was the fuckin' hottest thing ever. I had no choice but to grab her under the ass or she'd slip from my arms and I sure as hell wasn't letting her go.

I kissed her back, a thirst for her so powerful it was like I'd been without water for years. Unable to get enough. Unable to stop the want. The need. It had been denied for so many years that stopping it now was like trying to stop a herd of elephants.

"Baby," Georgie murmured against my mouth.

I fuckin' loved her calling me that. Never thought I would, thought it sounded pussyish, but from her lips, it was heaven. I drove my mouth into hers, sucking the air from her lungs, making it mine. I staggered into the wall and then quickly turned around so her back was against it and I had leverage.

"When Kai finds Robbie, I need to be there," she murmured against my lips.

"No," I growled.

"We can—"

"We? You mean you and who—Kai? Fuck, no. You're living on another planet if you think you're ever seeing either of those bastards again."

"I won't get hurt."

"Stop fuckin' asking."

"Put your cock inside me and I will."

I could've laughed at her, but I was too pissed and turned on to do anything but kiss her harder and shut her up. Her hands came between us and while I kissed her neck and bit her shoulder, she had my jeans undone and was trying to get them off me.

"Baby, help me."

I knew damn well we were past the point where I had any control to stop myself from fucking her. I carried her out of the office and into my bedroom where I tossed her onto my bed.

She was already taking her pants off by the time I was naked, condom on and climbing on top of her. She didn't even let me kiss her before she had a hold of my straining cock and was putting it between her legs.

She tilted her hips up and the tip went inside.

"Jesus, Georgie." I entered her slowly, not wanting to hurt her, but she had other ideas and she grabbed my hips, bending her knees while placing her feet flat on the bed. Then she thrust upward and I sunk into her hard and deep.

"Oh, God. Yes." She put her head back onto the pillow, her hands reaching above her to grip the rungs in the headboard. "Fuck me."

I was so taken back that I froze, watching her writhe beneath me while my cock was wrapped tight in her warmth. Her eyes flew open and then she smiled and my heart skipped a beat.

God, she was mine. I'd never thought I'd have the chance. Shit, I'd been careful to not break my word to Connor and then when the drinking and partying started, I knew I could never be with that girl.

And now … She'd have to accept everything about me because Georgie was locked in me and there was no way in hell she was ever getting the key.

"Deck?"

I'd never been so literally frozen. Just didn't happen. Too dangerous in my line of work and yet, staring down at her, feeling my cock nestled tight, her body stretched out like a cat … even her blue highlights against the stark-white pillow … everything. This moment was … perfect.

"Baby?" She reached up and stroked my head, her eyes soft and still smoldering with desire. "What's wrong? You okay? You don't want to do this?"

And that right there was the Georgie she'd kept hidden. That part of her I'd been wanting to see again. Her vulnerability, her caring, her

137

sweetness. It had lain buried beneath the lies.

Fuck, I loved her. Always had. I'd do anything for her and maybe it was crazy loving someone as much as I did her, but Georgie was the good in me. Without her, I was sure I'd sink into the darkness of my mind and never emerge. She gave me the light to keep coming back. To crawl away from the evil I was surrounded by, the nightmares, the coldness, and she made me human again. She kept bringing me back here—to her.

And maybe she was right and she needed to see Robbie again. I knew what it was like to need closure. I hadn't wanted to taint her life with that shit, but it was already tainted with me in it. The only thing I wouldn't allow was her to watch me torture the bastard. Because he was going to suffer for what he did to her.

"Fine. But it will be me finding him. Not Kai."

Her eyes widened with surprise. "Really? You're okay with it?"

I shook my head. "No, babe. I'm not okay with it. But you need it, then we'll work it out."

"Okay. Now stop dawdling and fuck me already. I'm throbbing and hot and you're heavy on top of me."

I shut her up by kissing her and then did what she wanted and fucked her—twice more.

CHAPTER FOURTEEN

Georgie

"**W**HAT THE HELL are you doing with that?"
I spun around and the gun went flying, hitting the floor then crashing into the wall. "Oops."

"Oops?" Deck, half-naked and wet from the shower, a towel slung low on his hips, strode across the bedroom and picked up the gun. I heard a few clicks before he tossed it on the bed then opened his bedside drawer and put the bullets inside. "A loaded gun. You were, what … seeing if you could shoot off your foot?"

I laughed, rolling my eyes, and then looked him up and down. The guy seriously didn't know how to look bad. "Baby, you look hot in a towel. I was thinking …" I lay back on the bed and stretched out. We'd spent the day having sex and not talking about any of the crap. He insisted I be on top because of my back, but no matter what position we did, we always ended with him over me.

Deck even brought me a sandwich in bed to which he promised a beating if I got any crumbs on his sheets. Of course I did, and the beating was of him thrusting inside me. "Maybe we could have a swim and do it in the pool."

His scowl deepened. "You had a gun in your hand, pointed at your foot and it was loaded with bullets."

"So, is that a no?" I purred then slid my foot up the side of my naked leg. I was wearing his shirt, which hung down to the cusp of my butt. It may hide my breasts, but I suspected Deck was a leg man anyway.

"Why the hell would you pick it up in the first place?" He threw his towel onto the bed, unabashed at his nakedness and I was happy to see he had one hell of a hard-on. The question was could I get him to let the issue go and concentrate on much more productive things.

I turned around so I was on my stomach, facing the end of the bed, propped up on my elbows with the shirt bunched around my waist. I was giving him a real nice view of my ass, as I still hadn't put on panties because I had intended on going for skinny-dipping sex. But Deck had taken a while in the shower and I'd been curious seeing his gun lying on the dresser.

I swung my legs back and forth, crisscrossing them. "You know, I was thinking I'd like to taste you. My fantasies can't even come close to the real thing. The salty taste of your pre-cum and then when you come in my mouth …" I trailed off as I stared at him.

He'd been pulling on his black cargo pants. Now, he was standing with them partway up his thighs, his cock jutting out and huge. He tucked himself in his pants, did them up and walked straight to me, yanking me up so I was sitting on his lap.

I smiled. "Do you think I can even get that in my mouth?"

"Georgie."

"Because it's monstrous." He was ignoring me despite my praise of his cock.

"We're sorting shit out now."

I sighed. It looked like I was losing this battle. "What guy refuses a BJ?"

"I love your sassy mouth, babe. Probably love it more around my cock, but let's get something straight. I ask a question, … I want the answer. No sass. No bullshit. This is so we don't have a problem. Have I been fair with you? Given you time to get your head straight?"

"Head's not straight. It's kind of in the candy land right now."

His brows rose. "Candy land?"

"Yeah, you know, sexy, sweet fantasy. You're my candy land. Finally I'm getting to taste it and I want more."

The tightness around his lips eased and his eyes went soft on me. Yeah, he was my candy land all right. "Come over here." He plopped me off his lap, pushed back further onto the bed, leaned back against the headboard, put his feet up and crossed his ankles. I crawled up beside him and he grabbed my thigh, put my leg on top of his, and then rested his hand on it. "Candy land or not, we need to talk, Georgie."

Talking position. Not sex position. He was unmoveable on this; it was like trying to get a tree trunk horny.

"We'll start simple ... how did you hook up with Kai?"

I laughed because that was the hardest one. "I wouldn't use the term 'hook up'—"

"You're right, bad choice of words. How did Kai find you?"

That was more like it. No one found Kai, he always found you. "Robbie." The stricture in my chest tightened as I thought of those months when I was so distraught and broken I gave in completely to Robbie. "It had been three months of him doing shit to me in the shed, but one day he grabbed me then took me to his house after school. I didn't fight him. I just walked along beside him like a puppy dog on a leash." I felt the tears prick my eyes at how weak I'd been. I'd hated myself so much.

"That's where I met Kai. He was talking to one of Robbie's brothers in the living room." Robbie had put his arm around my shoulders and pulled me into him then kissed the top of my head like I was his girlfriend or something. I almost vomited all over their carpet. "Robbie took me to his room where he cut me and then took pictures of his work. He had a binder. It was where he kept all the pictures. I wasn't his only one." I inhaled a shaky breath as the memory flooded back, the feeling of helplessness, of being separated from my body, of despair. "When Robbie let me go home, I was walking down the street when Kai pulled up and told me to get in. I didn't think about it. I just did it. It wasn't like anything could get worse. I think I wanted Kai to kill me, hurt me, anything to stop what I was already feeling. I missed Connor so much and I prayed for him to come back and help me. I know if he'd been alive ..."

I looked up at Deck and his eyes were on me. I expected anger, but instead they were calming, as if he was giving me that part of him to get

141

through telling him this. "But Kai knew. I don't know how, but he knew what Robbie was doing to me and he gave me a way out. At first I refused. I was so lost and immune to the pain I didn't care about anything. And I was terrified of Robbie finding out and going after my mom like he said he would. Connor was gone and you ..."

"... were overseas."

I nodded. "I hated you for a long time for leaving." He gently pushed my hair back and kissed the top of my head. "I know it was stupid, but I think a part of me had hoped you'd ... shit, I don't know what I hoped. But I know now you had to go back to your team."

"I would've stayed if I ..." He sighed, linking his fingers with mine. "I don't know if that's true. If I'd been given the choice to leave the JTF2 at that time ... babe, I wouldn't have stayed. I couldn't be near you. I needed time to try and forget you ... but fuck, I had no idea."

I nodded. Yeah, and I never blamed him for not saving me from Robbie. I blamed him for letting go of the something between us. "Robbie's brothers were in deep with some motorcycle club. Kai was hired by them to get their money back or ... " We both knew what the 'or' was. "But when he saw what was happening to me, he said he'd do pro-bono work." Deck's body tensed. "Kai set up Robbie for the fall with the drugs at school."

"So, he was arrested."

"Yeah, and he'd just turned eighteen."

"And the brothers?"

I shrugged. "Kai never said and I never asked."

"Kai's motive was to give you something that would make you trust him."

Yes. I trusted him because he saved me from Robbie when I thought no one could. "And he offered me a way to get back what I lost."

Deck didn't say anything.

"I was pretty fucked up after that." I'd felt like a cut-up piece of meat, bleeding and raw. "Kai helped me. I guess it was training of sorts. Mostly psychological. You know, learning how to hide your emotions, how people tick, reading movements, gestures, signs of weakness. He taught me self-defense and how to use a knife. And certain computer skills."

"Not a gun?"

I shook my head. "No. Kai doesn't like guns. He said they're dangerous." Deck scoffed at that. "And I'd never intended to have to use one."

"And Robbie?"

"He disappeared when he was released from jail. I think he was scared of Kai and the MC his brothers stole money from."

Deck took hold of my chin with his thumb and forefinger. "Why didn't you tell me, Georgie? Why, after all these years, did you keep this from me? You know I would've helped you. Shit, I'd have found Robbie and made him suffer for what he did to you."

"Kai. There was one condition. I could never tell anyone about him. He knew about you. About Connor dying. And he knew that … he knew you were my weakness." Deck let go of my chin and looked away. "But if I told you …" I paused. "Deck, if I told you, what would you have done?"

"You know damn well what I would've done."

I nodded, not saying anything. Deck would've tried to end it and Kai would've killed him. He still might.

"I did little jobs for him. Lionel was a job. I was to get into his computer and copy his hard drive."

"Fuck."

"I never know the details. Kai says it's safer that way."

"So, you went to some guy's house to steal from him?"

I nodded.

"Jesus, Georgie. You know how dangerous that is? What if he'd found out? What if he caught you?" He pounded his fist into the mattress. "Fuck."

"Lionel's a pussy, Deck. I could've taken him."

He snorted and then got out of bed and started pacing. "Kai was involved with the sex trafficking. I don't know how deep, but it was enough to get him into the compound in Mexico. You fuckin' know that."

I really didn't know the details of Kai's involvement in that. Shit, Kai kept all of what he did from me. "He wouldn't hurt—"

"He's dangerous as hell."

"And you're not?"

He didn't say anything.

"When you rescued London from that auction and brought her to my place …" Deck's eyes shot to mine. "I called Kai. Told him she was with me, but he already knew. He was trying to get info on the sex-trade transporter, Jacob. The only way to get close to him was through Alfonzo, so he made a deal with Alfonzo, exchanged London for money."

"Except he didn't want London."

I nodded. "He wanted to be led to the transporter."

"Jesus Christ. You were nearly killed. They drugged you and—"

"Kai wouldn't have let anything happen to me."

"You seem pretty damn sure of a man who has been using you. Fuck. And he's convinced you to keep it from me because he knows damn well I'd fuckin' never let this shit happen."

"I'm using him, too, Deck. I want Robbie stopped. I can't let him hurt other girls, and he's finding a way to get to him."

"And it's taken what … seven years?" Deck scoffed. "Bullshit. He's using you and dangling Robbie over your head like a fuckin' carrot. That's what he does, Georgie. He uses people. That's all he knows. You ever wonder what he'll do to you once Robbie is dead?"

I wasn't really certain because I'd asked that very question to Kai and he said we had to find Robbie first. "I don't know."

"Yeah, because he doesn't want you to know."

"Kai doesn't share much with us."

"Us? How many people work for him?"

I shrugged, because I honestly didn't know. "Tanner and I are all I know about. But I suspect he has others elsewhere. He doesn't stay put for very long, and sometimes I won't hear from him for months. When he was looking for London, he was gone a few months. I thought he was dead."

"And the drinking?"

"Kai thought I needed a cover … " I took a deep breath. "It kept you focused on my drinking and partying rather than what I was doing with the assignments. My targets."

"Jesus Christ. I'll fuckin' kill that bastard."

"He never forced me. I made the choice."

"If I hadn't fucked off, it would've never happened. None of it."

Probably not, but … "You didn't fuck off. You went back to your team, Deck." But two years was a long time and by then, I was so immersed with Kai that even when Deck came back, I knew stopping was impossible. This was exactly how I knew he'd react. He'd want to go after Robbie, Kai. And then what? Kai would kill him like he had always threatened to do. I wasn't ignorant to the fact Deck was capable of looking after himself, but there was no way in hell I'd ever chance losing him to something I could've prevented.

All the years I tried to avoid this very outcome, and it happened anyway. Except something had changed. Kai didn't want to kill Deck. Why? What did Kai want?

I said quietly, "I need Kai."

His eyes darkened as he glared at me. "Tell me I didn't just hear you say you need Kai."

"You heard me just fine. And you know what I mean." Needing Kai had nothing to do with anything other than finding Robbie and stopping him from hurting others.

I'd never give up, no matter how long it took. The sick bastard had to be found. There was a reason he was hiding. No chance was he some upstanding citizen, and if by some miracle he was … well, then I was going to be there to see it for myself.

"I can't believe you even said that after I fucked you." I did smile a little because Deck was acting jealous. "Georgie … this isn't a game. Kai doesn't give a shit about anyone, even himself. You don't fuckin' need him."

I sat up, putting my legs over the side of the bed. "He's been searching for him for years Deck. I know you have contacts and can look for Robbie too, but Kai will do what needs to be done." Kai will kill Robbie.

"And I won't? That's my fuckin' job."

"No, Deck. That's not it." Well, it was in that I didn't want any of this on Deck.

He turned and walked into the bathroom and I heard him smashing a drawer shut then the shower door slamming—violently. When he came back out, his face was shielded with a cold mask of darkness. He was going dark on me.

"You're not being tainted with this shit anymore. Whatever needs to be done, I'll deal with it." He paced and ran his hand through his hair. I'd never seen Deck so disturbed. He was rock solid … he was *my* solid, and I didn't like that I made him this way.

145

"Deck." God, I did this.

"My fuckin' girl is not going near any *men* who put cuts on her back."

I sighed then slid off the bed and came toward him. He ignored me. I wrapped my arms around his waist from behind and lay my head on his back. "I love you calling me your girl." I felt the stiffness leave his body as if he was sinking into me. He was trying to protect me where he thought he failed. "No matter what I did, you never left me. You protected me and put up with all my bullshit. Even now … the lies … you didn't leave me. You never failed me, Deck. You've saved me again and again. Please, let me try to keep you safe from this."

He was quiet, but even my words didn't take the tension in him away.

"Where's Kai? I've called and he won't pick up."

I sighed. He obviously didn't want to talk about it. "He changes phones constantly except for the number I have." Kai was always the one to call people.

I slipped away from him, walked over to the nightstand and picked up my cell. I entered the password and then another to get to Kai's number. I pressed call. When Kai answered, he wasn't his usual charming self; he was the hard, cold bastard who had demons in his past. I didn't even have to say anything before Kai told me to pass the phone to Deck. I did.

I'd been around Deck enough to know that trying to listen and find out what he was saying to Kai was hopeless.

I walked out of the room, and with every step I felt Deck's eyes on me. When I glanced over my shoulder I saw his face as he held the phone to his ear—pure, unadulterated wrath.

Tears pooled in my eyes as I closed the door behind me.

CHAPTER
FIFTEEN

AFTER TELLING DECK everything, I was pretty fucked up ... kind of like I'd been run over by a bull then ripped apart. I didn't like that my emotions were all scrambled up now. I'd been hiding this from Deck—from everyone—for so long that now I was overcome with so much guilt. It was acid staining my soul, a soul that had already been damaged, but I'd managed to live with it by doing what I did. However, I had doubts. Not of going after Robbie, fuck no. I wanted him to piss himself because he was so freakin' afraid. What I doubted was who I was now. I felt like I was part Chaos, part Georgie and part the innocent girl I'd once been. I didn't know who the real me was anymore.

Deck had walked into his office talking to Kai three hours ago. I watched a movie, finding out Deck had no television channels, only movies, and then I sat by the pool hoping he'd come out of his office and join me. I listened for crashing or shouting, but it remained quiet; not sure if that was a good thing or not. With Deck, sometimes being deadly silent was worse.

I had tried the door to his office and it was locked. After the movie, I tried again—still locked. Since I was really bored and nervous as to what the hell he was doing in there, I knocked. His reply? "Not now."

My reply? "When?"

"When I'm done."

So, I made dinner, a surprising feat for me considering I sucked at it.

The band Tear Asunder would come over every Sunday when they were in town and I'd help make brunch, but that was the most cooking I did. It was a pretty big group now that Kat and Emily were with two of the band members, Ream and Logan, it was like a big family gathering. Even my parents often stopped by. Crisis had a thing for my mom— well, Crisis had a thing for every woman. The guitarist was a sex God … at least he thought he was. A blond one with a sexy ass and devilish eyes.

I had hit on him … more to make Deck jealous, but that was when I was drunk, and that night it wasn't a pretend drunk—I was smashed. Deck ended up throwing me over his shoulder and taking me back to his place where the usual happened—nothing.

I pulled the tilapia out of the oven and sprinkled more lemon pepper on it then dished it onto the steaming green beans. I poured light garlic lemon butter sauce over the whole thing.

"You made dinner."

I hadn't heard him come out of his office or approach me and I dropped the sauce pan. It clattered onto the counter and remnants of sauce splattered. "If you want to call it that."

He grabbed my hips from behind then leaned down and kissed the side of my neck below my right ear.

I melted, sinking into his touch like a flimsy stem of a dandelion. Wow. He was being sweet. I didn't get why yet after whatever went down with Kai, but I was getting sweet Deck and after all the shit I just told him I was taking it.

He took the plates out to the terrace and I brought two glasses of ice water with lemon. When we sat and ate, it was still sweet and … comfortable. Deck actually opened up and told me about how he and Connor competed in JTF2 training. They were both the top of the class, and Connor excelled at everything involving water while Deck excelled at tactical planning. It was a toss-up with who had the better shot.

"And I bet he bragged about every single thing he did better than you."

Deck chuckled. "Hell yeah. Connor was the cocky bastard who made everyone laugh." Yeah, my brother had always been the easy-going one. Even when I was upset at something silly, he'd come in my room and within five minutes, he'd have me giggling. "When we were in deep on a mission … " Deck paused as if thinking about it. "He could put a smile on the guys' faces. Even Vic's."

I laughed, and the tension I'd been feeling slipped from my shoulders. I hadn't realized how uptight I still was. I looked at Deck sitting back in his chair, the tautness around his lips gone and it was like … well, it was like there were no shields between us. We were two normal people talking.

And I loved him even more for doing this. Giving me a piece of my brother I hadn't seen.

"Your brother was good at what he did, Georgie. The best man on the team. And he loved it, too. " I noticed a flicker of uneasiness in his eyes before it vanished and he grabbed a green bean and tossed it in his mouth. "We'd been in a covert situation for three fuckin' days. Sitting in the desert sweating our asses off. No communication except hand signals. Taking a piss was the most movement we did. Our target was inside a bunker and had yet to make a move, but we had intel that he never stayed in one place for longer than five days. So we waited." A flicker of a smile danced at his mouth. "Your brother, he fuckin' loved it. It was like a challenge to him to see how far he could push himself. While the rest of the men were on edge and just wanted to get this shit done, Connor was relaxed. It didn't even faze him." I saw the flicker of something in his eyes again. "He was good at his job because he loved it so much."

"Did you?"

Deck looked a little startled at the question as he placed his fork back down and looked at me. "Yeah, I did. It was my home, Georgie. They were my brothers. Now the guys at Unyielding Riot are."

"You're Unyielding and Connor is Riot. That's why you named it that."

He nodded.

"What about your real home? Brothers? Sisters?"

He shrugged. "Never had a real home. No family." He paused before he said, "I killed my father."

Holy fuck. I tried to keep the shock from my face, but I knew he must have seen my eyes widen with surprise because he was looking at me when he said it. Connor had said he'd gone to Juvie and then was on the streets before he joined the Army. Was that why?

"I was fifteen. He was beating up my mom like he always did. Fuck, it was a weekly thing in our house. He stopped hitting me when I hit him back the year before. He actually stopped beating both of us for a while after that. Then … he left us. Not sure why, but I didn't care. He just disappeared one day and we didn't see him for five months. My mother cried for weeks. Guess in a way she loved him; I mean, he *did* bring her presents all the time—after he beat her. Made me sick seeing him all sorry and shit while my mom's face was black and blue and she couldn't leave the house for weeks without a hat and sunglasses."

I knew what was coming. A guy like that didn't just walk away.

"He came back but this time with a gun. He shot her right between the eyes then kicked her over and over again. It was in the middle of the night. I woke to the shot and came running downstairs to see him beating on her dead, lifeless body." Oh, God. I felt sick to my stomach and put my hand over my mouth. I hadn't noticed I'd been crying until I felt a warm tear drip onto my hand.

Deck held out his hand. "Come here."

I didn't hesitate and took his hand, crawling onto his lap, settling my head on his shoulder. He tightened his arms around me and stroked my arm with the tips of his fingers.

"He was so focused on my mother he didn't even notice me come down the stairs. I jumped him and we fell to the floor. Then I just started pounding with my fists. I don't remember how long I did it, but when I finally stopped, he was dead."

I knew sorry wasn't enough or even appropriate. I was beginning to understand why Deck was so protective of me. He grew up trying to protect his mother and failed time and again. Even the last time he'd been too late.

"You were just a kid."

Deck's hand paused caressing my arm then started again. "You know, Connor kept a picture of you with him." He was done talking about his past. "Kept it tucked in his wallet. He never said it, but he worried about you all the time." He paused and looked directly at me. "I did, too."

My breath hitched as our eyes locked.

"You ever read his journal, Georgie?"

I shook my head. "No. It's his private thoughts and feels ... I don't know—wrong, I guess. But I used to sleep with it under my pillow. When the Robbie shit was happening, it was the one place I felt safe ... in bed with my hand on his journal."

Deck lowered his head and nodded.

"Deck." I waited until he looked up. "It was you, too. It was the last piece I had of you."

Then he kissed me. It was sudden and unexpected as he grabbed the back of my neck and pulled me further into him. His mouth took mine in fierce warmth. A blanket of tingles swept through me as I sagged into him, the invasion of his tongue feeding me what I'd been starved for. And now I understood. We'd both been starved for one another.

He pulled back and his fingers in my hair massaged slowly while he stared at me. He looked relaxed and content. I never saw this side of Deck; it was hotter than the badass side. Hmmm, maybe not. That was a toss-up because thinking about his office this afternoon had me shifting in my chair and aching to have his hands on me again.

"Turn, babe." He put his hands under my armpits and helped me shift around so my legs were on either side of him. My stomach whirled as I felt his cock hard beneath me. I put my hands on his chest, loving the feeling of his heartbeat beneath my palm. It was like it became a part of me, fed me, lit something up inside that couldn't be shut out.

Deck pulled me forward and kissed the tip of my nose. It was sweet and I liked it—a lot.

I looked down at his chest, slowly drawing circles over the hard slab of muscle. "I love being here with you."

"That's because of the multiple orgasms."

I laughed. "True." I trailed my finger down his chest to between his legs and felt him tense. His cock jerked against my palm and I bit my lower lip and smiled while I unzipped his pants. His hand tightened on my hip and I heard the slight rumble in his chest. I smiled. "I want dessert."

CHAPTER SIXTEEN

DECK

I WAS REELING from telling her that shit. The only other person I'd ever told about my father was Connor. But for some reason, telling Georgie felt … right. I needed her to see that side of me. There was no fuckin' way I was ever letting her go, so she needed to see the fucked-up parts, and those parts were pretty damn big.

There wasn't a day I regretted killing my dad. Not once. Maybe that was wrong in the eyes of the law or a psychologist, but I didn't give a shit. He deserved it.

Georgie slipped off my lap and all thoughts of everything except her and what she was doing went dark. She knelt between my legs and then her hands went to my jeans and she undid the zipper.

Her taking out my cock and that sassy expression on her face … Fuckin' hell, it was something I'd imagined her doing for years.

Her tongue darted out and touched the tip of me. I curled my hand in her hair. "Babe."

I closed my eyes and my head went back as she gripped my cock in a fist and then slid me into the warmth of her mouth. My hand tightened in her hair, trying to control the urge to force her deeper. Not yet.

She sucked while her tongue flicked over me and her hand, slow and hard, fisted my dick. She moved up and down a few times then pulled all the way out and my eyes opened. Her kneeling on the patio in front of me, cheeks flushed, eyes curious and smoldering … my control faltered.

She cupped my balls, her fingers tantalizing, stroking. I tried to bring her mouth back to my cock, but she resisted and I didn't like it. I hated not having control, and Georgie literally had me by the balls. "Put your mouth on me," I growled.

She tightened her hand on my balls while her other pumped me hard a few times. "Oh, baby, not the time to be giving orders." She smiled and her tongue darted out and licked the tip once.

Fuck. I shifted in the chair, fighting the urge to throw her on her back and push my cock down her throat.

Then she went deep and I could feel the back of her throat as she sucked. The tightness and warmth caused shivers to erupt and my chest to tighten. Just when I thought I'd come like I've never come in my life before, she pulled back and sat back on her heels.

"Teach me to use a gun."

"Jesus Christ." I was sitting with my dick hard as a steel rod, throbbing between my legs, in front of the girl I've wanted for so goddamn long it had become painful to be near her. Yet I couldn't ever walk away. Then she dropped the sass and put her hands on my thighs.

"Baby, please. I want to learn. And I want you to teach me. It's better than learning from some hottie at a gun range."

Shit. I never wanted Georgie near guns or the shit I had in my dark world, but seeing her fumble with my gun scared the crap out of me. "Fine."

She wiggled closer, her hands stroking up and down my thighs. "You saying fine because you want me to suck you off?"

"I'm saying fine because I don't want another man's arms around you teaching you how to hold a fuckin' gun."

She laughed then grabbed my cock at the base and squeezed. I groaned then watched as my girl put her mouth back on my dick.

Georgie

DECK AND I took the dishes back inside and he scrubbed the pot and pan while I dried. I was right; he was massive and my jaw was a little sore from taking him, but he tasted damn good and when he came down my throat, it was more than that. It was about Deck being vulnerable and he'd given that by telling me about his dad and when he let me take control sexually.

He handed me the last pan and I was reaching up to put it away when he grabbed me and pulled me in tightly to him. "Your brother said your bed was your imaginary island and that's where you and your stuffed animals lived."

Jesus, Connor had a big mouth. "Kids had monsters in the closet … I had sharks swimming on my floor."

His finger tucked my hair behind my ear. "I'd slay them all for you, babe."

"Mmm, a hot pirate."

"A pirate with a prisoner." Deck kissed the side of my neck and I shivered, the familiar ache building between my legs. "Who needs to walk the plank."

He turned me around in his arms and I was met with a playful smile. It was like the demons in both of us were being washed away just by being with one another. "Meaning?"

His smiled dropped. "Meaning I want you in the pool in two seconds."

I raised my brows and put my hands on top of his, resting firmly on my hips. "Well, a pirate doesn't always get what he wants, does he?"

"This one does." Before I could do anything but squeal that girlie sound, he had me thrown over his shoulder and was striding through the house to the terrace. Without a second's hesitation and still with my clothes on, he tossed me into the pool.

I came up sputtering. Deck was standing at the edge so I splashed him. He didn't move, nor did he smile, but he wasn't mad. There was heat in his eyes which made the butterflies in my stomach go bungee jumping. This was the office-Deck taking control.

"You going to stand there or is my pirate coming to fuck me?"

His eyes sparked like they had when I put my mouth on his cock.

My stomach splatted and sizzled like butter hitting a hot frying pan as he stood staring at me treading water. He was mine. After all the years fantasizing about him and trying to convince myself he would suck in bed, Deck was mine.

I swam to the edge of the pool and watched as he took out a small square silver package from his pocket and ripped it open. Then he slowly took off his jeans and his cock sprang free, already hard. He yanked off his t-shirt, put on the condom, then walked to the side of the pool and looked down at me.

"In the shallow end. Knees on the second step, hands on the top."

I swallowed. His eyes were dark and narrowed, watching me, bold and unyielding as he waited for me to obey. I wanted to sass and tease, but I held back. There was something about him that had me bite my tongue. And I was totally turned on by his order, thinking about what he was going to do.

His brows lowered further and his scowl was like it'd been in his office. I knew he'd walk away. Deck was in control, I was going to be his puppet and the thought heightened the throbbing as I swam to the other end of the pool.

I did what he asked and my ass was half out of the pool. I heard him approach, his bare feet slow and deliberate as he walked toward me. My heart pounded against my ribs and got faster as I looked up to see him standing at the edge of the pool in front of me.

"Head down."

I did. Only then did he come up behind me. He yanked my track pants down and I lifted each leg as he pulled them off and threw them aside. I looked over my shoulder and as soon as I did, I felt the slap of his palm against my ass. "Eyes forward."

Shit. That hurt. My skin was wet, his slap making it worse, but then I felt the warmth of his hand soothing where it stung. I sighed and relaxed, my head dropping forward.

I felt his finger lightly trace one of the cuts. I barely felt them now as they had scabbed over. "This doesn't happen again."

I didn't know what to say.

"I know why you do it, Georgie. Use the physical pain to take away the emotional. But we can find another way. Another outlet."

I sighed and closed my eyes. Yes. And I was already beginning to find it. This is what I wanted. Needed. It set me free, gave me the freedom to be who I was. Deck did that.

I knew he had to be still fighting himself for breaking his word to my brother, but I hoped in time that guilt would fade and he'd realize it was right. We'd always been meant for one another. Our paths had been running parallel for so long, trying to cross, yet the ghost of Connor and Robbie and even Kai kept us apart.

His hands gripped my waist—hard. Fingers digging into my skin and pulling me back toward him with a jerk as his cock rammed me. The water lapped at the harsh movement, splashing up the sides of us and onto the stair.

My knees hurt from the cement nodules in the step as they scraped the surface. He didn't seem to care and his body leaned into me as his hand shoved me down lower so I had to arch my back.

"I'm going to fuck you so hard, you're going to beg me to stop."

Holy fuck. A wave of desire spread through me. "Okay."

"No talking." He gripped the back of my hair and pulled. "But screaming … that's allowed."

I could feel his cock in the crack of my ass and wanted to push back into him, but didn't dare move. He let my hair go and slid his hand down my back until he came to my butt. Then his body moved back a bit and I sucked in air, not liking him moving away. I wanted to reach back, look at him, feel him, but knew he wasn't in the mood for me not following instructions. So I impatiently waited, slick moisture building between my legs as his finger slid down my crack into the wetness then came back up and hovered over the pink, puckered flesh.

"Going to fuck this one day." He circled and I moaned at the unusual feeling of a finger touching me there. I never thought I'd like it, but it turned me on even more as he started pushing. His voice growled, "Relax."

I couldn't. The feeling was odd and I instinctually resisted his intrusion. He moved away and I felt the water slosh at the sides of me. Oh, God, he was walking away. I knew I couldn't say anything, so I wiggled my butt and lowered my head until my forehead skimmed the surface of the water.

"You going to give me all of you? Every part, Georgie?" His voice was harsh and stern. A chill went through me and I nodded.

He didn't give me any warning as he put his finger at my tight, puckered ass again and pushed. I closed my eyes and battled the urge to clench, doing the opposite. His finger slid inside me and I sighed at the erotic feeling.

Then he started moving it in and out and my hips rocked back and forth with him. "That's it," he soothed, breathing against the side of my neck.

Without warning and in rhythm to his finger thrusting in my ass, he shoved his cock inside me and I screamed, titling my head back in shock at the sudden intrusion. He didn't stop. One finger in my ass, his other hand on my hip; he kept moving, the water slapping between us and making a loud noise. His thrusts got harder, faster and my need grew with each push and pull.

"You belong to me. All of you." Deck's finger slipped from me and he grabbed my other hip and thrust with more force.

I arched my back into his assault. Wanting it harder. Needing this, the pain and pleasure swirling around me. I wanted to beg him to touch me. To grab his hand and make him touch me until I came.

"Shh," Deck murmured as he slowed and the waves in the water matched the rhythm. He knew what I wanted, gliding his hand down over my hips then across my abdomen and sinking beneath the water.

"Ahhh," I moaned, the second his fingers touched me and started circling. My body jerked back against him and he stopped moving.

"Stay still!"

I nodded. Shit, I'd do anything he wanted at that moment. He waited several seconds as if to make certain I was going to do what he said, and then his finger pressed down hard on my clit and a jolt went straight through me. He did this several times then started moving inside me again, his cock so deep it was near painful when he jerked his hips forward.

"No one takes you from me."

He growled the words in my ear, but I wasn't sure if he was saying it more to himself than me. My breath hitched as his finger moved faster, back and forth, every muscle tightening. He wrapped his arm around my waist and drew me even closer to him.

My body screamed in pleasure as tingles and a brilliance of fire-works shot through me. His arm tightened and he thrust. Once. Twice. Three times and then he groaned low and shuddered around me.

The waves slowed as we remained still, me on my knees, him be-hind, holding me close. I'd never felt so—whole. Deck brought me back from the numbness and the lies and made me feel alive.

I put my hand back and slid it down his leg beneath the water. He kissed the back of my neck then sprinkled my spine with tiny kisses, which were sweet and seductive. Then without a word, he picked me up in his arms and carried me into the house.

I wrapped my arm around his neck and he had yet to look at me. It wasn't until he tossed me on the bed and stared down at me that I got a look at his face. His eyes were warm and filled with softness. The hard lines on his face were gone and his lips relaxed, and it made me want to kiss him even more than I already did.

I reached up.

Deck knelt on the bed and straddled me.

Then he kissed me and I was lost to the most soul-touching kiss a woman could ever have. It was filled with years of need and want and never being able to take. It was him and me finding our peace together. It was our demons being joined and burned to ash.

It was his promise of tomorrow and demand of today and every day after.

CHAPTER SEVENTEEN

I WOKE TO Deck's splayed fingers on my stomach, his naked body pressed against my back, one leg over the top of mine and his chin resting on my head. He breathed steadily and I closed my eyes again as the comforting feeling washed over me. I wanted to lie here for days in his arms and soak up every part of him.

The moment of purity was quickly interrupted as my cell rang. I tried shifting to reach over and grab it off the nightstand, but Deck's arm tightened, tugging me back. "Baby, my phone."

"Let it ring," he grumbled.

"What if a herd of pink elephants are running through the coffee shop and Rylie is freaking out?" I smiled when I felt the rumble in his chest as he chuckled.

"Josh is watching the shop. Something's wrong, he'll call me."

Figures. "Maybe Emily is freaking over her man not being able to perform anymore and she needs to talk."

"Logan not being able to perform on stage isn't an emergency."

"Oh, I wasn't talking *that* kind of performing."

Deck grunted. "Doubt that's ever going to be an issue for Logan." He settled in closer to me and his words whispered in my ear, "And if it is, it's not your issue. I don't even want you thinking about that shit."

My phone stopped ringing then started again. "Oh, I bet it's that sweetness on a stick, Crisis. I was thinking that—"

I squealed as Deck flipped me onto my back and was on top of me, his weight pinning me down. "You remember what I said to you the first time we had sex?"

"That you were going to make me come?"

"That this," he grabbed my chin, his thumb stroking back and forth, "this entails everything. I asked if you're ready for it. What did you say, Georgie?"

"I said hell yeah, sweetpea."

He nodded then reached over and grabbed my phone. "Everything," he repeated. I thought he was going to pass the phone to me, but instead he answered it. "Yeah."

"He's kidnapped me," I yelled, "and is giving me copious amounts of orgasms." I giggled.

Deck said into the phone, "Yeah, second part is true."

I really hoped it wasn't my parents on the phone. Shit, I hadn't talked to them since the hospital. But I was betting Deck had. The guy left nothing undone. No wonder why he excelled in tactical.

"Yeah, Emily. She's good." He paused and I could hear her muffled words in the background. "Did I say she's good?" I was guessing Emily found out about the overabundance of alcohol and the hospital stay.

He passed the phone to me then slipped from bed, tagged his cell and was already talking to Tyler before he disappeared into the bathroom. Which was a disappointment, because I watched his naked ass walk across the room and I wanted him to walk slower. Much, much slower. I heard Emily calling my name and stopped staring at the closed door.

"You and Deck? Really? Like, as in together-together?"

I laughed and lay back on the plush white pillow. God, I missed her and Kat. I missed all the Tear Asunder guys. It kinda sucked them being famous now and they were always gone. I'd known a couple of the guys since they started coming to the coffee shop before I even owned it. High school boys trying to make it with their band. "Like, I'm no longer a virgin."

Silence, then, "You were a virgin?"

She said it loud and then I heard the guys in the background, which sounded like Crisis and Ream. I laughed. We chatted about the band's tour and how Ream was being a super control freak over Kat. Then how crazy it was now the band was so popular. They had to hire security and Logan insisted Emily have a personal bodyguard, but he quickly got rid of that idea when he saw how attractive the guy was. He ended up hiring a female bodyguard.

I asked about Crisis, the bass guitarist, when the shower turned off. Then I wasn't really listening to Emily as I was thinking about Deck, soaking wet. When he came out of the bathroom, still naked, water droplets gliding down his glistening skin …

"Gotta go, Eme. Love ya." I tossed the phone aside as Deck strode toward me. Suddenly, he stopped short, his back stiffened and his eyes narrowed. Then I heard it, the scratching of something like …

He made it to me in two strides, grabbed my arm and yanked me off the side of the bed, hidden from the bedroom door. I landed with a loud oof and a sharp pain in my right hip. He put his hand over my mouth and kept me locked up against him as he whispered, "Stay down and don't move." He grabbed his jeans off the end of the bed and slipped them on, before grabbing my track pants and t-shirt and handing them to me.

I heard the distinct click of a bolt turning.

"Shit," I mumbled beneath his hand.

He took his hand off my mouth then grabbed me behind the neck and before I could say anything, he kissed me. It was hard and fast and over before I could take my next breath.

I was a little freaked at who the fuck would have the balls to break into Deck's penthouse. They were either super brave or super stupid.

He quietly opened the nightstand drawer where he'd placed the bullets when I'd been playing with his gun and then kept low as he went to the dresser, grabbed his gun and came back.

I watched as he popped the bullets in place then slid the barrel back and handed it to me.

He put his hands over the top of mine. "Both hands." His voice was low and steady, completely in control. This was why he was great at what he did. "Anyone comes toward you, …" he curled my finger on the trigger, "shoot."

"That's my lesson? Jesus, Deck. Don't I get some target practice?"

"Yeah, the asshole who's breaking into my loft." Deck pulled me back so I was leaning up against the bed. "Don't move. I need to know where you are at all times. Shoot anything that moves."

"What if it's you?"

"You won't shoot me."

"How can you be so sure?"

"You won't shoot me." Deck was edging toward the end of the bed.

I said in a loud whisper, "But I could if you surprised me and—"

Deck glanced at me and his expression was fierce. Not a fierce I could work through. No, this was immeasurable and severe. This was the Deck who went after the scum of the Earth. "Then don't be surprised." Then he was gone.

I didn't know how to handle a gun, but I wasn't stupid and I had been around Deck all my life. Guess I was getting a lesson earlier than I thought.

I moved to the other side of the room behind the door and peeked through the crack. I did still have an issue with following instructions.

DECK

WHO THE FUCK was breaking into my loft and how the hell did they get past the concierge? I slipped into my office, grabbed my spare gun and crept down the hall.

Tyler was on his way over, but he'd have knocked. Never had he just walked in my place even though he had a key. My house cleaner I'd cancelled for two weeks until all the shit settled.

I crept into the spare bedroom, which was closest to the front door. I didn't hear anything. Nothing. Fuck.

I waited another two minutes and then slid along the hallway wall again, peering around the corner into the living room. I noticed the front door wide open and …

I felt him behind me a second too late and by then he had the cold, sharp edge of his knife on my throat.

"And you're supposed to be the best."

Fuck. I dropped my hand to my side and took my finger off the trigger as he took the knife from my throat. Jesus, I was too focused on Georgie and not on what the fuck I'd been trained to do. "You owe me a new lock."

"What lock? All I did was click and turn. Ever hear of security? My girl is a rather valuable asset—"

I swung around and punched him in the face, although I was rather disappointed he didn't go down. I would've punched him again if Tyler hadn't come running in the door and grabbed me. I think I would've actually killed him and the bastard knew it.

My finger, however, was back on the trigger of my gun and pointed at him.

"Easy." He lowered his knife, leaned over and put it in a holster strapped to his leg. Kai stood up straight and nodded. "Guess I deserved it—once."

"Deck, man, we need him." Suddenly I wished I hadn't called Tyler to come by this morning. Bad timing. Another two minutes and I'd have a dead body to help get rid of.

All I could think about were the cuts on Georgie. Her words, 'I asked him to', ravaged through me, eating up my control like termites. I knew why she'd done it, as a way to deal with her past. To feel the pain and walk away strong, not weak like she used to feel when she was sixteen. It was a classic way to cope with shit fucking with your head. Feel the physical pain in order to deal with the emotional.

Fuck. I should've been there. I should've been the one to help her and fuckin' Kai was there instead. I was filled with fury, but I did lower my gun.

As soon as Tyler stepped away from me, I swung again, this time catching Kai unaware and landing him flat on his ass. He shook his head as if to clear it then came to his feet and our gazes clashed. "You done now?"

The guy had no fear. I was the one with the fuckin' gun. Christ, even worse than dangerous was not caring whether you lived or died.

Kai was a lethal weapon in the sheep's clothing of a rich gentleman. Pretending to be someone he wasn't, just like he made Georgie do. His slight English accent was the final touch to his bullshit persona.

Kai strode across the room and opened the sliding glass door as if he owned the place and was a welcomed guest. *Cocky son of a bitch.*

When we talked last night, I'd told him we'd meet today, although I hadn't intended it to be here or with Georgie around. Kai obviously had other plans.

The bastard headed out onto the terrace, completely at ease. I followed. "Where's Chaos?"

I raised my gun and pointed it at him, my hand steady as a rock as I tried to stop myself from killing the asshole.

She was sixteen when Kai met her. Sixteen when he pressured her, a vulnerable girl who was being abused by a boy at school and had just lost her brother. The fucker deserved a bullet between the eyes. My finger twitched on the trigger.

"Deck." Her voice came up behind me and her hand settled on my waist. I lowered the gun. I tried to keep her safe from shit like this all her life, and the irony was she was around it the entire time anyway. "Hey, Tyler." She paused, her gaze on Kai and she raised her brows, cocking her hip. "Ever think of knocking, asshole?"

I felt the pull at the corners of my lips. I wasn't sure how Georgie would be with Kai, whether she'd fear him or sass him. The latter was a point for me.

"I like the dramatic," Kai said, pulling out a chair from the patio table and sat, stretching his legs out. He grabbed Georgie's coffee mug from earlier, sniffed it then took a sip and set it down.

She huffed. "That's bullshit."

"More like traumatic," Tyler said and yanked a chair out across from Kai and sat.

I kept my hand on my gun resting at my side. Kai glanced at it and a mild smirk emerged. "Not very trusting, are you?"

"I find out my girl has cuts on her caused by you. No, I want to blow you to pieces at the moment." But that was too clean; first, I'd torture him and make him suffer for oh, about ten years. I felt Georgie's hand leave my waist. Okay, she had her reasons for letting him do it, but I didn't have to fuckin' like it. It sure as hell wasn't happening again. I had demons, too, except I beat them out by killing the scum of the Earth. Well, I'd fuck her demons out of her.

"Why?" I knew Kai would know exactly what I was asking. Regardless of how much I hated him at that moment, we thought alike.

"If you'd stuck around, you'd know."

164

I went for him and Georgie's grab on my arm did nothing, nor did Tyler's attempt to pull me away. Kai fought back; the table was pushed over and slipped into the pool as Kai charged me, and we both landed hard on the patio stones. We rolled and I felt the hard clip to the side of my face and elbowed him in the chin before I managed to plow my fist into his nose. I heard the crunch and a satisfied grunt emerged. It didn't last as his fist slammed me in the lower back and I arched in pain just as he kicked me in the back of the legs. I went flying forward, grabbing out at his shirt and taking him with me as we both crashed into the pool.

It was the cold water and Georgie's shouting which finally got me to stop. She stood on the edge of the pool, her hands on her hips and her face furious. Tyler was on his phone and I was guessing it was to Vic who was more than likely in the car waiting for Tyler, having no idea Kai was here.

I slapped the water with my hand while looking at Kai. "She no longer works for you." I climbed out of the pool. "Kill him if he goes near her," I said to Tyler and went inside to change.

Georgie

I WATCHED KAI get out of the water, looking cocky and confident even with a bleeding nose and soaking wet jeans hanging off his hips. His white t-shirt was what caught my attention though as I stared at his chest, mouth agape.

Scars crisscrossed his flesh. There wasn't one inch that didn't have a scar, and they were obvious even with the tatts he'd had inked over the top of them. He must have known Tyler and I could see them, but he remained stoic as he righted the chair he'd previously occupied and sat.

"You done staring?"

I nodded. Shit, I didn't know what to say. I knew he had something dark in his past, but the scars were … even through the wet t-shirt they looked painful.

He smiled, flashing his pearly-white teeth. "So, he finally fucked you."

"Hey, man, you see we're on the thirtieth floor here," Tyler said. "Might want to cool it before you're on the ground floor real fast."

Kai laughed then kicked out at a chair beside him. "Sit, Chaos. You're making me nervous standing there." It was my turn to laugh because the idea of Kai ever being nervous was hilarious. "Need a favor."

Tyler snorted.

Shit. Kai's favors usually involved me flirting with some guy and getting info out of him. If I ever had to go back to his place, I was fake-drunk enough to pass out before he took off his pants and he wouldn't get suspicious. Once he crashed, I could search his place and be gone before he woke. The only one I had considered sleeping with was Lionel and that was purely because I had been tired of saving it for Deck.

There was a guy I'd taken to my friend, Kat's, art gallery showing who I'd actually been interested in ... well, interested in having sex with. Hottie turned into a meatloaf with lots of money and no charm past the public eye.

I heard Deck come up behind me then he rested his hands on my shoulders. Vic arrived and nodded to me and there wasn't the usual glare of what I took as hatred. Now, he actually smiled at me and his sexy, milk-chocolate skin against his white teeth made him look super-hot. Then he looked at Kai and the smile dropped, all business again. Deck obviously told his boys about my extracurricular activities.

"I was just telling Chaos about a ... favor I require."

Shit. Deck's hands tightened on my shoulders and he moved in closer so his body was leaning into the chair.

"Chaos?" Vic said.

"Nickname," I clarified.

Vic grunted.

Kai looked rather relaxed, considering he was outnumbered and didn't even carry a gun.

"Lionel—"

"She isn't going near that guy again," Deck shouted. He actually shouted. Deck rarely shouted.

Vic leaned up against the glass window and crossed his ankles. Tyler looked from Kai to Deck and then to Deck's grip on the gun.

I raised my hand like in school to which Kai laughed. Deck slipped

166

his hand in mine and lowered my arm. "Kai, bad timing," I said. "You should've knocked or called, not showed up here." I tilted my head and looked up at Deck. "And Lionel's harmless."

"No." Deck was unwavering and I would've stomped my foot if I was standing, but since I wasn't it would've looked silly.

"Sugar, it's not happening." Tyler winked at me and I sneered. "Give it up."

Kai sighed while tapping his fingers on the table. "You fucked that scenario up." His words were to Deck and he was probably right. Lionel nearly pissed his pants when Deck broke into his place. "Have you told her what you've been doing overseas for the last few months?"

It was Vic who lost it and came at Kai, but Deck stopped him, blocking him with his hand on his chest. "Not now."

"What's overseas?" The men were quiet and Tyler wouldn't even look at me.

"Get her out of here," Deck ordered Vic.

"What?" I shouted as Vic hooked my arm. "What the hell? What is it? Kai? Deck?" Vic effortlessly swung me off my feet and carried me inside. I yelled the entire way into the bedroom.

DECK

I WAITED UNTIL Georgie was out of earshot before I spoke. "I want her out."

"You said that already."

I had on the phone last night after I gave him a detailed report on how I was going to torture him.

Kai wasn't easily shaken, if at all. I suspected he had no family, nothing to give him a weakness and by the look of the scars under his shirt, the man knew pain and was numb to it. "Who do you work for, Kai?"

There it was. The slight shift in weight, not actually moving, but like an inner jerk that only someone as advanced as my men and me could read. It was all I needed. Kai worked for someone and that meant they were way more powerful than him.

"And I think it's not up to her or you … is it? It's up to whoever you work for." Kai met my eyes and didn't say anything. That cocky smirk was gone, and all I saw were blank, numb, dead eyes. It was the look we hated to see when trying to extract info from a person because you knew no matter what you did, you'd never get him to talk.

"Why did you really come here, Kai?" I kept my voice steady and calm, watching every shift in Kai's movements, which were barely any.

"Lionel's dead."

"Fuck." I knew what that meant and so did Tyler. We looked at one another.

"Place was ransacked. Police say it's a burglary gone wrong."

I didn't believe in coincidences. Not a chance in hell it was a burglary gone wrong. More like a murder gone right.

I felt the tension rippling in my muscles and my heart pumping so hard it felt like there was a riot inside me. Lionel was dead. Georgie had been at Lionel's. They'd been seen at Avalanche together according to Matt.

"You fuckin' put Georgie right in the middle of this?" I had my gun at his temple in half a second and Kai never moved. Even the rhythmic turning of the empty mug remained steady. I cocked the hammer and still Kai did nothing. I hated men like this. He had no qualms if I pulled the trigger. I even wondered if he wanted me to. Men like him had nothing to live for and everything to die for.

"Boss," Tyler slowly put his hand over top of the barrel of the gun.

I knew damn well Kai had a knife drawn under the table ready to slit the femoral artery in my inner thigh the second it looked like I'd pull the trigger. Tyler saw it, too.

"She needs to finish an assignment."

"For you or for whomever you work for?"

"Does it matter?"

"You really are a cold-hearted son of a bitch," Tyler said. He snorted and kicked at the empty chair beside him. "Shoot him, Boss. I have no problems cleaning up the mess."

Kai uncrossed his ankles and leaned forward in his chair, lowering his voice. "The consequences of her telling you about me—your life. She knew that. Those I work for won't be as … understanding as I am."

I snorted. "You're not understanding, Kai. That is fuckin' bullshit.

Let's make this simple for you, Kai. If you or any of your little friends even breathe on her, I'm coming for all of you. Every single one of you."

Kai gave a single nod as if with respect. I didn't like it. Shit, I didn't like any of this because I had no control over it. I researched. I planned. I got in and out of a situation before they even knew my men or me were there. Suddenly, I was in the dark and I fuckin' hated it. What was worse was that Kai was a fuckin' mystery. I didn't know whether he was good, bad or indifferent.

"Why do you think I was given the task to gain Georgie's trust? You're not the type of man to believe in coincidences. Nor am I."

What the fuck? Suddenly, my brain began to put the pieces of the puzzle together.

Connor dying, or so we were made to believe.

A few months later, Kai showing up in Toronto right after.

Kai *bumping* into Georgie at Robbie's place.

Kai taking a menial job to kill a couple drug dealers who stole money from a MC club.

But where did this all start … My jaw tightened as I said, "Connor."

Tyler groaned. "Shit storm."

Kai said, "Yes. They have him. The people I work for."

"Who are *they*, Kai?" I asked.

He ignored me. "Everything you thought you knew about Connor is dead. He will even kill her if he has to." I saw the scars on Kai and I knew without a doubt Connor now wore similar ones. Who the hell was Kai affiliated with? "Georgie won't be free of them now that they have Connor. I give her minor assignments so she'll stay safe. She's just lucky they haven't taken her in, too." Kai chuckled. "My guess is they didn't want to have to deal with you if Georgie disappeared." He sobered again. "Or a tactic to help Connor … see things their way. My guess is that is why they let you live instead of killing you right from the beginning. Despite how this looks, killing is not how they generally go about things. Coercion—yes. Torture—definitely. Death is too final."

Who the fuck were these people? How did they get to Connor? Why him? Most of all, how the hell could I keep Georgie clear of this?

"And Robbie?"

"Dead. I killed him the second he walked out of jail," Kai said.

"Jesus Christ. She thinks he's alive. That you're trying to find him.

You've been lying to her."

"And you're not?" Kai huffed. "Come on, Deck. You've known Connor is alive for months and yet you haven't told her."

"You're keeping her on a leash by telling her Robbie is alive. You're using her." I'd have to tell her about Robbie and Connor. Fuck, neither was going to be a good conversation.

Kai shrugged. "You can look at it whatever way you want. Bottom line—I'm saving her from them." Then his voice lowered and lost that slight accent. "I was there when she was sixteen and damaged by that fucker. You weren't." Now, *that* was a fuckin' stab right in the gut. "I saw what he did to her, what it still does to her, and I wasn't letting him walk free after that."

"The cuts." I closed my eyes, a wave of sickness breaking through my usual steady calm. Then in a sudden abrupt movement, I hauled off and landed Kai on his ass with one punch. This time, Tyler stood back and watched. "I don't care if she begs you. And fuck whoever you work for and fuck Connor. Georgie doesn't get involved in this."

Kai lay on the ground a second then reached out his hand. Cocky bastard. I yanked him to his feet and he smiled. "Too late for that. She's been involved for ten years."

"Get her uninvolved."

Kai shook his head back and forth. "Lionel is dead. Who do you think is responsible? Don't know for sure yet, but I'm thinking it's who I work for." Shit. "Georgie stops doing assignments, they'll know and they'll send someone after her. My guess will be Connor. You can imagine what that will be like for her, having her dead brother showing up to kill her."

"Jesus Christ." Tyler got up and walked away, his hands in his hair as if he was pulling it.

I didn't say anything. I fuckin' couldn't; my throat was locked up tight.

Kai stood and the scrape of the chair against the stone echoed. "And just so you know how serious these people are." I noticed his jaw clench and his hands curl into fists at his sides, not gestures Kai usually displayed. "The girl, London, who I asked you to find in New York ... is now theirs. They didn't like it that I hired you guys to find her."

Fuck. That was why Kai wouldn't try to find her himself. Why he brought us to New York and asked us to look quietly for London and then, if we found her, to hide her until he contacted us. He didn't want whoever he worked for to know he was looking for London. Shit, was that why he'd left her in Mexico when he could've easily gotten her out himself? "Why do they want her?"

Kai shrugged.

But I knew why. I knew how people like this worked. Kai showed a weakness for the girl, and that wouldn't be taken lightly. Weakness led to failure.

There wasn't much of a choice here. Whoever he worked for was more powerful and had more contacts than I did. There was no chance I could begin to put a dent in some organization that faked the death of a JTF2 officer.

"I won't keep this from her, Kai."

"And I won't kill you."

I snorted and shook my head. "Why tell me this? Georgie seemed to think if she told me anything, you'd *try* to kill me. Was that a lie to keep her in line?"

"No. I would've. But now I want something."

"London," I said beneath my breath.

Kai nodded. "Yes. But if there is any indication I told you about them … that Georgie knows more than she should, we're all … I'd like to say dead, but it will be more wishing we were dead." Kai's hand smoothed down the front of his shirt and the scars accentuated through the material. "And it won't be pretty."

CHAPTER EIGHTEEN

Georgie

HALF AN HOUR later, Deck came in the bedroom. He nodded to Vic who'd been silent the entire time I was pacing the room and shooting him dagger eyes. The guy had the gall to laugh at me then dared me to try him when I eyed the door.

I didn't, of course. No matter that Deck and I were together now, I wouldn't have put it past Vic to tie me up and throw me in the closet. After he'd shut me up by putting my head in the toilet.

Vic did, however, smile at me when he left, but his smile reminded me of a hot boogey man.

Deck shut the door behind Vic and I didn't waste any time. "So, you going to tell me what Kai was talking about?"

Deck took his time before he answered. "Yes."

I waited.

Deck didn't look happy—at all. Actually, he looked uneasy and tense. Shit, something was off. Badly off. I preferred when he was angry because then I could easily sass him and try and get him to bend. This … this was a Deck I didn't know. I started for him and didn't stop until

I was pressed against him. "Baby, what's wrong?"

He tilted his head down, lifted my chin with the tip of his finger and met my eyes. They were soft and gentle, the warmth of milk chocolate swirling in the depths. "I can't fix this."

"Deck—"

"Georgie." Shit. Just the way he said my name made me tear up. "I can't fix this," he repeated. Then he leaned closer, snaked his arm around my waist and kissed me.

It was a beginning of something new between us. A truth lay in the way our mouths met and became linked. It was nothing like how he'd ever kissed me before. No, this was purity and it made me his that much more.

"I can't fix this," he said again between kisses.

I wrapped myself into him, feeling the pain in his words. Knowing that whatever he couldn't fix was bad—really bad, because Deck thought he could fix everything.

He pulled back and rested his forehead against mine. "We need to sort this shit out."

Yeah, I figured that, but feeling the torment in Deck was like I was being pulled apart, limbs left hanging weak and unable to bring him into me. I needed that. I had to have that before whatever torment he was dealing with became mine.

"Do you love me?"

His eyes closed and it was as if he was letting go when he sagged against me and I held him. "I've always loved you, Georgie. Always." In one swoop, he picked me up in his arms and carried me to the bed. He laid me on the mattress and followed so his weight was on top of me. Then his hand tucked my blue strands behind my ears. "You're my rainbow. The brilliant colors of you make me whole. Without your colors, I'm just a man living in the dark."

A tear slipped from my eye and he leaned forward and kissed it then drizzled sweet kisses down my cheek, across my nose and to my lips where he lingered.

I put my hands in his hair and pulled him closer, deepening the kiss. His tongue swept into the warmth and we melted into one another in an orchestra of a soft melody. It was beauty and an awakening. It was discovering a part of one another kept veiled behind curtains of hidden

173

secrets.

My hands went under his shirt and lifted. He shifted to the side and yanked it off, throwing it on the floor. Then he pulled mine over my head and my bra followed. His hands stroked a path up my arms, which I had above my head.

His head lowered to my breast and I shivered, arching into him as his mouth took hold of my nipple and sucked. The warmth spreading over me was like a heated blanket of home.

"Baby," I moaned as he nipped the sensitive nipple then soothed it with his tongue. He did the same to the other then trailed kisses down the center of my core. "What about Kai, Tyler and Vic?"

"They left." He yanked down my track pants and I lifted my butt to help. The touch of his hands on the bare flesh of my hips sent an intense ache between my thighs and I arched toward him, closing my eyes, hands curling into the pillow. I expected him to touch me.

He didn't.

I opened my eyes and looked at him hovering over me. It was as if he was seeing me for the first time as his eyes roamed over my naked body, inch by inch. I felt … yeah, he made me feel beautiful.

Robbie made me an abstract of confusion and darkness with my back as his canvas. Deck couldn't erase the embedded emotional pain of who I became from that, but he made it better.

His eyes met mine and the torment I saw earlier was pushed back to be blanketed by desire. "I'm never letting go."

I knew why he said that. Whatever torment lingered wouldn't be pretty and he was making it clear no matter what happened, he was never letting me go.

I gasped as his finger slipped into my wetness and then his tongue followed. I moaned. "Deck."

He drove his finger inside me as he suckled on my clit. His other hand stayed on my hip, pushing me down so I couldn't move as he tortured me with his mouth. The ache built and built until I was squirming beneath him.

He drove his finger into me harder and harder. My legs opened wider. It was when I opened my eyes and saw him between my thighs that sent me over the edge.

"Deck. Deck!" I screamed as my body shattered into a brilliance of pleasure. He didn't stop with his tongue until my body stopped trembling and lay limp.

I heard the rustling of clothing as he took off his jeans, then the wrapper of the condom, and anticipation filled me again.

I reached for him just as he came back to me. My hand curled into the back of his neck as I pulled him down to me and kissed him. It was me giving him what I'd hidden. It was an apology. And it was me loving him for everything he was. "I'm sorry, Deck. God, I'm so sorry."

"I know you are. But you have nothing to be sorry for."

I felt his cock hard against my inner thigh and reached between us to take hold of it. "I need you." He jerked in my hand, the thickness swelling even more. "I'll always need you."

Deck groaned as I placed him at my wet entrance. He grabbed my hand, pulling it away from his cock and putting my arms above my head again. I was getting he liked that. A power position. Control, and yes, it turned me on. Not because he controlled me but because it released me. Was it possible Deck gave me what I needed? That the physical pain I sought could end? Deck was giving me that. He let me be free.

"Wrap your legs around me." He was nudging at my opening and I wanted to push him inside me so badly I was trembling.

"Please. Deck, I need—"

He shut me up by taking my mouth in a fiery passion. This was no longer sweet and gentle. It was an assault of Deck's mouth until I felt him arch away, then in one thrust of his hips, shoved his cock hard inside me. I screamed beneath his kiss, making a muffled sound.

He pulled out and did it again. This time, he wasn't kissing me but staring down at me. "Keep your eyes on me," he ordered.

He drew back again and I tensed, holding my breath just before he thrust back into me. The intensity of his stare heightened the passion, held me and wouldn't let me go. He moved faster and faster, the link between us endless as he kept one hand locked on my wrists above my head and the other flat on the mattress to give him more power to drive into me.

"Hell," he said as he pushed harder. Faster. Deeper. Until I was meeting each motion with my own. I fought against his hands holding me down, wanting to touch him, but he wouldn't let me go.

"All of you." Deck pounded. It was as if he couldn't get deep enough.

His eyes were closed now, tightness around his lips as if he was in pain. Then his grip loosened and he let me go. My hands instantly went around him, and I felt the straining of his muscles as he held onto control.

His hand slid between us and he touched me. "Now, babe. Now."

He flicked his finger over me several more times until my body let go. He put both hands on the mattress on either side of my head, giving him leverage and then he violently pumped into me a few more times before he joined me in the whirlwind of brilliance.

Deck took off the condom, tossing it aside before shifting onto his back, taking me with him so I was laying half on top of him. His arm was around me, the other linking our fingers together and resting on his chest. Both of us were silent for a few minutes, our chests rising and falling with our heavy breathing.

"I love you, Georgie."

I tilted my head, looked up at him and smiled. It was a real smile, one which lit me up from the inside. "I've always loved you."

A tiny flick of a grin before he said, "I know, baby."

I tried to smack him in the chest, but his hand locked in mine and he wasn't letting go. Then he did chuckle and brought me in closer as he hugged me. It wasn't the hard, cold and unemotional Deck; this was the one who let me in to see a part of himself he hid from others.

And yeah, he probably *did* know I loved him from the beginning, even that day he broke my world apart. I had a feeling it was going to happen again, except this time, I had him.

I felt it before he even said anything. The way his muscles tensed, how he held me tighter to him, how his heart picked up speed beneath our hands locked together.

What I never expected were the words he spoke next.

"Connor's alive."

CHAPTER
NINETEEN

A ROAR OF emotions exploded all at once as I tried to comprehend what he'd said. I didn't believe it and yet … Deck never lied.

I couldn't control my breathing as I started hyperventilating. Deck sat up and brought me with him so I was facing him, straddling his lap. He cupped my chin and forced me to meet his eyes. "Breathe, Georgie. Deep breaths."

I stared into his calm, steady gaze as he stroked my back and forced me to keep our eyes locked until I was breathing better. "Where is he?" It wasn't 'how was it possible' or 'why'; all I could think about was having my brother back. When could I see him? Hear his voice. Feel the touch of his hand as he ruffled my hair. I didn't care how this was possible. Nothing mattered except that he was alive.

"I don't know," Deck said.

I scrambled for words, thoughts pounding me in drums of confusion and disbelief. "My parents. I have to call—"

He shook his head. "No, Georgie. They can't know." I went to argue, but his hand tightened on my chin and his eyes grew dark. "No."

"But—"

Deck's eyes said it all and I felt my stomach plummet. There was nothing good about Connor being alive.

"Oh, God. Deck. No. Please tell me he's okay." Tears filled my eyes as I imagined him burned beyond recognition, sitting in a hospital somewhere for the last ten years with no one with him. "You saw him die. You said he was in a vehicle you saw blown up." I shivered as the questions and urgency to find answers swarmed me. "How did you find out?" Then I realized the timing of Deck telling me and Kai being here. "Kai? Kai knew about Connor? He told you?"

Deck looked a little uneasy as his hands stopped stroking my back. "Yeah, Kai knew. I had a suspicion for a while, but I wasn't sure until a few weeks ago."

I froze. "For a while? You've known for a while? You've known my brother has been alive for a while?" I repeated. I pushed on his chest and tried to climb off his lap, but he was ready for it and flipped me over onto my back so he was on top of me. "Get off me. Get the fuck off me, Deck."

"No."

I glared. He glared back.

"Damn it." Tears filled my eyes. "God damn it, Deck. Why didn't you tell me?"

"You're questioning me about not telling you shit? You hid shit from me for years. Years, Georgie."

I clamped my mouth shut. Fuck. He was right, but I was reeling with confusion and so many questions, I wasn't thinking straight. "I couldn't," I said quietly. "Kai said … he'd kill you."

"And you think a threat like that would matter to me?"

"Damn it, Deck. It matters to me. You're all I have."

"That's not true, Georgie."

I had my parents and Emily and Kat and the band, but Deck … he was part of me.

Deck was silent. I think he was contemplating what to tell me next, because I knew there was more. Suddenly, his weight left me and he was off the bed and walking to the bathroom. I sat up as I heard the taps turn on.

Connor had been his best friend, his brother. This wasn't just me hurting, this was us hurting. I crawled to the side of the bed and got up, throwing on my panties and a t-shirt. Then I padded across the room to the bathroom and saw him looking in the mirror, his hands on the edge of the sink, his face dripping wet.

I walked up behind him, wrapped my arms around his waist and leaned into him. "We'll find him."

He stiffened. "No, Georgie. He doesn't want to be found."

"What?" I pulled away and he took the opportunity to walk back into the bedroom where he sat on the edge of the bed, putting his head in his hands. I crossed my arms and leaned against the doorframe. Then I waited for him to tell me. It was the longest wait ever and yet it was mere seconds.

Deck started talking and it was after he told me about Connor being taken by the people Kai worked for that I slid to the floor, curling my legs into me. He told me everything, how he and his men had been overseas because an acquaintance of theirs, a Navy Seal, told them they thought they saw Connor while they were on a mission.

Deck and his men had been searching for nearly a year until they found a guy who also said he knew of Connor. That was when the guy was delivered dead with the note taped to his chest written in his own blood.

I was shaking with disbelief. I couldn't believe it was the same Connor I knew who wrote something like that, who threatened my life. Deck didn't stop and give me time to breathe or take in what he was telling me. He kept pounding me with truths as he told me about Robbie.

I stopped shaking as my gaze darted to him. "He's dead?"

Deck nodded. "Kai killed him the second he was released from jail."

"But that was ... seven years ago."

Deck didn't say anything. Fury erupted in my stomach like a volcano as I thought of all the times Kai told me he had a lead on Robbie, where he might be. Why? Why the hell would he do that? Why keep me thinking Robbie's alive hurting other women?

"Bastard." I darted to my feet and was out the bedroom door before Deck could stop me. I made it to the elevator and pressed the button before I realized I only had my panties and a t-shirt on. Deck stood at the front door with his hand outstretched.

When I didn't move, he sighed and lowered it. "Babe, he did what

I would've done. Should've done. Robbie never deserved to walk free and if Kai had let him, he would've hurt other women."

"He used me all these years. Made me believe he was trying to find him," I yelled.

Deck nodded. "Yeah. It's who Kai is, baby. But I don't think you finding Robbie is what you've been chasing after all these years."

I sighed and looked at my feet. I really didn't know what to think right now. Robbie was dead, and that was what I wanted. But there was no satisfaction knowing that. I'd thought I'd feel this immense relief … but there was nothing.

"You want to find yourself, Georgie? Get that part of you back that you lost? Then stop running from it. All Kai did was teach you how to survive. But, baby, now I get to teach you how to live."

A tear slipped from my eye and slid down my cheek. "How do you always do that?"

"Do what?"

"Make me love you more."

He grinned and then the elevator dinged.

"Babe, get your ass in here. I don't want to have to beat some guy because he saw you half-naked."

I smiled.

He scowled.

I quickly walked to him and he pulled me inside and shut the door. Then he picked me up and carried me out onto the terrace where he told me the rest of what Kai had revealed, while I curled up in his arms.

"WHAT WILL THEY do to London?"

We were in Deck's black Audi on the way to the Unyielding Riot office where Vic, Tyler and Josh were digging up anything they could on every secret organization known throughout the world. Of course, the job wasn't so easy. I'd tried calling Kai to try and get more information out of him, but he wasn't picking up.

"Torture her until she breaks, most likely."

I asked for it. Deck didn't give bullshit or make things look prettier than they were. I was a little, okay, that was bullshit, I was a lot freaked out that I was under the thumb of some powerful secret organization I knew nothing about and neither did Deck. "Do you think Kai will try and get her out?" Shit, he was the one responsible for her being targeted. London had been through enough already.

Deck parked and shut off the car. "No. And he'd be stupid to try." I closed my eyes, feeling my heart cracking as I thought of the broken girl who refused to meet anyone's eyes and trembled at the sound of a man's voice. "Then that means Connor ... " I couldn't finish. Was he lost to us forever, too?

Deck reached across the space between us and took my hand and squeezed. "Probably. But I'll never give up on him."

I nodded. Yeah, that was Deck.

"But keeping you safe comes first, Georgie. Not only because I love you, but because Connor asked it of me." I opened my mouth and then shut it again because we'd already been over this. I argued that Connor was more important and Deck refused to listen. There was no discussion. No leniency. No give. Deck wouldn't go after Connor if it meant my safety.

He let me go and opened the car door.

I got out and we strode into his office where his men were sitting in the glassed-in boardroom. It looked odd, three hot men wearing jeans or cargo pants and t-shirts sitting around a dark mahogany table in an office building.

When we walked in, all eyes went to me and I knew they were looking to see if I was still freaking over the news about Connor.

I wasn't. I had my shit together and I knew that had to do with Deck. He grounded me. "Sweet, three cupcakes *and* a fancy coffee maker." I went over to the machine and started making a cappuccino. I could feel their eyes on me and turned. "I'm good. Stop staring at me. Jesus."

That got a snort out of Vic, a laugh out of Tyler and Josh merely looked away. Deck, on the other hand, shut the door harder than necessary, then walked over to me, picked up the cappuccino I'd just made then sat me down beside Tyler, He placed the mug in front of me then went and sat at the other end of the table.

Tyler snagged my mug and took a sip.

"Hey."

"You think I'm hot, eh?"

I rolled my eyes. "You are until you open your mouth." I grabbed for my mug, but he lifted it in the air out of reach.

"Nice get-up." He eyed my track pants and sweatshirt. "Easy access, I guess."

"Tyler," Deck warned in a quiet tone. It was instant. Tyler's laughter died and he was serious again as he passed me my cappuccino. "What have we found out?"

Josh slid a sheet across the table to Deck. "List of organizations which we know of. Seven we've had dealings with which I scratched off. Two are affiliated with hate crimes, also scratched off. The last one is a possibility, but unlikely. According to what I found out, it was established ten years ago and wouldn't have been around to pull off something so elaborate as kidnapping a JTF2 officer while on a mission in the Middle East."

Where Connor had supposedly been killed in a car bomb explosion. Deck had seen it happen. At least he'd thought he had. To pull something off that well-executed, these people had to have men who were just as good as or better than JTF2's.

Tyler pushed back his chair and stretched out his legs. "We dig deeper, we raise red flags which—"

"Puts Georgie at risk," Deck finished. "Okay, what about the guy, Tanner? Who is he? Where did he come from?"

I sat up straighter. "Deck, Tanner doesn't know anything. Kai brought him in to watch out for me when he was away."

"Yeah," Tyler said as he looked at me. "But why him? Why a kid Connor used to know?"

I shrugged. "Because he knew me. When I found out Tanner was also working for Kai, it made me trust Kai even more because I had familiarity with Tanner."

"And how long was Tanner involved with Kai before you were brought in?" Vic asked.

I didn't know. Well, not really. When I didn't answer, Deck said, "Bring him in quietly."

I froze. "What does that mean? Are you going to hurt him?"

"Not if he talks," Vic said.

I looked to Deck who wasn't looking at me. "Deck? Damn it, Deck.

Tanner's my friend. Connor knew him." I knew by the silence in the room what they planned to do and it was a reality check of what these men did. Of what we were involved in.

"Friends don't let you be cut up while they wait outside." Deck's words plowed into me and it took me a moment to catch my breath. How did he know Tanner had been there? Who told him? Kai? But why would Kai do that? And from the look on the men's faces they didn't know about the purging. I guessed it was something Deck had kept to himself. He chin lifted to Vic and the scrape of his chair sounded on the hardwood floors as he came to his feet, snagged his cell and walked out.

Deck turned all his attention to me and his eyes softened a bit; not much, but they weren't as menacing as a few seconds ago. "You have two choices, Georgie. I tell you nothing and you ask nothing. Or you're on board with what we have to do here. Which is it?"

Whoa. Okay, I understood what he was saying, but shit, hearing it so harsh and in my face set me back. I suspected that was what he was trying to do. I didn't say anything for a second, a little shocked at Deck's abruptness, although I shouldn't have been; it *was* Deck, after all. Tyler kicked me under the table and I jolted. He raised his brows and tapped his hand impatiently on the table.

"Okay."

Josh huffed and hung his head as if I'd said something wrong. Tyler kicked me again and I looked at him and mouthed, "What?"

"Okay, what, Georgie?" Deck asked.

"Okay, yeah. I'm on board."

"Now, that we have that shit cleared up, can we get back to business?" Josh asked and then shoved his tablet across the table to Deck. "I've compiled a list of jobs Kai has done that we know of. The graph shows the links to people we know about and who they're affiliated with."

Deck was quiet as he looked it over. I watched his intensity. The way he sat at the end of the table looking as if nothing could touch him. Focused. Concentrated. Fuck, I'd brought all this shit down on him and he still loved me. He still wanted to protect me from it.

The men talked about the different contacts for a while and then Deck tried calling Kai again. When he received no answer he asked me to call, but Kai wasn't picking up.

Deck stood and looked at Josh. "Keep trying the number I have for Kai. Tyler, call Rylie at the coffee shop. Tell her Georgie will be back in tomorrow. We need to keep things as routine as possible. Contact me if you find out anything else."

He walked over to me then took my hand and tugged me to my feet. Then he hauled me out of the board room. I thought we were going to the car, but Deck ushered me into another room down the hall, this one with no glass except for a window to which he went and twisted the hanging white rod and closed the blind.

Then he stalked toward me and it was totally a stalk. Like I was his prey and he was going to devour every inch of me. I was trapped with nowhere to run. Except I didn't want to run.

"I can't be in the same room as you and not want to fuck you." He reached me and I felt the tingles erupt into a violent storm of lightning strikes.

I had no time to take a breath as his mouth crushed mine, hands on either side of my head, holding me still as he kissed me. But it was over quick as he pulled back to yank off my track pants and panties, one arm holding me up while he pulled them over my feet.

My stomach whirled and my knees weakened as his dark, smoldering eyes met mine. Then he undid his jeans and pushed me against the wall—hard. "Legs." He lifted me up by my butt and I wrapped my legs around his waist. The second I did he slammed inside me.

"Oh, God," I yelled, my head falling back and hitting the wall.

I was already wet and I could hear it as he violently pushed inside me, the wall giving traction to make his thrusts harder. The sound was rhythmic, like a hammer being pounded. Only it wasn't a nail, it was me and I was guessing if Tyler and Josh were down the hall, they heard exactly what was happening.

His lips were on me again, sucking my neck and nibbling before moving up my throat until he took my mouth again. It was everything feral and irrational and out of control. I felt the tightness in my belly and moaned. He pushed inside me harder. Faster.

I screamed against his mouth as I went over the edge. "Oh, God, Deck. Deck!" I quivered around him and within seconds, he joined me. His deep groan roared from his chest and pushed the final wave from my body as I breathed heavily into his shoulder. I had no strength as he held me between him and the wall, his cock still throbbing inside me.

When he pulled out I felt the warm wetness slide down my thigh. I froze, smacking Deck in the chest. He dropped me to my feet, frowning. "Condom. Deck, we didn't use a condom."

"And?"

"And? Jesus, Deck, I could get pregnant."

He stepped back, looking not the least bit worried that I could get pregnant. He casually did up his jeans and without looking at me said, "I don't have a problem with that."

"You don't have a problem with that?"

He raised his brows. "No. Do you?"

"Ummm ... Deck. We're talking about a baby. And you're supposed to be the responsible one. Having a baby would be—"

"What, Georgie?"

I put my hands on my hips and tried to look fierce with no pants on and legs still shaking from the spectacular, amazingly hot sex against the wall. "Irresponsible. And plus, you've also been with other women. You should get checked before we have unprotected sex." That sucked, but it was reality. I had no misconceptions that Deck had slept with plenty of women.

He leaned over, picked up my track pants and then passed them to me. I quickly slipped them back on while he walked over to the desk, leaned against it, and crossed his ankles and arms.

I bit my lip. Shit, he looked sexy all satisfied and relaxed. I was also thinking despite the soreness between my legs that I'd like to wrap myself around him again.

"I was checked."

"What? When?"

"When I left you at my loft after you told me about Robbie." I spent hours sitting in his hallway waiting for him to come back. Band-Aid. He'd had a Band-Aid on his arm and then he fucked me for the first time. "You pay enough, you can have your results within hours. And Georgie, I'd never fuck you without being checked. You should know that."

"Oh." Wow. How could I love him any more than I already did? But I did.

He was standing in front of me and his hand was curled around the nape of my neck. He was gentle as he moved in and kissed the tip of my nose. "I'm not worried if you get pregnant. You're with me and that isn't ever changing." He sighed and I felt his warmth ease my argument. "You don't want kids, then we won't."

"Really? Just like that?"

He nodded. "Just like that."

"I want to use condoms—for now."

He nodded. "I'll buy condoms." He took my hand and headed for the door. "I'll take you home. I'd keep you at my place but we'll have to play our relationship down a bit. I don't want this organization having a suspicion that I know about you working for Kai."

I snorted. "Yeah, won't be much of a play down if I'm suddenly fat and waddling around."

He stopped dead and pulled me hard up against him. "Jesus. That image … my baby growing inside you … you fat and complaining about your feet." His kissed me and it was sweet and warm and curled my toes. "I want that with you, Georgie."

I stared up at this man I'd loved my entire life. I wanted that too, but not now. Not when everything was all fucked up. "Okay."

He grinned and it was as if I gave him the light to his darkness with one word.

Then we were walking again.

CHAPTER
TWENTY

DECK DROPPED ME off at home and for now, I was to do what I normally did and that meant pretending to drink while in public, go to work and flirt. I laughed when Deck said the word flirt as it came out in a ragged growl. I stopped laughing when he scowled, because he really looked in pain saying it and I liked my sweet Deck. There was one rule that came with the flirting—no touching. Not even a hand touch. Then he leaned over, opened my door and told me he loved me.

I watched him drive off, wondering if I'd ever get used to idea we were together. I opened the front door, plopped my bag of sweats and t-shirts on the floor and walked into the kitchen.

I turned on the light and stopped, the air sucking from my lungs. "Tanner. What are you doing here?" He never came here; it was too risky. Well, it had been too risky when Deck didn't know about me. Did Tanner know that Deck knew? Would Kai have told him? I really didn't think so.

He sat at the island, beer in hand, eyes glazed and red. He raised the bottle and tilted it slightly. "Ahhh, she finally comes home. Been waiting a while."

There was a white dusting on the counter that looked like icing sugar, but there was not a chance Tanner was here baking a cake. From the look of him, his legs tapping up and down and his eyes red and a little wild, he was high on cocaine. Shit, he hadn't touched the stuff since he was a kid. "Kai know you're here?"

He shook his head and his untidy hair fell haphazardly over his eyes. "Nah … he doesn't like us being friends. Says I'm too close to you."

Yeah, that was something Kai would say, now more than ever. I sat on the stool beside him, touched his shoulder and squeezed. I had no idea what was going on with him, but it was bad. "You shouldn't be here." Jesus, Vic was looking for Tanner right now. I'd have to call Deck. I didn't want to because I knew damn well what they'd do to him. But I also knew if Tanner was in the dark just as much as me, then they wouldn't hurt him.

I was never afraid of Tanner. He'd always been good to me, but I also knew something was off with him and it wasn't just the drugs. He was freaked out over something.

"That target you were getting info from his hard drive?" Tanner said.

"Lionel."

He nodded while he stared down at his beer. "Dead."

"Kai told me." Actually, it had been Deck.

"I killed him."

A wave of unease hit me and I swallowed then shifted so my feet were on the floor and not resting on the stool's foot bar. Something didn't sit right. Tanner's hands on the beer were unsteady when he took a pull from it then set it down again. "Maybe I should call—"

He jerked up so fast, his barstool toppled over. "No."

I jumped to my feet and took a step back. He looked at me, eyes wide and dancing from side to side, the whites lined with red. "What's going on with you, Tanner? Why would you kill Lionel?"

"I finished your job for you."

"Tanner, my job was to get his hard drive, not kill him."

His breathing was ragged and he tapped his fingers insistently on his thigh. He was high as a kite and whatever he was scared of was making it worse. "They're going to kill me. I'm next, you know."

"Tanner." I kept my voice soft and calm while giving a half-smile. "No one is going to kill you." But an oil stain of dread started spreading in my stomach and I knew I had to call Deck ASAP. Tanner must know about the organization. But why would they come after him? Why now? Had they asked him to kill Lionel? "Let's go sit down and I'll make you something to eat." And call Deck.

I led him into the living room and urged him to sit on the couch. I turned to go in the other room and make the phone call when he grabbed my arm. I looked down at his hand then up at his eyes, fear pounding through me. "Sweets, let me go. I'll be back in a sec."

His eyes hardened. "You're calling him. Aren't you?"

"No, I swear. I won't call Kai." His fingers tightened and I gritted my teeth. "Are you trying to break my arm, because you're well on your way." I yanked. He pulled—hard—and I fell into him.

"Deck. You've been with him since the hospital." His hand went into my hair at the back of my neck. I tried to push away, but he curled his hand in the blue-tipped strands and yanked. "I smell him on you. Now, you're fucking him? After all these years?"

What the hell was this? "Tanner, let me up." His grip tightened and I didn't think he really knew how hard with the drugs pumping through him. "Jesus, ease up."

Instead of easing up, however, he pulled me closer and then his mouth slammed onto mine so hard our teeth hit. It was a sloppy, bruising kiss and my stomach churned, tasting the beer on his breath. My shoving him in the chest did nothing, and the hold he still had on my arm was so tight it felt as if he'd melded my skin and muscles to my bone.

His tongue pushed past my tight lips and he groaned. I bit down as hard as I could and Tanner vaulted back screaming, blood dripping from his mouth. I reacted, using the heel of my hand to jab him hard in the throat.

His eyes widened as he let me go, holding his throat and gasping for breath. I scrambled off his lap and fell to my knees. I got up and made it two-feet before I felt his weight crash into me and we both went sprawling to the hardwood floor. I kicked out for his kneecap and hit his shin, then I punched for this throat again, but he jerked back, ready for it. Tanner had been trained, too; he knew what I was going for and he also knew how to get the power position.

Tanner punched me so hard in the side of the face my vision blurred, and I froze for a second trying to get my bearings. He straddled me, his hands going for my throat and squeezing. My instinct was to react, but I relaxed in his hold, hoping he'd ease up so I could breathe.

He did and I wildly sucked in gasps of air.

"I'm the one who's been there for you—not him. I know your secrets. I know what Robbie did to you."

"Tanner. What the fuck are you doing?" I held onto his wrists. "Tanner, damn it. Don't do this. We're friends." Well, not anymore. Kai was getting an earful about this shit.

He slammed my head into the floor and I hadn't expected it, not that it would've made a difference. The jolt of pain shot down my spine right to my toes. He leaned in close and I gagged as his breath hit my face. "I watched you drool over that piece of shit for years. He's nothing. He doesn't even know who you are. I do. Me. He doesn't deserve you. I do. I've watched out for you. I'm the one who made sure Robbie didn't go too far. I'm the one who protected you. I'm there for you when you purge. Not him."

Bile rose in my throat as his words echoed in my head over and over again. He'd made sure Robbie didn't go too far? He was fuckin' fourteen. "What the hell are you talking about?"

I lay limp beneath him, shock stalling my fight as I stared up at him. He killed Lionel. He had known about Robbie hurting me?

A slow smile emerged and my fear shot to another level. "It wasn't easy for me either, knowing Robbie was cutting you and just standing on the sidelines—watching. But it had to be done. They needed you broken."

"You bastard." I tried to get away, struggling beneath him as fury ripped through me.

"Settle down. It wasn't that bad. You have no idea what bad is, but soon you will." His eyes were calmer now, breathing slower, almost rhythmic which was a good thing. "They sent Kai in when I told them you were ready."

"Ready?"

Tanner nodded. "Yeah, broken. Ready to do anything to stop it. Even to trust a complete stranger."

"Kai," I breathed. I closed my eyes, my body shivering beneath him as the betrayal sunk deep. He set me up for the fall.

"Robbie's brothers needed the money and Robbie was paid a lot of cash to do it." Tanner laughed. "The kid was a sick bastard. He wanted to rape you like he did the other girls he fucked with, but Kai wouldn't let him."

Tears spilled from my eyes as I broke. Everything was a lie. Robbie was paid to hurt me. Tanner knew what Robbie was doing to me. It was all a lie in order to get me to break. To trust Kai and join them for what … so Connor was easier to coerce into working for them because I was in their grasp? To keep me close?

"They have your brother, you know. He's alive and well." He chuckled. "Well, I don't know about well, but he's alive."

I faked a gasp of shock and hoped like hell he believed it. I didn't need him knowing I had already been told about Connor.

Tanner shrugged. "Don't know why they risked taking him. Deck would've been a better choice. No family. No ties." He sighed and his grip around my neck loosened. "But now … now, Georgie, things are all screwed up because of you. You told Deck about Kai and I, didn't you?"

"No," I lied. "Tanner, that's ridiculous. You know I'd never do that." I kept my eyes directly on him, knowing he'd be able to tell I was lying if I looked away.

He paused and I felt his hands tightening on my neck as he thought about it. "I saw you kiss Deck in the car, Georgie."

Double-fudge-fuck.

"If you told him, they'll kill him, you know." I nodded. "I know you'd never want that to happen to him." Okay, he was going to believe me. "Kai doesn't agree, but you're weakening. I saw it when you were drinking after the purge. Do you know how many times you called out for Deck?" Shit, I couldn't remember anything. "You need to be brought in now, Georgie. It's too risky, you being on the outside." I thought of London; Deck said she'd be tortured until she broke.

"Tanner. No. It will ruin everything. If I disappear, Deck will start a war."

He laughed, throwing his head back. "War has already started."

It was my moment. I grabbed his wrist with my opposite hand, the other above his elbow and I hooked my foot around his, raised my opposite hip at the same time as I pulled on his elbow.

It was one solid movement and it knocked him forward and off-balance. We rolled, so I was on top of him, and I didn't stop as I jabbed my fingers into his eyes. He screamed and writhed beneath me, hands going to his eyes. I scrambled to my feet and at the same time reached into my back pocket and pulled out my cell while I dove for the front door.

I heard him yelling as his footsteps thudded after me.

My hand was on the doorknob and turning when his body slammed into me, the momentum pushed me hard against it, knocking the wind out of me. My cheek pressed to the door, I pulled my arm out enough to glance at my cell still clutched in my hand. I hit redial then dropped it to the floor before he realized I'd placed a call.

"You fucked him. Didn't you?"

I felt his cock hard against my ass and he held me trapped between him and the door. "Tanner. Let me go," I shouted. I needed whoever I'd redialed to hear me. "You're hurting me. Get out of my house." I hoped like hell someone had already picked up the phone and was listening.

Tanner knew exactly what I'd done and yanked me back, with his arm hooked around my neck then smashed his foot into my cell, the plastic shattering. "Who did you call?"

"I don't know." I was trying to think of the last person I talked to, but my mind was in escape mode and not on thinking things through.

His fist barreled toward me and I shifted to the right and it smashed into my forehead. "Who did you call?"

"Fuck you, Tanner."

He had me by both arms, his body close to mine. I didn't have enough room to knee him in the balls, and my head was still reeling with pain from the blow to the head. "It doesn't matter. We're leaving and we won't be back for a long time. When they're done with you, you'll be good. And Deck ... " He chuckled in my ear and cold shivers raced through me like stabbing icicles. "He won't want you. You'll be so damaged, no one will." He kissed the side of my neck. "Except me. I will, Georgie. I'll look after you like I always have."

Rage gripped me at his words and I wanted to shout at him that he was a lying, disgusting piece of shit. Instead, I kept my voice calm and controlled. "I won't leave you. We can do what we've always done. Nothing will change. Think about what you're doing. You'll ruin everything." Whoever these people were, they must have had him in their grasp since he was fourteen, maybe younger. He'd been watching me for ten years. I was his *assignment* since Robbie.

To think Connor was in these people's control. Why? What purpose? How many did they take like Connor? How many children, men, women disappeared? When had Kai been taken?

"Deck will come after them, Tanner. They don't want that, right? They'll be mad you've put that on them. We can just let this go. Forget it ever happened." Like hell. If Kai or Deck didn't kill him, then I would.

"So, you do know about the organization?"

Fuck.

I recognized the cold, smooth surface when it touched my cheek. Shit, I had Robbie's haunting memory to prove it. I also knew Tanner was really good with a knife; Kai had trained him and I was beginning to wonder who else had. Did he have scars on his body like Kai?

"Kai has been too easy on you. Look what's happened to that London girl. He should've brought her to them when he was told to instead of hiding her."

"Hiding her?" I wanted to keep him talking as long as possible. If we moved locations, whoever I called wouldn't find us. "What do you mean, Tanner?"

He laughed. "Kai showed up at the auction because he was going to get her out of that shit. Then Deck got her out and Kai thought she'd be safe. But they found out about him being there." What? Holy shit, my mind reeled and I felt sick as I realized how powerful these people were. "Kai was ordered to bring her to them. Funny thing is … she ran away. Coincidence? No. I think Kai took her and hid her from them. Until she escaped him and we found her. Of course, this is only me guessing, but they will know soon enough."

"Why do they care? She's harmless."

He grunted. "Kai cares about her. That makes her deadly." His breath wafted across my ear as he leaned into me. "And I know what you're doing. Time to leave."

I reacted, not carrying if he cut my face or stabbed me. I wasn't going with him. But he was ready and slammed the butt of the knife down on my head so hard I crashed to the floor then nothing.

CHAPTER TWENTY-ONE

DECK

"WE HAVE A problem." Hearing Kai's voice was a reminder of the sharks we were now swimming amongst.

"Yeah, a shit load. And you're the one who brought this hell down on us. Where is Tanner?" Vic had been looking for him for hours. Even with Kai's possible locations, the guy had vanished, leaving me with an uneasy feeling that he knew something was up.

"Call came in from Georgie. He has her." My hand clenched the phone as a cold wave gripped me. I immediately put my hand up and signaled to the guys. Josh and Tyler shot to their feet and we were already running from the office while Vic went to the cabinet on the far wall and entered a combination. A click sounded on the opposite side of the room and he strode over, pressed on the wall and a door popped open revealing a walk-in closet.

"Where?" I said as I joined Vic and began dressing for war. I put on my holster with my guns and knife then grabbed Josh's while Vic did the same and grabbed Tyler's. They'd have the car running and waiting for us outside the door.

"I'm on my way to her place. That's where she'd said on the phone, but I suspect it won't be for long." Kai's voice didn't have the usual cocky tone to it and that fucked with my head.

Fuck. Vic and I ran for the car as I kept talking. "Where would he take her?"

"In," Kai said.

I stopped with my hand on the door, the car idling outside the window. Tyler watched me as I stood frozen for a second. "In?" Fuck, no.

"Best guess … he found out about you and her hooking up. I warned *them* he was too close to her. I tried to get him off the assignment, but she trusted him, so it was easy for him to keep an eye on her."

I slammed my palm into the glass door and ran out to the car. "Who the fuck is *them*, Kai?"

Silence.

"Kai. Jesus. You know better than anyone what will happen if she's taken to this organization." I jumped in. "Georgie's." Tyler shot out of the parking lot.

"I'm here already." I heard Kai's car door shut and he sounded like he was running. A loud bang and then, "it's too late."

It was as if pieces of my soul cracked then bled as his words hit me. I closed my eyes as I inhaled the fear. "Fuck." I had to pull my shit together or Georgie would be just as lost to me as Connor. I had no misconceptions of who these people were. Even with all my abilities, contacts and power, trying to get anyone out … chances were pretty fuckin' slim.

"Kai," I said quietly. "I know you're not like them. You tried to save London. You know what they're capable of. Don't let them have Georgie, too."

"If Tanner's told them anything, it's too late to stop." He sounded resigned and it pushed the fear into my stomach, churning like a cyclone. "We're all finished."

"Where would he take her?"

"The shed maybe? But he'd know I'd find him there." Kai was silent a few seconds and I could hear him getting back in his car. "The school."

"School?"

"Georgie's old school. Tanner was taken by *them* as a kid. He was

195

trained, if you want to call it that, and Connor was his first assignment. He hung out at the motorcross track where he met Connor and Georgie. Became friends. When Connor died, his new assignment was Georgie. Tanner used to watch Robbie cut her."

"Jesus. Fuck."

"He was to tell us when Georgie was … vulnerable enough to trust me."

I was pulsating with so much fury I thought I was going to break. Vic must have seen it because he leaned over the seat and squeezed my shoulder.

We knew one another pretty damn well and right now, I was volatile as hell.

Kai gave me the directions and I repeated them to Tyler who had turned around and headed for the highway. "Deck. I suspect Tanner killed Lionel. He set this in motion."

"And that means?"

"It means he wants them to bring him and Georgie in."

"Why would he do that?"

"So you can't have her."

"Fuck." I ran my hand over the top my head, back and forth then down my face.

"Meet you at the location." The line went dead.

I threw the phone on the dashboard. "Tell me you've found something on this Tanner kid? Anything, damn it." I stared out the window but saw nothing. The fear had changed to rage, and the rage was now a cold-steel determination to destroy and conquer anyone or anything that stopped me from finding Georgie.

Vic sat forward so each elbow rested on Tyler's and my backrests. "I narrowed it down to one missing boy a year before this Tanner kid showed up at the motocross track where he met Connor and Georgie. A ten-year-old Michael Donald vanished from his Toronto home, never to be seen again. No leads, nothing. He fits Tanner's description with the compilation. Time frame is right. I'm guessing whatever organization we are dealing with took him in, tortured him, trained him, brainwashed the kid."

Tyler shook his head. "Jesus, he was a kid."

I glared at Tyler. "Yeah, who can make Georgie disappear."

"I know, Boss. But whoever these people are, they're taking in children. They need to be stopped. Fuck, Connor would do whatever it took to take these guys down."

Yes, he would. Connor was the guy who always helped the kids wherever our missions took us. And now he was part of an organization that destroyed them. "And we will."

Josh spoke from the backseat. "Why would he want to bring her to them? Kai says he has a thing for her. I'd think he'd want to get her far away from these assholes. Not a chance would I let those fuckers near my girl." Josh cleared his throat. "Sorry, Boss."

"If he knows her and I are together, the only way to get us apart is to bring her in. If Kai is right, there is no escape from these people, so trying to run would be stupid."

Our advantage, they had no idea what Kai had told us. If Tanner had yet to make contact with the organization, then there was a chance we could stop everything from snowballing into a total cluster-fuck of a nightmare.

We drove for a half hour before Tyler pulled over on the shoulder and nodded to a school down the block. "Looks like this is it."

It was two minutes later that Kai pulled up behind us. Tyler reached over and put his hand on my arm. "I know you'd like to blow Kai's brains out right now. Fuck, Boss, I do, too. But he wants London, that gives him a reason to go after them."

I wouldn't kill him, but fuck, I wanted to. Just the thought of Kai's involvement in this … I unclipped my seatbelt and got out. Kai was standing with a knife in hand and without his usual air of cockiness.

"We bring her home," I ordered. Because if we didn't, my darkness would smother the only good parts of what I had left and I'd never come back from that—nor would I want to.

Georgie

"YOU KNOW, I used to stand on a milk crate outside the shed and look through that window." He nodded to the left at a dusty window at the back of the shed. "I'd watch Robbie with you. Hear your sobs. I wanted to soothe you, hold your hand, but *they* wouldn't let me."

I whimpered against the black rag he'd shoved in my mouth. "That's how I knew what to do when I cut you at the shed. Then Kai refused to let me do it again. But I knew I was better at it. I knew how to help you, Georgie." He reached out and I flinched away, but he managed to stroke the side of my face. "We're connected, you know. We share the same pain. We're the same."

My eyes widened. I had no idea what the hell he was talking about. My knees ached from kneeling on the hard, plank floor and he had my arms behind my back and tied with a belt—just like Robbie had done.

"Have you seen Kai's scars? They're bad. He must have fought them a long time. Me … I was only ten, so I didn't fight them for very long, kind of like you didn't with Robbie."

That's because I was already broken, you bastard. Connor dying, Deck leaving, had destroyed me already.

"They won't like it that Kai failed to keep you and Deck apart. You know it was why he couldn't leave JTF2 for those two years? They pulled some strings, made sure he was kept in the military until Kai had you completely immersed with us." I moaned against my gag. He tilted his head to the side. "Kai … he'll be brought in, too. They won't kill him for it, but he'll be tortured. Or maybe they'll just torture the girl while he watches. He should've done what they asked and brought the girl to them when he was supposed to. They will make him suffer. He probably already knows it." He chuckled as he ran a finger down my back. "Vault will be pleased with me for bringing you to them as soon as I found out you were with Deck. And if they're not … " he shrugged. "At least Deck will never have you."

Vault?

He crouched down in front of me, holding out a carving knife. He tilted it back and forth, sliding his finger down the edge of it. "We'll be here a while. My message won't reach France until it goes through the channels here." He ran his hand over my head like I was his puppy dog. "But I can help you. I'll take away your pain like you want, Georgie."

"You fucking bastard," I shouted against the gag, but all that came out was a roar of moans. I rolled to the side, but I couldn't get up with my hands tied behind my back. He yanked me back up to my knees and came up behind me, pressing down hard on my back until my cheek pressed into the floor.

The knife punctured my lower back on my side and started to drag up. I felt my skin separating, the blood leaking down my side and I tried to move, but his weight wouldn't allow it. It didn't feel deep, just enough to make me bleed. What I didn't know was how much worse it was going to get.

"Oh, it's not that bad. Wait until Vault have you. *Then* you will know pain." He ran his finger down my spine like a soft caress and I felt his lips brush against the small of my back. "I'll erase him from you. Make you forget him, Georgie."

Like hell, he could ever do that. No matter what was done to me, I'd never stop loving Deck.

"When we go—"

There was a loud bang as the door flung open at the same time as the small window shattered and glass flew everywhere. The door ripped off the rusted hinges and swayed twice before it fell to the floor, just missing Tanner and me.

My eyes widened when I saw Kai and Deck standing in the doorway and Vic and Tyler climbing through the window, all with guns pointed at Tanner. Except Kai, he had a knife but it was as good as a bullet. He could throw it quick and accurately and Tanner knew it.

Tanner looped his arm through mine and dragged me backward two steps until we hit the wall, a shovel and spade wobbling on their hooks. He held the jagged knife to my throat and his other arm locked around my chest.

I was drooling from the gag in my mouth and trying to inhale large breaths through my nose. My gaze hit Deck, but he wasn't looking at me. He was locked on Tanner.

Kai lowered his knife, slipped it back in his holster and took a step

199

forward. Tanner's grip tightened and I felt the slight puncture of the tip of his knife.

"What are you doing, Tanner?"

"More like what are you doing, Kai? Did you tell them about Vault? Looks like you did or they wouldn't be here right now. No matter, they will deal with you as soon as they get my message."

I noticed the muscles in Deck's arms twitch and yet he remained completely stone-still, eyes on his target, waiting for the moment he could take a shot.

Kai chuckled and it sounded odd in the tense situation. "And you think they'll let you live? You've kidnapped one of our own to what ... bring her to them? If they wanted her 'in' they would've done it years ago. They don't, Tanner. They won't kill her. And if you do, they'll make you beg for death." Tanner's hand shook and the knife scratched my neck. I tried to lean back into him as far as I could to avoid the blade, but he wasn't paying attention to me; he was looking at Kai and I knew he was scared.

"Let her go and we can stop this," Kai said taking another step toward us.

I inhaled sharply as he yanked me closer. "No. He can't have her." Tanner looked at Deck. "I've been the one looking after her."

"No connections, Tanner. You know that. They'll never allow it."

"You should talk. I heard about that London girl. Heard she hasn't begged yet. I wonder how much longer it will take them to break her."

Deck stepped forward and grabbed Kai's arm.

Tanner laughed. "Yeah, I guess that's why they don't like us forming relationships, because you react foolishly."

I glanced over at Tyler and Vic who stood on either side of the window. I knew they weren't blocking it because Josh was a sniper and most likely outside, waiting for the right moment when he could one-shot Tanner. I just hoped if he did, Tanner's knife didn't slice into my neck as he fell.

"Lower the guns," Tanner ordered. Deck nodded to his men and they put them on the floor. There was no chance they'd barge in here without a plan. They were operatives. "Kick them over here." I heard the scrape of metal gliding to Tanner. He was careful to keep me directly in front of him. "Knife, Kai. It's just as deadly as their bullets."

"More so," Kai said. There was the cockiness he always had and in a way, it made me feel better. He wasn't worried—not that Kai was ever worried. Kai bent down then slid his knife across the floor.

I looked at Deck, begging him with my eyes to look at me, to tell me this was going to be all right. But he wouldn't. His gaze was pinned to the figure behind me and I knew why. Deck was the killer right now. The hunter. The assassin.

Kai straightened. "What are you going to do? Wait here for hours until they make contact?"

"Keys," Tanner ordered.

I noticed a change in position as Deck now stood ahead of Kai and then he finally looked at me.

He didn't have to say anything. He barely had to move. I read him like his men did. His eyes shifted to the right and then his fingers started curling into his palm one by one.

Five.

Four.

Kai reached in his pocket and pulled out his keys. "Here."

Three.

Two. Kai threw the car keys to Tanner.

One.

It happened so quickly. At the same time as Tanner reached for the keys, I shifted my head to the right as far as I could which threw us off-balance. The sound of a knife whooshed through the air and embedded right in his chest, missing my arm by an inch. Tanner dropped and I went with him.

Within seconds, I was dragged off him and the rag was ripped from my mouth. Deck's arms came around me as he cradled me to his chest. I could feel someone's hands on my wrists, undoing the belt, and the instant I was free, I wrapped them around Deck's neck and sobbed into his shirt.

I sobbed for what I'd done. For the lies. For the purging. For bringing Deck and his men into this. I cried for us; for the years we'd lost. But most of all, I cried for my brother because I was finally realizing how bad this was and the hope I had when Deck told me he was alive was now drowning in the fear of what he was involved with.

Vault ... they owned me. They owned Connor and Kai, and now

London.

"I can't get out. Can I?"

Deck stiffened as his hand stroking the back of my neck stilled. "No." And that was Deck. He wouldn't give me false hope. He knew what I was involved with was too big for him. "But I won't let them have you. If we need to disappear, I'll make it happen."

Yeah, and that was Deck, too. He'd do whatever it took. Tanner was dead. He was the only one who knew that Kai told Deck about them. That I knew the truth. Until the message Tanner sent was read. "Tanner sent a message."

"Kai said he would. Come on, baby. Let's get you out of here."

The men moved around us and I smelled gasoline then Deck lifted me in his arms and walked out of the school's shed.

Halfway down the parking lot, I heard a loud explosion and then Kai, Vic, Tyler and Josh were beside us.

Grey clouds billowed in the air. Fire crackled. I breathed in the smell of smoke. It was the burning of all the lies. It was the purging I'd been seeking all along. I finally felt free from Robbie. From the parts of me I hated that were weak and still lost to the pain of what I'd kept alive.

The ashes of that part of me were swirling around us and then were lost to the breeze. I looked up at Deck and stroked the side of his face. "I'm only a rainbow because you make me that way." His eyes were still dark and haunted by what just happened, but there was a hint of the sweet I'd found in Deck and I smiled. "Love you, baby."

CHAPTER
TWENTY-TWO

DECK KEPT ME locked bedside him in the backseat, while Tyler drove and Josh sat in the front. Vic went with Kai.

I winced when the cut on my back rubbed on Deck's arm and he immediately loosened his grip and looked down at me, brows low over his eyes as concern etched his face. I reached up and touched his chin like it was the most delicate, expensive diamond. "Did I ever say thank you for saving my ass, sweetpea?"

I think he was too worried about me to take to my sass because he just looked at me. I sighed and rested my cheek against his shoulder.

"Boss?" Josh looked over his shoulder at us. I noticed him give me a once-over as if he was checking to make certain I wasn't bleeding to death. Like Deck would let that happen; I gave a half-smile when his eyes reached my face. He grunted. Josh was a weird guy. Quiet and no sense of humor and yet I saw something lingering in him as if he was fighting the need to laugh or smile. "You want our guy to look at her?"

That got my attention. I was the only *her*.

Deck nodded.

"Hey, wait a sec. Who is our guy, Deck? And why is he looking at me?" Josh turned back around.

"Rick," Deck said. "A doctor. And you're being looked at because I said so."

"You know, sometimes it would be nice if you weren't so damn … direct. Couldn't you ask me how I feel about it? Maybe threw in a 'babe, I love you but … '"

Deck huffed, obviously not in the mood for even a slight grin. "Josh, get him over to my place ASAP."

"I'm fine, Deck. It's a couple scratches and bruises."

"You see your face?"

"Well, no. It's not like I've been too concerned about what I look like at the moment."

"You need a doctor."

I leaned forward and looked in the rear view mirror. I met Tyler's eyes who pursed his lips together and shook his head. I knew what it meant—I wasn't winning this one. I had a minor scratch on my neck and a pretty bad bruise on my forehead.

Deck watched me, eyes narrowed. I knew he was waiting patiently for my argument.

I crossed my arms and stared out the window. "Fine, but you owe me copious amounts of orgasms."

Tyler burst out laughing. Josh grunted. Deck was silent.

He put his arm around me then pushed my head down on his shoulder. I reached over and linked my fingers in his. He squeezed and it was all I needed to feel his comfort seeping into me.

Within a half hour, Kai's car pulled over on the side of the road and he and Vic got out looking really unhappy. And Vic looking unhappy was pretty damn scary.

Of course, everyone got out. Deck told me to stay put, which I didn't. He scowled at me but didn't interrupt Kai who was giving the bad news that he was unable to intercept Tanner's message through the internet.

"Shit," Tyler said and kicked the tire at the same time as he hit the roof of the car. Seeing Tyler react like that somehow didn't suit him.

"Alternatives?" Vic asked.

"Manually go in and delete it from the main computer before it's reviewed then sent to France."

"France?" Deck asked.

"Where Vault is based."

I knew Kai giving us the location was huge.

"What is it that Vault does, Kai?" Deck asked. "Besides, kidnap and torture people."

"Everything," Kai sighed. "Vault is like a religion. It runs off beliefs that were set up by a group of nine people many years ago. Power. Money. Drugs. Corruption. We go after some of the worst criminals. We also protect some of the worst. It's all about control and information."

"Fuck," Tyler said.

Kai nodded. "And they will send someone after all of us if I don't intercept that message."

"And I'm betting none of us can get close to the main computer. At least not fast enough," Josh said.

Kai didn't need to say anything because we all knew the answer. The question was did any of them really trust Kai? Was it even possible to trust a guy like that? He'd been involved with a secret organization which kidnapped men, women and children to use for their own purpose.

Kai spoke directly to Deck, eyes unwavering. "They get that message—I'm eliminated or worse, taken 'in' and so is Georgie. It's in both our best interests to make certain that doesn't happen." Kai nodded to me. I met Kai's eyes and they held steady on me. I knew exactly what he was going to say. "I just received a message from Vault; they want her to go out on an assignment tonight."

"No," Deck immediately replied.

I put my hand on Deck's arm. "It makes sense. I have to."

"No," Deck reiterated.

It was Vic who objected, crossing his arms over his broad chest. "She disappears, it's a red flag. She's right. You know it, too, Boss."

He stood stiffly beside me and I watched his jaw clench then unclench before he finally nodded.

But when Kai told him who I had to make contact with … that was another fight. Kai did have Deck's men on his side now, though. I needed to go to the bar, drink and do the usual. Kai would go into Vault's residence here, and delete the message from their secure computer before it was approved and distributed to the organization's leaders in France. And it had to be tonight as every morning someone went in and went through the correspondences to see what was important to be sent to France.

"Percentage of success?" Deck asked.

Kai shrugged as he walked to his car and opened the door. "Depends if my mother's there." I gasped and the men's eyes widened. "Goes down exponentially if she's in town. Bitch hates me."

I hadn't realized I had my hand over my mouth until Deck took it in his and lowered it. I thought of the scars on Kai and couldn't imagine a mother ever allowing that to happen to her own son. Kai was more fucked than I realized and that scared me, because if a mother could watch her son go through something like that, then what had they done to Connor?

CHAPTER
TWENTY-THREE

MY TARGET—TRISTAN. I was to meet up with him at Avalanche.

When I called him, he didn't sound surprised to hear my voice and agreed to meet me for drinks, which was perfect for me, since I was to appear tipsy to get him to loosen up and Tristan needed loosening up. Eventually, Vault would ask me to get something from Tristan, whether files from his computer or to tap his phone, but they were obviously in no rush with Tristan.

I did this plenty of times. But somehow … now I didn't want to do it. I wasn't scared—I was pretty confident in my ability to play my part. It was the fact I had to flirt with another guy. But I didn't have a choice and Kai was risking his ass to erase Tanner's message. I could meet some guy for a few drinks to help keep Deck and everyone else safe.

Of course, Deck was not happy. "The doctor said you should rest."

Deck's doctor had been waiting for us at the loft. He checked me over, said I could have a concussion then treated and cleaned the cut on my back. There were no questions asked as to who I was or how I was hurt. I suspected the doctor got paid a lot to not ask questions.

"You agreed to this."

"That was before the doctor saw you."

"I'm perfectly fine. I've done it before. Not a big deal. Besides, we don't have a choice. No red flags, remember."

"I don't fuckin' like it."

He was worried and I liked that he was worried about me, but there was no choice. "You know I have to do this, Deck. You of all people understand what this is about."

He looked me up and down, his lips tightening. He knew I was right. This argument had gone down in the car with the boys earlier. "You're not wearing that. Change."

Here we go. The top was like a second skin, blue sequins with a V-neck and spaghetti straps. I wore tight black leggings with it and blue flashy high-heels. "He likes blue."

"Then wear that blue pajama top." He strode out of the bedroom as if it was the end of the conversation.

He remembered my blue puppy dog pajama top? It gave me a warm, fuzzy feeling, like whenever I saw the brown bunny rabbit Connor had given me and still sat on my bed to this day. It was just … nice he paid attention considering it was years since I'd worn it.

I went after him, my heels clicking on the hardwood floors. He was in the kitchen—looking completely at home as he grabbed the dishcloth and began wiping down the counter. He wasn't wearing a shirt, and his jeans hung low on his hips revealing that trail of scattered hairs leading down to his cock.

I swallowed. He ignored me standing a few feet away, his muscles flexing as he moved, tatts glistening over them. Jesus, I wanted him to strip me down and fuck me on the kitchen counter.

"When you're done staring, go change."

Shit, did he have eyes in the back of his head? Yep, he was Deck. He had eyes everywhere.

"If I don't look sexy, he won't like me."

"Good."

I sighed. Yeah, this assignment shit was going to be an ongoing issue. I came up behind him as he tossed the cloth in the sink. "Baby." I felt the tension in him, caressing his arms and then down his back. "I know what I'm doing. You have to trust me."

"I trust you, Georgie. I don't trust him." Suddenly, he snagged me around the waist, picked me up and went and sat on the barstool. I put my legs on either side of him and his arm kept me from falling back. "You're changing."

"Shit." I gave up because getting my way with Deck when he was like this wasn't happening. "I'm smashing the piggy bank and buying myself something with your coffee money. Maybe some handcuffs to keep you in line."

He didn't chuckle as I expected him to; instead, he ran his finger over my collarbone, expression serious. "Thinking about you doing this … babe, I've tried to protect you for years. Now, I have to willingly let you go into a situation, which could get you hurt. It's going against everything I am." He tilted my chin up and his thumb caressed it. "I love you, Georgie. I won't lose you."

Jesus, and then he had to say shit like that and I knew exactly what he was saying because I felt the same way. "You have protected me, Deck. And you'll never lose me. I'm yours. Always have been." Then I kissed him until I felt the tension ease from him.

When he pulled back he tucked a blue strand of hair behind my ear. "The pink elephant under the counter?"

I smiled. "Yep. I've emptied it five times already. The money is tucked away for our wedding day."

He laughed and it shocked me. The seriousness was replaced with a smoldering burning. "Our wedding?"

I shrugged.

"Fuck, I love you," he said. Then he kissed my neck and I moaned. "Buy some sexy lingerie for our wedding night," he whispered in my ear then nibbled on the lobe.

I rested my head on his shoulder. "Deck?" He didn't say anything, merely tightened his hold on me. "Thank you for always being there for my brother." I felt his breath hesitate then exhale. "And for me."

Then he kissed me hard and we were pulling at each other's clothes. He was careful not to hurt my back. But he wasn't careful about fucking me. It was hot and quick and probably had a purpose because Deck ripped the sequined top right off me.

DECK CONCEDED WITH me wearing a black top, which was less revealing, less tight and less sexy. Of course, I'd gone through five other tops before he finally agreed to one, and that was because I was a half hour late to meet Tristan.

Tyler and Vic were already at Avalanche and had texted saying Tristan was there at the bar. Deck wasn't allowed inside because we all knew he'd fuck it up. Instead, he was waiting outside in his car.

Kai texted me on our way over to make certain I was meeting up with Tristan. Then he said he was on his way to delete the message which made me nervous for him. For Deck. For all of us. Kai was fearless and yet I sensed in him something before he left us earlier. It wasn't fear exactly, but it was as if his composure was off.

"One drink then you leave," Deck ordered.

I nodded. "An hour—tops."

Deck grabbed my hand before I got out of the car. "I'm proud of you, Georgie. You are the person I always knew you were and couldn't find." He sighed. "I won't ever give up. I'll find a way to keep you safe."

Goose bumps rose and I felt my eyes fill with tears. Jesus, how could I love this man more than I already did? But another piece of me was glued back together at his words. I kissed him and it was slow and heated with a promise of never letting go. Then I went into Avalanche and did what I had to do.

DECK

I LASTED A half hour waiting in the car. I knew what it would do to me, seeing Georgie with another guy. Fuck, I'd watched her with other guys for years and it ruined me. Now, she was mine and I still had to watch it.

"Not a good idea, Boss." Tyler came up beside me. "Vic and I got this."

I knew they did, and I trusted them, knew they'd never let anything bad go down. But I was a controlling asshole and had to have a visual. "I'm not leaving."

Tyler chuckled. "Yeah, well, you should've been here sooner. I lost fifty bucks to Vic. I didn't think you'd last this long. I gave you ten minutes before you had your ass in here."

Fuck, these guys knew me too well. He passed me a beer and we made our way through the crowd to a booth with a good vantage point to the bar where Georgie sat next to Tristan.

I watched my girl touch his arm, the lightness of her fingertips on his skin. And it wasn't jealousy I felt because in order to be jealous, you had to be insecure. Georgie was mine. There wasn't a chance in hell another man could ever take her from me. I was obsessively protective.

I was also aroused. My cock strained at my jeans, threatening to break free from its tight confines. I knew what her fingertips felt like on my skin, on my cock, and I had the urge to go over there and fuck her on the bar.

"You good?" Vic asked.

I nodded. Fuck yeah, I'm good. I was the one taking her home tonight and sinking inside her wet pussy. I held the beer in my hand, although I didn't drink it. I wanted every single molecule in my fuckin' body ready to react.

Tristan was high profile, meaning he had a lot of money, was in the news often whether it was about his development company or his bachelor life. He was generous with several charities that involved helping children and on paper was an upstanding citizen, but Vic couldn't find anything on his family. No past. And no past meant it was hidden

What I really didn't like was the fact he came to Georgie's coffee shop when there were two others closer to his office. But there wasn't anything to indicate he was involved in illegal activity of any kind.

Then why did Vault want Georgie to get close to him? What purpose? And why did Kai receive a message for Georgie to meet up with Tristan tonight?

That didn't sit well with me. As a team, we went into every situation with as many details as possible. We had a plan for every possible outcome and we knew what to do if things went bad. This was a crap shoot. We had no idea who was involved with Vault, what they wanted or if Kai was on our side or Vault's.

I watched Georgie … no, Chaos. She was playing a part and yeah, she was hot. Fuck, I hated that Chaos was part of her, but it was something I had to accept, as it was part of who she was now. And any fuckin' guy would be turned on by his girl bold enough to do what she's done all these years. I didn't have to like it—shit, I *didn't* like it—but my girl was tough and that was fuckin' hot as hell.

Georgie

TRISTAN WAS A hard nut to crack. He didn't drink from his beer and he didn't react to my slight touch on his arm. He was stone cold and it reminded me a little of Kai. Well, my job tonight was just to make contact and he was obviously interested because he'd agreed to meet me here.

We chatted about the coffee shop and his company, Mason Development, and got into how I knew the band members of Tear Asunder. Then he hit me with, "He was a liability." Tristan's grip on his untouched beer was light, not a flicker of tension in him.

"Who?" A shiver went down my spine. I was uncertain what he was talking about, but I didn't like where this was going.

Tristan didn't look over at the booth where Deck, Tyler and Vic sat, but he gestured with his head, tilting it in their direction. "You know exactly who I'm talking about, Chaos. And so do they."

Fuck. Double-fudge-fuck. It took everything I had to remain relaxed and not react.

"I assume Tanner's dead?" Tristan said. "Did Kai kill him or Deck?"

Jesus. How did he know? I didn't have to fake taking a sip of my beer because I needed it. I also knew when to shut the fuck up. There was no hiding from this. Tristan obviously knew about Vault. Shit, was this why I was given orders to get to 'know' Tristan? Did they already suspect that he knew about them?

"Kai won't be far behind him, despite who his mother is." He shrugged. "They'll know soon enough who his loyalty is with."

"And yours?" Because I was wondering why he'd tell me this. He must know I was part of Vault, although it wasn't willingly.

It was the first time I witnessed a slight grin as if he was impressed

I was keeping it together. Well, I was good at pretending because right now I was freaking out big time.

"My loyalty is to myself." He leaned forward, placing both arms on the bar, beer between his hands. "They find out your boyfriend over there knows about Vault, they'll kill him … and you … you'll be taken to them and shown what happens to those who betray them."

I really didn't give a shit about me, but I still felt the fear settle.

He was quiet for a second before he looked at me and I met the cold, unfeeling eyes again. "I'm pretty sure they know by now you're with Deck and for now, they're allowing it."

Allowing it? Shit. And fuck. Because they'd wonder why Deck would allow me to date Tristan if I was with him. Deck wasn't the sharing type.

"They'd know I told Deck the second I called to meet you tonight. Deck would never let me date another guy when I'm with him. That's ludicrous."

He grinned and I caught a glimpse of his pearly-white teeth. "Ah, but they don't know I'm meeting you. The order Kai received to meet me tonight was from me."

It was that comment which made me lose my composure and my eyes widened as I turned to meet his eyes. "How? Why? And how do you know about them? About Tanner's death?" I had so many questions flying around in my head I didn't know which one to start with.

"It was unfortunate what happened to you."

"To me? You knew Tanner took me?"

He nodded. "It had to happen. Tanner was very loyal to Vault and him kidnapping you gave Kai a reason to take him out. Although, I suspect it was your man over there who killed him. And before he loses his cool and comes over here, it's better we end this now. What you need to know now, *Chaos*, is we're taking them down." He smirked at my shocked expression then got up and put a fifty on the bar. "Lay low for a while, would you? We need this shit with Tanner and Kai to settle. I'll be in touch."

I stood and grabbed his arm before he could leave. From the corner of my eye, I saw Deck get out of the booth and stand, but he didn't come toward us. "Tristan." He looked at my hand on his arm, but I refused to back down. "Who the hell are you?"

213

His brows rose. "I'm exactly who I say I am, Tristan Mason, owner of Mason Development."

"If you're telling me the truth, then give me something to make me believe you. For all I know, you're Vault trying to set me up."

He was quiet a minute then boldly turned and looked straight at Deck. "He's good at what he does, and we'll need that." Tristan leaned in closer, his chest barely touching mine. "I know someone in Vault. It was my contact who suggested to them to keep an eye on me."

"What? Why would you do that? They'll kill you if they find out."

"I needed to meet you and I needed it to be their idea, not mine." He glanced back down at my hand still holding his arm and I let go. "I'm high profile. They won't touch me unless absolutely necessary. I have nothing—at the moment—that would make them come after me."

"Except your contact." He trusted someone in Vault? He knew someone in Vault that meant— "My brother? Do you know anything about him?" I held my breath waiting, heart pounding. *Please say he's still alive.*

"Connor. He's in France. Alive." I closed my eyes and took a deep inhale. "I'm sorry, that's all I can tell you right now."

I nodded, looking down at my feet trying to hold back the tears. A conflict of emotions pooled inside me. I wanted so badly for my brother to be alive, but at what cost? What had they put him through? What were they doing to him now? "I want him back," I whispered more to myself than to Tristan.

"You won't get him back." My gaze darted to him, chest tightening. "If he gets out, he will never be the brother you knew."

"You don't know that."

"I do." Tristan tensed and his jaw twitched. "Because I was never the same."

"What?"

"The Vault kidnapped me when I was eight. Destroyed any child-hood I would've had. To this day, my parents and sister don't know I'm alive. They can never know. I lost that the second I became part of Vault."

"But you aren't now."

"No. I escaped when I was fifteen. Someone from Vault helped me—my contact." Tristan's brows lowered further over his darkened eyes. "Now, I have the money and the resources to get my contact out and rip Vault apart." He nodded toward Deck. "Your man and his men have a reason to go after Vault. You have a reason to go after Vault and now Kai has a reason to go after Vault. It's time."

"Do you think we can really do this?"

"No, but I'll die trying." Then he walked out.

CHAPTER TWENTY-FOUR

KAI

I HATED COMING here.

It was as if I was stripped down and forced to walk naked into a place where they had magnifying glasses and were looking at every part of me. And no one was even here. The real fucked-up part was that if they didn't like something, they had every right to do something about it. And that something always sucked.

Immunity didn't exist even for the son of one of Vault's board. Shit, Mom killed my father after having him beaten until he vomited blood. She made my sister and me watch—we were five and seven. Then she walked up to him, hanging by his wrists in the middle of the room where the members of the board stood around and watched. And she drove her knife up under his ribcage and killed him.

A few years ago, my sister was brought to France where she was tortured publicly for days. She had attempted to escape Vault. I warned her not to do it.

They found her. Now she sat in some filthy cell in their dungeon of horrors in France. Death was too quick. Too easy. No, they'd make an example of her. She'd rot to death and then they'd show us all what happened if we tried to leave.

Nothing was simple here. Death came with a price. Death was a privilege. I learned early on to block out the faces, the screams, and the smell of blood, piss and vomit.

And I survived because I was good at it.

Until her.

The girl.

London.

It was the first time in my life I felt.

I pressed the security code and strode through the massive house from room to room until I came to the oil painting. I hated it. So ironic, two lovers embraced together, the sun beaming down between them. Fuckin' sick bastards.

I shifted it to the right then pressed in a code on an alarm pad. I heard a click and the door opened beside the painting. I strode through it and it slid closed behind me. It was like sealing myself in hell.

I rarely came here except once a month for a meeting with Brice or when Mommy dearest was in town and wanted to see me. The woman could read a lie before you even spoke it. I practiced for years as a kid in front of the mirror, being careful of my gestures, of my muscle movement, keeping my eyes dead. Breathing was paramount, steady and even. I'd lied to her about the girl London.

Told her I hadn't seen her when she ran away. Of course, that was a lie.

Lies were everywhere. The art was whether you could make them into truths.

My dress shoes clicked down the cement floors to the basement. I wore my suit and tie like I always did when I came here. It would be disrespectful to look anything but your best.

I stopped at the grey steel door. "Glen," I addressed the guard.

"Wasn't expecting you."

I smirked. "Better you don't expect anything. That way you won't ever be disappointed." I lowered my voice and lost my grin. "Open the door."

Glen did and I strode into hell. The dark corridor was one I'd never get used to. No doubt, they designed this place so if any of us had to walk down the corridor, we'd be reminded of what would happen to us if we made a mistake.

The cells of torture. Five of them and each had its purpose. We were lucky if we came here instead of France, though.

I put my finger on the scanner. It beeped then went green and a door clicked open. I walked in and went directly to the computer. They'd know I was here and I had to have a good excuse as to why. I was hoping one would come to me—eventually.

It took only a few minutes to get into the emails. The trick was making certain any trace of it ever being sent was cleaned up, and I spent forty minutes tracing backwards until I was sure Tanner's message was deleted from all possible links. Well, I was betting some hacker could find it, but unless they were suspicious then they wouldn't be looking.

I shut off the computer, got up and walked out.

It had been easier than I thought. Explaining Tanner's death, I'd have to go to France and face my mother, but they wouldn't be upset at his loss. Besides, telling them I killed him because of his relationship with Georgie would only strengthen their trust in me. That had been a little shaky ever since London.

I shut the door and started walking back.

Then I heard her.

It was faint, but I'd never forget the slight lilt to her voice. Fuck. I closed my eyes and forced myself to keep walking. With each step, my heart thudded louder. My mind expanded into a fit of rage and agony.

I didn't expect her to be here, but now I knew why she was.

Because I was.

A test.

Loyalty.

They knew I came here once a month to meet asshole Brice. That I had to walk down this corridor. That eventually I'd hear her cries. Notice her.

Jesus. Their cruelty was endless.

I stopped at the door, my hand curled into a fist, raised and ready to knock for Greg to let me out. I could do this. I could leave and not look back. I could forget. I knew how to stop the nightmares.

But not this one.

My head dropped forward as I lowered my arm. I turned. What was

I doing? I knew I couldn't get her out. What was the point in seeing her? They'd want me to do this.

Like I told Deck, there was nowhere to hide from Vault. My sister was proof of that.

My feet continued down the corridor to where I'd heard her voice. I knew what I'd see. I knew how they broke them. I was one of them.

They drove all hope out of you until you became dead—nothing.

I couldn't enter the cell as they were all fingerprint access. They'd know it was me.

I stepped closer. Then I raised my head and looked through the tiny barred window.

I had to grab the bars to support my weight as my knees weakened when my eyes hit her.

I'd thought I'd been broken once before, but now—

Now it was complete.

As if sensing someone was looking at her, London raised her head, the curtain of hair parting to reveal haunting eyes and dried, caked blood on her forehead and mouth. I couldn't swallow. I had trouble breathing and the agony in my chest hurt so much I winced. At that moment, I prayed for the dead man I'd grown up to be, because feeling this pain was worse than any torture they had ever done to me.

"London," I breathed.

Then the haunted look died and I saw dead. She'd given up. Another day and she'd do or be anything they asked of her for the rest of her life. They'd zapped all hope of being saved.

Her head fell forward again as if she was too weak to look at me anymore. "Jesus." I had to walk away. I had to.

I couldn't escape with her. I'd be bringing down on her something far worse if I did.

But I knew how to end the pain. How to help her.

It was the only kind thing to do—for now.

"You're nothing, London." She didn't move and I raised my voice a little. "Look at me." I saw her fingers twitch and she slowly raised her head again. I felt sick to my stomach as I forced myself to harden and glare at her. *I am dead. Don't feel. Don't let the monsters in.* But the monsters were already in me. I felt them living and breathing. Monsters they trained us to slay—emotions. "You will never escape them. Better to know that now. You belong to them and the faster you accept it, the sooner the pain will end. Give up."

For a second, I saw a glint of anger hit her eyes and then her head dropped and she hung like a dead carcass.

Fuck. Fuck. Damn it.

But I had to do it. I had to cut her cord to any hope of leaving. Because if she lost hope, then it would stop the torture.

I closed my eyes then turned and strode down the corridor. *I'm coming back for you, London.*

CHAPTER
TWENTY-FIVE

Georgie

AFTER TRISTAN WALKED out of Avalanche, Deck, Tyler and Vic came over, and without a word, we left, Deck's hand at the small of my back as he led me outside.

Then we sat in the car and I told them everything. Word for word.

"You think he's for real?" Tyler asked.

I shrugged. Deck didn't say anything as he kept his fingers linked with mine and looked out the windshield.

"Does it matter if he is?" Vic said. "He obviously has someone on the inside that's loyal to him otherwise Vault would've killed him by now. He also is pretty confident they have no idea who he is. He had his insider get Vault to start watching him. That was brave as hell or stupid as hell. I vote we do what he says. Let the storm calm."

"I agree," Deck said. "But we dig deeper into Tristan's past. Vic, you make contact with him. I want to know who his parents are and if they think he's still missing. Any police reports of when Vault took him as a child. Everything he told Georgie must be checked into. If he cooperates with us then we will start planning our next move."

"And Kai?" Tyler asked.

"He texted me ten minutes ago. Tanner's message is deleted." Deck's voice was tight and I knew there was more to it. With the way the guys looked at one another, they did too. But no one said anything— except me.

"What's wrong?"

Vic got out of the backseat and shut the door.

Tyler's hand came down on my shoulder. "You did good, princess." Then he slapped Deck on the arm. "You, too, Boss. Thought you might lose it when she touched his arm."

Deck grunted.

Tyler chuckled then winked at me, hopped out and jogged to Vic's car.

"Deck?"

"Kai saw London."

I didn't want to know, but I knew it was important to face whatever we were getting into with my head clear. Burying the bad shit wouldn't do me any good. "Is that all he said?" Deck may try to protect me, but he wouldn't lie.

"No. We don't have much time. She needs out soon."

"Oh, God." That wasn't good.

Deck reached over and squeezed my hand. "Kai is going to France. He says he needs to do something before we go after Vault. I don't know what, but until he returns we keep who Tristan is under wraps. I don't trust either of them."

Neither did I.

Deck drove us back to his loft and it was quiet. I think we were both thinking about London and Connor and what would happen to them. Wondering if we could get them out and if we'd be able to stop Vault. I did feel a little more hopeful with Tristan on our side. If he escaped, then maybe others could.

I changed my clothes when we got back then came out to the living room to see Deck standing looking out onto the terrace. I came up beside him and he pulled me in front of him then wrapped his arms around me.

"You were good tonight. And looked sexy as hell."

"Surprising since someone made me wear a baggy, black shirt." I smirked, he growled and I could feel his hard cock pushed into my back.

"I lost fifty bucks tonight, too."

He turned me around in his arms then pressed me against the sliding glass door. "What?"

I ran my finger over his tense jaw. "Vic won. I had you at three minutes, tops."

"Jesus," Deck muttered.

"You weren't jealous?" I had expected Deck to keep his cool because … well, Deck was damn good at keeping his cool. But I had anticipated a bit of jealousy in him. From what I got so far, he hadn't even been affected.

He grabbed my chin and it was harsh, mimicking the look in his eyes. "When are you getting that nothing touches this—us? There isn't a man in this fuckin' universe who could take you from me." The darkness in his eyes changed and smoldering heat flared. "I didn't get jealous because it will never happen. You'll never leave me and I sure as hell won't be letting you go."

I smiled. "Pretty sure of yourself."

He ground against me. "I'm sure of us."

I curled my hand around the back of his neck. "So am I, baby."

Then his mouth took mine in a forceful kiss and I submitted to it—to him. There was gentle, sweet Deck and hard, ruthless Deck.

This was ruthless. I craved every part of it as his hand tangled in my hair and yanked my head back so he could kiss my neck and then bite my skin so hard I cried out. His tongue quickly soothed it with a warm, velvety touch.

He yanked me away from the door and we crashed in a mess of limbs on the floor, Deck being careful to take the brunt of the fall. He ripped off my top and my hands tore at his. There was no gentleness in what we both needed; it was wild urgency. It was only with trust in one another we could let go like this. I gave every part of me to him and he was doing the same.

I loved that we had that. The fierce and the tender … the crazy need in us refusing to be sated. I heard the tear of his shirt as it finally gave way to my hands and it hung open so I could run my hands over his chest.

"Baby, jeans." I had my hands down his pants, hand gripping his cock and pulling upward.

He groaned. "Easy." He was off me in a second as he yanked my black pants off and threw them aside. My pink thong went with them and he stared at me for a second before he grabbed my legs and put them on his shoulders. "You good?"

"Fuck, yeah." I collapsed back as his tongue swept over my clit and then he started suckling and tasting as intense quivers soared through me. "Deck. Fuck me." I was falling fast and so turned on I was teetering on the edge.

"That's it." His drove two fingers inside me and I arched in pain at the sudden intrusion, but at the same time, I loved every second of it. "Come for me, babe." He suckled hard on my clit and I screamed out as my body released, legs trembling as wave after wave shot through me.

He slowly pushed his fingers in and out of me while I came back down, the twinges like electrical shocks still pulsing inside.

"Fuck." He pulled his fingers out of me and I opened my eyes, still breathing hard as he moved up to run his glistening fingers over my lips. "Taste yourself. It's fuckin' heaven."

I didn't hesitate and opened my mouth so he could slip them inside, the sweet scent of me on them. "Mmmm."

"Fuck, Georgie. That's hot as hell." He yanked his fingers out of my mouth, and then pushed back and had his jeans off in seconds. He grabbed my hands and wrenched my arms above my head so I was stretched out like a cat. "Your back?"

"Damn it, it's fine. Just fuck me."

Then he was kissing me again, our mouths harsh against one another, both of us tasting me on our lips. It was so erotic and hot and I wanted him to fuck me so badly.

I was quick and he wasn't expecting it as I pushed up hard with my right hip and sent him forward, loosening his grip on my wrists. Keeping with the momentum, I rolled so I was on top of him.

"I'm fucking you tonight." Then I took hold of his cock and held it while I slammed down on top of him. He groaned. I did it again and again until he forced me to stay down on top of him, rocking my hips.

"Georgie. Babe." His fingers dug into my hips as I moved up and down on his cock, the slapping of our skin, the panting, our moans pushing us faster and harder.

"Enough!" Deck yelled and within a second, he had me on my back again, trapped beneath his weight. He grabbed my chin and I met his eyes. "You and I … this doesn't end. Ever."

"I know." I smiled. I knew he was saying it because he was feeling what I was at the moment—disbelief that after so many years we got our real. Then my smile turned into a gasp as he shoved his cock back inside me.

"Scream for me," he ordered as he thrust fiercely, his eyes locked on mine.

I didn't need him to tell me as I felt my body's release at his thrust. "Deck!" I cried out as a burst of ecstasy swam through every inch of me to settle deep between my legs. Deck pumped three more times before he joined me, groaning loudly. I felt his body quiver and shake over me and watched as his expression tightened, eyes closed, head back as if in pain.

He lazily slipped in and out of me a few more times while I stroked up and down his arms. When he opened his eyes, my breath hitched.

It was the lightness I rarely got to see. All the shit he had seen, the loss, the deaths—it was wiped away for those few seconds he was in my arms. Then he was kissing my bruised lips again, but this time it was gentle and sweet, a slow warmth bringing us back down to where we needed to be.

When he stopped kissing me, he rolled onto his back, one hand beneath his head while the other brought me with him and kept me locked against his side. We lay still and silent, while our breathing slowed and we got our emotions back in control.

I lay my cheek on his chest, my hand resting on his abdomen, drawing little circles. "I got us in some serious shit."

He huffed and I felt his hands in my hair as he caressed me. "None of this is your fault. They handpicked Connor. You're collateral. No matter what decision you made, it would've been the same outcome. All of it was to make certain Connor became theirs and to make certain it stays that way. What we need to find out is why him."

"You think we can ever bring him back?" I knew Deck wouldn't lie to me and I held my breath waiting for his answer.

"Even if we did, I don't know if you'd even recognize the man anymore, Georgie. Connor was a good guy. He cared about every innocent life in this fuckin' harsh world. He'd have given his life for a perfect stranger. Shit, he risked his life for strangers every day. Countless times he risked his life for some kid caught in the middle of a shit storm. That was him." He hesitated and I tilted my head to look up at him. "Babe, chances are he doesn't want out now."

I tried to swallow, but my throat was so tight it hurt. Tears filled my eyes and it was for the loss of Connor because he had died the second they took him. My brother was dead and that was what Deck was preparing me for if we ever saw him again.

"We need to read his journal."

"Yeah," I whispered as I kissed his chest.

"We lay low for now. We plan. Then when the time is right, we go after them."

I moved up his body until my mouth was inches from his. "Promise me you won't let them have you, too."

"Can't make that kind of promise, Georgie."

I closed my eyes and nodded.

He kissed the single tear that escaped. "Babe, I waited ten years for us. I'll do what it takes to keep us together." He kissed the tip of my nose. "And only one person can ever truly have me, Georgie, and that is you."

EPILOGUE

Sunday brunch, four weeks later

"SWEETPEA?"

"Rainbow," Deck replied.

I laughed and smacked him in the chest. He started calling me that when I dyed my hair again. I knew he didn't like the blue, so I surprised him a few weeks ago. Now, I had pink tips with a few stray strands of purple. "You need a bigger terrace."

Deck's brows rose and his mouth twitched which had me standing on my tiptoes and kissing the corners. His arm hooked around my waist and he drew me hard against him. He whispered in my ear and shivers sprinkled like blooming wildflowers across my skin. "Penthouse with a plunge pool not big enough for you?"

I was being sarcastic and he knew it. I pretty much lived here now. Actually, we were looking to rent out my place since I was never there. There hadn't really been a discussion on where we'd live. It was Deck telling me I was moving in and me conceding because shit, who wouldn't want to live in a penthouse with a plunge pool? "Not really. Is there something above a penthouse? Something a little nicer. More … I don't know, classier."

He snorted and bit the lobe of my ear. "Yeah, it's called Heaven. And you're not going there anytime soon. You'll have to make do with our lowly penthouse." I loved that he called it ours. He nodded to the terrace where our friends were. "And they don't mind the new location of our Sunday brunch."

"That's because they're too scared of you to say anything."

He growled, but it turned into a chuckle.

"Sweet mother of fuck. Deck chuckles? I need to blow a horn. We need an announcement." Crisis, the bass guitarist of Tear Asunder, sauntered into the kitchen grinning ear to ear. "Guess no more grabbing her perfect ass. Have to make do with Haven's, only single chick left in the group."

I laughed because touching Haven was off-limits. First of all, Ream would kill him because Haven was his twin sister and Crisis was a cocky, arrogant womanizer. Secondly, from the limited times I'd met Haven, I was betting she'd snap his neck if he even tried it. The girl was cold, like ice cold, although it was deceiving considering she looked like an angel.

"I dare you to try it, smarty-pants," I said.

Crisis wiggled his brows and his arrogant grin broadened. "Oh, I did when we got back a few days ago." He pointed to his slightly bruised cheekbone. "She has one hell of a punch. But I'm good with a little rough and tumble. I'll be tasting her before the week …" His voice trailed off when he noticed Deck shaking his head and me wincing.

Crisis swore beneath his breath and sighed.

"You fuckin' go near my sister, you're dead." Ream slammed his fist into the back of Crisis' shoulder. "Shut the fuck up about it, man."

"Need any help …" Kat came in and stopped abruptly as she looked from Crisis to Ream. Then she sighed, went up to her fiancé and slid her arms around his waist from behind before she kissed his neck. "Baby, get the orange juice."

I smiled when I saw the tension ease out of Ream. He shot Crisis another glare before going to the fridge, taking out the orange juice and walking back out to the terrace where Logan, Emily, Kite, Vic, Tyler and Matt were. Josh opted out on the invitation and this was the first time Vic and Tyler had come.

Deck kissed me on the mouth then let me go, picked up the tray of fruits and brought them outside. Kat sank down onto a bar stool, smiling with a glimmer of laughter in her eyes. "Girl, I never thought I'd see the day. You and Deck … holy smokin'. Deck always scared the shit out of me. Shit, he still does, even when he kisses you like he's all sweet 'n stuff." She jumped up and down in her seat. "Oh, my God, Vic …" She lowered her voice. "You see those arms? I swear he must have an eight-pack beneath that t-shirt. Almost willing to push him in the pool so I can see them against his wet shirt." She lowered her voice. "But Jesus, I swear he is—"

"Scary as hell," Emily finished as she came out of the bathroom. Her arm came around me and she kissed my check. "I don't even want to know what that guy does for Deck."

It was great having Kat and Emily back, especially now that I felt … well, free to be myself. They'd never know about Vault or Connor—that would only put them at risk—but we'd curbed the drinking cover story. Kai wasn't pleased, but Deck told him too bad.

"I asked him to fuck me in the shower."

Both Kat and Emily's mouths dropped open and stared at me as if I had two heads.

"You think he looks scary now … damn, that cupcake made my vagina shrink up and hide. He shoved me against the wall then put his hand around my throat and squeezed." I had their rapt attention. "I'm thinking he doesn't like teasing."

"Shit."

"Jesus."

"Deck know?" Emily asked.

I shook my head. "Are you kidding me? Deck threw a punch at Tyler because I …" I winced, thinking about my stupid remark. "This was before we were together and I was pissed at him."

"Like usual," Kat said.

I smiled. "So, I said something about Tyler and me fucking."

Emily gasped. Kat laughed.

"Tyler landed on his ass."

"Mouse, you coming?" Logan popped his head in from the terrace. He winked at me and I smiled.

"Girl gossip, Logan. You and Ream stole my girls for months. We're busy comparing dicks."

"Fuck," he groaned. Then he slammed the screen door shut and I heard him say, "They're comparing our fuckin' dicks in there."

Tyler and Crisis laughed their asses off and I saw Deck scowling, but when his eyes met mine, he grinned.

He knew me. He knew I spewed bullshit and he loved me anyway. Deck loved me. He always had. I bit my lower lip as I thought of his cock inside me this morning. That was how I woke up: him behind me, pushing inside. It was so hot waking up to him like that.

"Earth to Georgie." Emily squeezed my shoulders.

"She's thinking about Deck's cock," Kat said. "So, is he controlling in bed?"

"Is Ream?" I knew the answer. Ream was crazy obsessed with Kat, to the point of needing therapy kind of obsessed, but it worked for them.

Kat moaned. "He plays me like a hard rock song and that's all I'm telling."

Emily and I laughed.

"Babe. Now. Meat is ready." Deck was at the screen door now. He raised his brows then walked back to the BBQ where Logan and Ream were pulling the meat off the burner.

I sighed as a wave of heat hit me. I needed a dip in the plunge pool. I didn't think I'd ever stop wanting or needing him. Shit, I'd wanted him since I was sixteen and that had never faltered despite my best efforts.

Emily walked over and grabbed the carafe of coffee. "I don't care if he looks less uptight now he's with you. That guy scares me and I'm not pissing him off."

Kat got up and grabbed plates. "And Vic looks hungry."

That got us all moving as we laughed and went outside to join the men. It was Tyler and Crisis who hit it off, probably because they both wouldn't shut up about themselves: Tyler and his ability to pick up women and Crisis with the way he *stroked* his guitar. We all knew he wasn't talking about stroking a guitar.

We ate and laughed, and even Vic managed a half-ass smile—or maybe it was a twitch. "So we finally get to see Deck's place. Been holding out on us, Deck," Emily said.

"Yeah, man. Seriously, we could have some serious parties here." Crisis said.

"We live on a farm," Kite said. He was playing with his eyebrow piercing as he sat relaxed with his legs out in worn-out jeans and bare-foot. He was head to toe tatted up—well, not his face, but he did have one crawling up the back of his neck into his hair. Kite was quiet and sexy as hell. Kind of the mysterious unknown because he rarely spoke and yet it wasn't because he was shy. Actually, I had the impression Kite was more confident than any of the guys in the band.

"And I own a bar," Matt added. "Sis, convince Logan to play at Avalanche again. For old times' sake. He owes me."

Kat laughed. "Yeah, well, you did punch him in our driveway once for dating Emily. Then attacked Ream in the parking lot of my doctor's office. Not really a good way to get a band to come to your bar by beating up the band members."

"Babe, he didn't beat me up," Ream protested, grabbing her around the waist and hauling her onto his lap. "If I recall, I kicked his ass."

Matt scoffed and shoved his plate away then leaned back in his chair, crossing his arms over his broad chest. "You kicked shit all."

"Shit all is right. Might want to beef up a bit, buddy. Next time, I might not be so kind." Ream laughed.

Matt was tall, a runner, and had huge arms. Ream was quick, agile and when he wanted something, he was damn tenacious. "My beef is where it counts. And I know how to use it."

Tyler barked out a laugh, joining Emily giggling and Logan rolling his eyes.

I slid my hand under the table onto Deck's thigh and slowly stroked up until I came to his cock, already hard by the time I reached it. "You guys want to throw down your dicks on the table, I'll be the judge." By Deck's grunt, I knew he didn't like the idea of me looking at any cocks. Except his, of course.

"Georgie," Deck whispered in a controlled husky tone, which sent my tingles to scatter like wildfire over my skin.

I continued rubbing him while I sipped my coffee and listened to Matt and Ream go back and forth about who could kick whose ass. Kat sat back against Ream's chest and told her brother to give it up. Matt was just as stubborn as Kat, though, and he'd never back down from an argument.

"Babe," Deck growled.

I felt him get harder and I bit my lower lip, silently laughing because I knew he was trying desperately to hold it together.

"Out," Deck said.

"Huh?" Crisis said, putting his hands up. "Out? Like get out?"

I winked when Crisis looked at me, completely offended he was getting kicked out of anyone's place. Crisis thought he was loved and wanted everywhere. And he was by most of the ladies.

Tyler and Vic were the only ones who got up right away and I suspect because they could read Deck so well. Emily and Kat looked at me, smiling, knowing exactly why they were being asked to leave. It seemed like the only one who took offense was Crisis.

"Why can't you go fuck her then come back? We don't mind." Crisis got a slap in the head by Kite. "Georgie, I haven't even taken a swim yet."

"It's a plunge pool. And we've been here two hours, time to fuck off," Matt said then got up, kissing his sister on the cheek then Emily and me.

After a round of goodbyes, Deck and I were alone and I was co-cooned in his arms, flat on my back on the coffee table. He was above me, looking down.

There were no lies between us. Just the raw truths that had brought us together.

"Going to fuck you now."

I smiled. "Okay."

"Wasn't asking."

Then he did more than fuck me, he made love to me.

Two Hours later.
Txt msg: **Back from France. We need to make our move.**

Perfect Ruin

The Vault Story continues with:
Kai and London.
Coming 2015.

Perfect Rage
Connor's Story.

Little interesting notes from the author*

Thank you so much for reading Perfect Chaos. I hope you enjoyed Deck and Georgie's story.

A couple interesting facts:

My brother owned a coffee shop called Perk Avenue and this is where I took the idea from.

I had a hamster named "Fiddlehead" who was my first pet when I was nine years old.

Subscribe to the Newsletter
http://nashodarose.us7.list-manage1.com/subscribe?u=1e800ef9a8a22
144c14399928&id=b12d168284

ACKNOWLEDGEMENTS

THERE ARE SO many I want to thank for this book as it has been a long complicated journey.

Sarah … **dude,** you held my hand and were there for me every step of the way. Plotting, pre-beta reading, proofing … love you.

Yaya and Midian, as always your pre-beta reading rocked! Short and to the point and as always brutally honest—you know I love it!

Paula, you did it again, found the issues in the book I was blind to (Deck does that to me). And as always your comments made me laugh—thanks sweets.

Susan, you bring a smile to my face with all your enthusiasm each day. Thank you so much for beta reading and being there for me.

Becky from Hot Tree Editing, this was the first time working with you and your crew and damn I love you all. I feel so lucky to have found you.

As always my content editor Kristin, you took my twisted path I put these characters on and made it so much better.

To all the fantastic girls in the "Unyielding Tear Asunder Book Babes" group! I love chatting and laughing with all of you. Thank you for all your advice and support. It has been amazing! And Michelle New … yes New, not Ryan! Hope you liked Deck's story.

Stacey, Stacey, Stacey … I was late. I hate being late. And you're so patient and sweet—thank you. You make my books beautiful with your brilliant final touches.

Thanks again Kari for another great cover!

Elaine, you've become a great friend through all this. Can't wait to meet up at the Tampa signing.

Authors that I've met on this incredible journey and who are so supportive, Penelope Ward, Ilsa Madden-Mills, M. Limoges.

There are so many dedicated bloggers that I've been fortunate to have met. You girls are so fabulous. Thank you so much for supporting me and sharing in my excitement of my books. I'm so lucky to have found some incredible friends …. HUGS.

My family, I love you. Thank you for being there for me.

Oh and of course Gimli … welcome to the family. You give me that perfect calm when I step away from writing.

Also by  Nashoda Rose

Tear Asunder series – Dark Erotic Contemporary Romance

With You (Tear Asunder .5)

Sculpt is an illegal fighter.
He's also the lead singer of a local rock band.
No one knows his real name.
And from the moment I met him, he made me forget mine.

In order to convince Sculpt to give me self-defense lessons, I had to follow his one rule—no complaining or he'd walk. I didn't think it would be a problem. I could handle a few bruises. What I hadn't anticipated was landing on my back with Sculpt on top of me and my entire body burning up for him.

I tried to ignore it.
I failed, of course. And having a hot, tattooed badass on top of me week after week, acting completely immune to what he was doing to my body—it was frustrating as hell. So I broke his rule—I complained. Then he kissed me.

*Novella with a huge cliffhanger. Like huge.

Torn from You (Tear Asunder #1)

Love is like an avalanche. It hits hard, fast and without mercy.

At least it did for me when Sculpt, the lead singer of the rock band Tear Asunder knocked me off my feet. Literally, because he's also a fighter—illegally of course, and he taught me how to fight. He also taught me how to love and I fell hard for him. I mean, the guy could do sweet, when he wasn't doing bossy, and I like sweet.

Then it all shattered.

Kidnapped.
Starved.
Beaten.
I was alone and fighting to survive.
When I heard Sculpt's voice, I thought he was there to save me.

I was wrong.

***This is a love story with very dark elements. CAUTION- Dark contemporary romance.*

Overwhelmed by You (Tear Asunder #2)

Love is ugly and secrets will destroy you.

KAT

I don't beg.
I don't cry.
And I don't give second chances.
Ream, the lead guitarist of the rock band Tear Asunder, deserves a gold medal for best dick move ever when he ran the moment he discovered my secret after two days of hot sex. Then he brings some chick to my coming-home party from the hospital—after being shot.
I hate him.
Until …
Ream's six-foot-two frame unfolds from the car after being gone on tour for eight months. I stared. And in my defense, any girl would stare. It would almost be rude not to because Ream was the type of guy who stood out. Not because he was loud and obnoxious. No, it was because he was the complete opposite. Subtle and dangerously quiet. If

he spoke, you'd better hope he liked you because otherwise, you'd be falling at his feet begging for mercy. Except me … I don't beg—ever. But when our eyes locked, it was Ream's steady confidence that had my nerves shooting off like jet sprinklers.

Then …

Ream told me he didn't need a second chance because he was still working on his first.

REAM

Sex is ugly. It's using someone for your own narcissistic pleasure. I did it, but hated it—until her. She was un-fuckin-expected. Then I had to wreck our beginning with my screwed-up past. I don't deserve her, but I'm selfish and I'm taking her anyway. This is who I am and it's too late to change me.

Warning: contains violence, sexual content, and coarse language. Some scenes may be triggers. Mature audiences 18+

Nashoda Rose's supernatural romance series coming soon.

Scar of the Wraiths

Ardent
Stygian
Tyrant
illicit

ABOUT THE AUTHOR

Nashoda Rose is a New York Times bestselling author who lives in Toronto with her assortment of pets. She writes contemporary romance with a splash of darkness, or maybe it's a tidal wave. When she isn't writing, she can be found sitting in a field reading with her dogs at her side while her horses graze nearby. She loves interacting with her readers on Facebook and chatting about her addiction—books.

Facebook: https://www.facebook.com/pages/Nashoda-Rose/
Twitter: https://twitter.com/nashodarose
Website: http://nashodarose.com/
Goodreads:
https://www.goodreads.com/author/show/7246093.Nashoda_Rose

www.ingramcontent.com/pod-product-compliance
Lightning Source LLC
Chambersburg PA
CBHW020638260626
47157CB00008B/2797